In

Dear Jane by Yvonne Lehman invites you to sit back and listen to classical music. Gloria Holmes has become temporary assistant to the world-famous concert pianist, Dr. William Robert Clayborn III. His musical talent and depth of character inspire her, but when he dedicates each concert to a mysterious "Jane," she is convinced that she must keep her thoughts of him on a professional level.

The Language of Love by Loree Lough takes you on a trip of discovery. Shannen Flynn has to travel to Italy to meet Joe Morgan, a man who is practically a neighbor back home. Touring the sites together gives them a whole new perspective on life, but will the challenges that await back home overweigh the joy of newfound love?

Candlelight Christmas by Colleen L. Reece sets you down in the middle of a hospital emergency. Seattle has been buried in a winter storm, and twins Allison and April are on duty at Shepherd of Love Hospital. But the stress of numerous medical emergencies and a regional blackout only serve to cover up their emotional stress. April is planning a wedding and Allison is in love with April's fiance. The twins have always told each other everything, but will they be able to communicate what is really in their hearts?

Renewed Love by Debra White Smith ignites old flames. Jake and Katelyn Grant divorced due to his marital infidelity. Now that Katelyn has become a Christian, she feels the Lord is telling her to forgive Jake and admit her own faults in their marriage—but she must do it in person. When Jake agrees to meet with her and quickly informs her that he still loves her, the true test of Katelyn's forgiveness begins.

Winter Wishes

Four New Inspirational Romances
from Christmas Present

Yvonne Lehman

Loree Lough

Colleen L. Reece

Debra White Smith

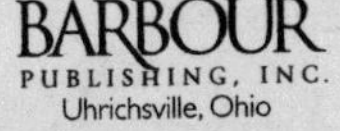

BARBOUR PUBLISHING, INC.
Uhrichsville, Ohio

ISBN 1-57748-596-3

All Scripture quotations are taken from the King James Version of the Bible unless otherwise marked.

Published by Barbour Publishing, Inc., P.O. Box 719, Uhrichsville, Ohio 44683 http://www.barbourbooks.com

Printed in the United States of America.

Winter
Wishes

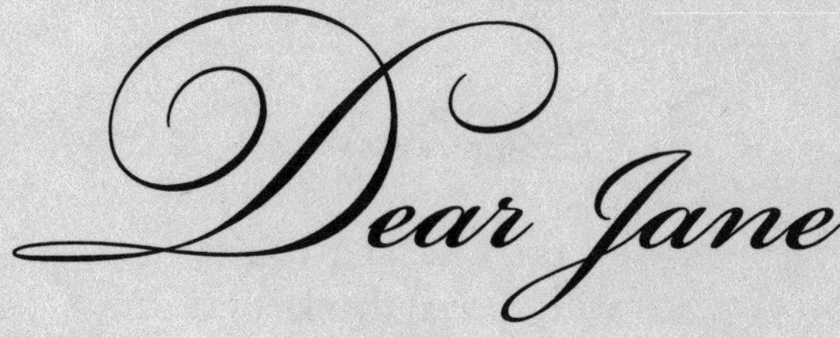

Yvonne Lehman

Dedication

To Lori, Lisa, and Yuliati,
with special thanks to
Diana Wortham, clinical specialist,
Mission Hospital

There is a time for everything, . . .
A time to be born and a time to die, . . .
A time to love.
ECCLESIASTES 3:1–2, 8 (NIV)

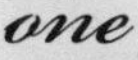

The first time Gloria Holmes saw William Robert Clayborn III, he strode across the stage in his black tux, white shirt, and bow tie. He bowed deeply, acknowledging the audience's applause, before crossing over to the piano. There he stood at a microphone until the ovation abated.

Gloria glanced at the conductor, whose baton should have been suspended in air. It wasn't. He stood at a side angle, facing the featured soloist.

Gloria had attended a couple of symphony concerts in the past and had seen opera's famous three tenors on TV, but she had never seen a featured pianist stand at a microphone as if he were going to sing. The audience seemed to hold its breath. The dark-haired soloist lifted his chin slightly, and his rich deep voice announced, "This performance is dedicated to Jane."

He then switched off the microphone, turned, and positioned himself on the piano bench. The conductor lifted his arms, and the concert opened with Brahms' *Piano Concerto No. 2*.

Gloria didn't know Brahms from Mozart from Tchaikovsky, but she had come primarily to see the man, not just to enjoy the music. Music? No! The genius. Gloria sat transported into another world for the next hour, her mind echoing with every note the musician coaxed from the piano. She appreciated what could only be the result of a God-given talent and years of hard work.

During intermission, twenty-six-year-old Gloria and her silver-haired friend Tess, who was almost seventy years older, stood in line in the restroom. Gloria checked out her appearance in the mirror. She pushed a couple wayward locks of her medium-length, wavy, light-brown hair away from her face. Her blue-green eyes picked up the blue-gray color of her silk blouse, which she was wearing with a multi-print mid-calf-length skirt. She applied a small amount of lip gloss and smiled, exposing her pearly whites. She was presentable, Gloria concluded, and then sheepishly admitted to herself that Dr. William Robert Clayborn III would not likely pick her out of the audience of hundreds.

Tess joined in comments with others about the wonderful concert and the talented pianist. Gloria's mind was shouting, *I'm going to meet him tomorrow. In fact, he's going to interview me for a job!* It wasn't easy, keeping her lips zipped.

Like all the audience members who appeared to be eager for the rest of the concert, Gloria and Tess soon hurried back to their seats for more of the beautiful music.

Gloria read from the program. The second half of the concert would open with Tchaikovsky's *Piano Trio in A Minor*, followed by the entire orchestra playing his *Symphony No. 2 in C Minor.* The program stated that Tchaikovsky had been inspired to compose the work while listening to Ukrainian peasants singing folk tunes as they worked.

The next thing Gloria knew, the lights went up, the curtain closed, and the standing ovation lauded the performance, initiating an encore. Not until the concert was over did the soloist's words of dedication again come to mind. *That wondrous performance was for Jane?* Gloria marveled.

Gloria and Tess walked from the civic center and out into the bright, late-summer evening. They reached Tess's little green bug, and Gloria unlocked the door on the passenger side for Tess, who didn't like to drive at night. The trim, elegant older woman, wearing a classic black dress, settled herself on the seat. "He doesn't look a lot like his grandfather," she said, then gazed straight ahead, lost in memories.

Gloria shut the door and walked around to the driver's seat. She knew that Tess was proud to have gone to public school with the concert pianist's grandfather, before he went off to study music and Tess went to Korea as a missionary. Tess still remembered William Clayborn I as a nice young man from a respected Christian family.

As Gloria pulled out onto the road, the conversation turned toward the phenomenal concert itself. The little bug sped along the interstate toward Highland, where Tess shared her home with Gloria. That had been an answer to prayer. Tess asked only that Gloria pay half the utilities and buy her own groceries. She also said it would be a sin to buy another car. Gloria could drive the little bug as long as she kept gas in it.

The thick growth of leafy oaks, maples, and evergreens blocked out much of the bright moonlight as the car wound higher up in the mountains of North Carolina. Gloria parked in the driveway next to the small frame cottage with its wide front porch that Tess had bought after her husband died on the mission field and she retired. Retired? Gloria laughed inwardly at that thought as the two women entered their home. Tess had retired from serving in Korea, but she still adamantly served others.

Both women were tired and quickly got ready for bed. Gloria closed the door of her bedroom, across from Tess's, and prepared to get a good night's rest. However, she lay awake half the night too wound up by the concert, too excited about the next day's interview to fall asleep.

She wondered how Dr. William Clayborn III had found time to become so accomplished, yet have a personal life with a special person. Gloria, herself, hadn't had many opportunities to meet available men when in Indonesia, and then she had busied herself with getting a higher education once she returned to the States. Now her life was at a slower pace, and she had wonderful friends and acquaintances. But. . .no one special. With a trace of longing, she wondered, *Does God have a special person out there somewhere for me?*

How romantic it must be to see your name on a road sign or on a banner behind a plane high in the sky or hear it announced to an audience of hundreds. What kind of man makes such a romantic gesture?

Gloria drifted off to sleep, the concert still reverberating through her mind. How fortunate was this Jane to whom such wonderful music had been dedicated.

Jane must be an extraordinary woman.

"Jane is sleeping peacefully, Dr. Clayborn," came the response to his telephone inquiry as soon as he could politely get away from the reception in his honor at the Radisson. "She's looking forward to your visit in the morning."

"I'll say good night then," he replied and hung up.

The phone call revealed that nothing had changed. This left William Clayborn's emotions in limbo. He could thank the Lord that things weren't worse. . .but neither were they better. He took the elevator down to the ground floor where the limo driver was waiting, as he had requested earlier.

After William got into the backseat, the driver closed the door. . .symbolic of the doors William had closed on his life and on his career. Tonight marked the last concert of this magnitude for. . . He didn't know for how long. Only God knew.

As the limo made its way along the interstate toward the mountain above the community of Highland, William leaned his head back against the seat. He was always drained after such a concert. It required total concentration and complete dedication. Fortunately, he could compartmentalize his emotions enough so that when his fingers traveled over the keys, all that occupied his mind and heart was the music.

The ability to compartmentalize was an asset to an artist. William had learned it early. When just a boy, his mother and father had encouraged him time and again by saying, "You must concentrate, William. Allow no outside distractions."

He had no problem with that as a young boy. His family was musical. He traveled all over the world and was accustomed to sitting by his grandmother while his grandfather and his parents entertained audiences. He'd heard the applause. He'd never thought he missed anything by rarely going to movies or by not playing rough games like football and soccer. His life was a movie, and his fingers were at home on the piano keys.

His father compared practice and performance to being a doctor, saying a surgeon could not operate if he allowed emotion to control him. He must be in control. "You cannot afford the luxury of allowing your emotions to control you."

His mother admonished, "You must learn to perform when your heart is breaking, when your body is aching, your mind is troubled, or your soul is sick. Your obligation is to your audience. They have their troubles too."

William had been able to take their advice and perform for thousands at his parents' memorial service after the fatal accident when his father had pulled out in front of a semi on a busy interstate.

He'd performed well during and after his grandmother's battle with cancer that eventually claimed her life. He'd wondered how Grandpa would fare with his beloved Cora gone and then when his arthritis got so bad at times that he couldn't even play the violin. He reasoned his grandfather's ability to continue lay in the words of the song the old man often sang: "Take your burdens to the Lord and leave them there."

Grandpa had apparently done that. *I'm trying to, Lord,* William prayed silently. *But I long for the day that I can see clearly. For now, I relate to the apostle Paul when he wrote, "We see through a glass darkly."*

two

Early Monday morning, Tess was up and making breakfast when Gloria got out of the shower and came into the kitchen in her robe and with a towel wrapped around her head turban-style.

"Oh, Tess. I hope that's not for me. I'm too excited to eat."

"I thought you might say that." Tess spoke in her motherly way she'd adopted. "That's why I fixed your breakfast. Now, you don't want to faint around midmorning, do you? Your Dr. Clayborn might get the wrong idea."

"Tess, he's not *my* Dr. Clayborn," Gloria chided, then laughed at the mischievous twinkle in the older woman's soft gray eyes and the grin on her face. Tess was a kidder, but sometimes her kidding bordered strongly on truth. How could a woman, young or old for that matter, sit and stare at a fine specimen of a man like Dr. Clayborn for over two hours and not feel. . .something? Especially when the sight was accompanied by heartfelt music!

Gloria sat down at the table, in front of the plate of ham, scrambled eggs, and toast that Tess set before her. Tess set her own plate opposite her in the warm yellow kitchen where sunlight began to shine brightly through the windows. They held hands, and Tess gave thanks, asking God's blessings on Gloria during her job interview with William Clayborn.

After the "Amen," Gloria looked across at her wonderful friend. "Thanks for the prayer," Gloria said. "I need it."

"Oh, bosh!" Tess said. "All the Clayborn boy asked for was a glorified secretary. And look at it this way: President Hunt hired you to teach a college class. William Clayborn's needs aren't nearly as demanding as that."

Clayborn boy? Gloria swallowed a bite of scrambled eggs. *That "Clayborn boy" is an accomplished thirty-four-year-old man!* Her eggs settled in her stomach like a fish splashing around in water.

"It's not the work that bothers me, Tess. It's the interview. You know how clumsy I get when I'm nervous. Remember when I tripped on the step before I talked to the women's group about missionary work in Indonesia?"

Tess waved her argument away. "That can happen to anybody. And once you got to talking about missions, nobody cared about that little stumble. Just pray and take a deep breath."

Gloria had been doing that for months—ever since President Hunt had said that William Clayborn had reviewed her credentials, was impressed, and was looking forward to a personal interview.

So, Gloria, she said to herself, *think positively. Don't fall on your face or put your foot in your mouth.*

Gloria exited to her bedroom and carefully chose her outfit, wanting to look her best when she met Dr. Clayborn face-to-face.

She was not one to be overwhelmed by anyone, believing that all people are created equal and that whatever talent the man had was from God. She told herself firmly that she would not feel daunted, yet a feeling she called anticipation washed over her as she guided the little green bug past the library and parked in her faculty spot at the back where she could walk right into the adult studies offices, located beneath the library.

Of course Gloria knew that what she was like inside was most important, but she believed she should do her best to make a good appearance too. Past compliments and her mirror revealed she was no raving beauty, but she was definitely attractive with her golden-brown hair that curled naturally. Her blue-green eyes could become almost any color, and this morning she'd worn a smart blue suit, having heard that all men liked blue. She did want to impress this man, who had so impressed her with his musical ability.

She took a deep breath, straightened her shoulders, and strode into the anteroom. William Robert Clayborn III and the gray-haired president of Highland College stood at the chest-high counter, both in business suits, white shirts, and conservative ties.

"Good morning, Cathy," Gloria said to the secretary at the computer in the office surrounded on two sides by the tall counter.

The secretary responded, and the president interrupted his conversation. "Here's the young lady now," President Hunt said with a congenial smile, "punctual, as usual."

She murmured, "Good morning," to the two men and smiled. She was grateful for any small compliment. President Hunt demanded the best from his staff, and she appreciated having been hired to teach English one night a week in the adult studies program.

Upon their introduction by President Hunt, Gloria extended her hand to Dr. Clayborn. She felt like strands of music traveled up her arm and spread throughout her body, lodging in her heart and mind—as if his talented fingers had elicited from her skin the same response they had gained from the piano keys during the concert.

He looked younger than he had on stage or even in the publicity photos she'd seen. But he'd been serious at those times. Now, he smiled, and his dark brown eyes reminded her of warm chocolate. His classic Italian good looks would have been inherited from his mother's side of the family.

His rich baritone voice resonated as he greeted her.

"My pleasure, Dr. Clayborn. I attended the concert last night. You were. . ." She cleared her throat, realizing she shouldn't say that he was wonderful. He wanted a competent assistant who wouldn't act like a giddy school girl, star struck by a pop or rock star. At twenty-six, she was far from being a school girl. And a thirty-four-year-old concert pianist was far from being a pop or rock star.

With what she hoped was a smooth transition, she corrected herself. "The concert was wonderful."

"Thank you," he said politely.

"If you two will excuse me," President Hunt said, "I have another appointment. If there's anything I can do—"

Dr. Clayborn extended his hand. "You've done more than I could have expected, sir."

President Hunt smiled, shaking his hand warmly. "I'll be in touch." He nodded at Gloria, then turned to leave.

"My office is right down this hall," Gloria said, as Dr. Clayborn picked up a leather briefcase from the counter.

He walked beside her as she led the way down the hallway and casually commented, "I've never interviewed anyone before."

Her head turned toward him. "Really? I would have thought you'd have a large staff."

"That's true, but I inherited them. I have the same PR man, financial advisor, and agent that my parents had. I've dismissed them until further notice."

Gloria stopped at a closed door, laughed lightly, and flashed a teasing gleam in her blue-green eyes. "So that's all this position requires—a PR person, financial advisor, and agent wrapped up in one person. Not to worry. But I suppose we must follow protocol and have the interview anyway."

Dr. Clayborn smiled back, and Gloria was relieved that he seemed to respond positively to her light bantering. She understood quite well that the position only required part-time secretarial duties.

Gloria opened the door and walked into her small office, one of several identical rooms in the building set aside for adult studies teachers who weren't part of the full-time faculty, who had offices in the faculty building. Out of habit, she took her seat behind the desk, then gestured for Dr. Clayborn to sit in a nearby chair.

Suddenly she sprang up like a jack-in-the-box after someone had released the lid. "Oh! I'm sorry, Dr. Clayborn. You sit here." She started walking around the desk and caught her hipbone against the corner of the desk. Her hand immediately went to her side, and a small groan escaped.

"Are you all right, Miss Holmes?"

"Oh, yes. Just a little bump," she assured, but it hurt like anything. She'd undoubtedly have a good-sized bruise. At least, no blood was coming through on the blue suit—yet! She gestured toward her chair. "Please, sit there."

"You sit there," he said. "It's your office."

"Right." Oh, well, if blood came through it would simply match her face, hot enough to burst into flame. "But *you're* interviewing *me*. Not the other way around."

Oh, how ridiculous. She had asked herself every conceivable question he might ask and had gone over her answers several times. But she hadn't thought to consider where they would sit.

"It really doesn't matter where we sit, does it, Miss Holmes?"

"Of–of course not, Dr. Clayborn."

Since he was still standing and she'd have to pass by him to get to a straight chair, she simply retraced her steps, being careful to avoid the corners, and took her seat in the swivel chair behind the desk, reminding herself not to inadvertently turn in circles. Wow! Wasn't she making a terrific impression of a competent assistant!

After she sat down, Dr. Clayborn took the chair beside the desk. "President Hunt informed you of my requirements?" he asked.

Gloria nodded. "His impression was that you want someone to work part-time, take care of correspondence, schedule a few concerts in the surrounding areas, and get brochures and programs printed."

"That, and chauffeur when I have concerts that are

scheduled any distance from the local area," he added.

"I think I could handle that." Then she grimaced. He was at least six feet tall. "But I'm not sure you could fit into the little green bug I drive."

He had an answer for that. "I have my own car."

Ignoring the pain in her hip, Gloria smiled. "There is one thing. I teach a class every Tuesday evening."

He spread his hands. "I have other commitments too. We can work around those. That is, if you take the job."

She assumed President Hunt had sent her résumé to Dr. Clayborn months ago. "You have my résumé?"

He nodded. "It's quite impressive." He paused. "Why do you want this position, Miss Holmes?"

She stared into his deep brown eyes for a long moment. She hadn't anticipated that question. She mustn't say it would be a great honor to work with such a talented performer, a handsome man, a fine man that President Hunt said had great faith and excellent morals, a man in whose gaze she could almost become lost. Realizing she was staring, she looked down at a paper on her desk. She did want the job for all those reasons. When she had been approached about it, she hadn't known William's age or his personal appeal. But now she knew—and she also knew there was a Jane.

That thought brought perspective. Her motivation was still what it had been before she'd seen Dr. Clayborn.

"There are two reasons, actually. The job is temporary. I don't want to tie myself down to a job since I'm not sure if God is calling me to the mission field or if I should seek a permanent job in the States. The other reason is because I want to send my salary to Indonesia."

As she talked, she described the drought in

Indonesia, caused by El Nino, which had brought such devastation to the islands that made up the Asian nation. Children were living in areas where water was contaminated, resulting in terrible skin diseases and deaths due to diarrhea. She spoke of her parents who served on the mission field in Indonesia and how they were involved in a program to raise money to bring clean water to five hundred families.

"I sponsor a little girl named Yuliati," Gloria explained. "She's doing so well in school. Can you imagine," she asked, "that some children who should be in the third grade still can't read or write or speak the national language?"

She didn't wait for him to respond. "Many children as old as ten have never attended school." Her eyes and voice softened. "With the help of those who have so much, are so blessed, this is changing. But I can't ask or expect others to give sacrificially," she explained, "if I'm not willing to do that myself."

Suddenly she stopped talking. She could feel her cheeks flush with embarrassment. How had she let herself go on like that? Taking a deep breath, she sank back against the chair at a loss for words.

"That's most commendable, Miss Holmes. It sounds like a worthy cause."

"Oh, it is, Dr. Clayborn. If you could see the conditions in Indonesia where my parents serve and how the drought has devastated the area, you would know that nothing here in this country can compare with it." Gloria stopped and shook her head as if to clear it. "I could go on forever about those needs. But that's not what we're here for, is it, Dr. Clayborn?"

His gaze shifted to beyond the window behind her, but she felt he was looking at something within himself, rather than the view. "Perhaps it is, Miss Holmes. We need to be open and attentive to whatever surprises the Lord may have for us each day."

Gloria smiled broadly. "That sounds very much like something my friend Tess would say."

"Frankly," Dr. Clayborn admitted, "It's something my grandfather used to say a lot."

"Oh, by the way," Gloria said, "Tess went to school with your grandfather."

"No kidding?"

"That's what she said. They went to the same high school."

Dr. Clayborn nodded. "He lived in the valley. In later years he built a summer home up the mountain. I'm staying there with him now. Um, who is this Tess?"

Just then, a knock sounded on the open door. The two looked up. There stood a radiant Tess wearing a string of pearls and a summer print dress.

Gloria stifled a laugh. She knew what Tess was up to.

"Oh, I'm so sorry if I'm disturbing you," Tess said sweetly.

Sorry, my foot! Gloria thought. Tess's Bible studies always lasted until 11:30, and then she stood around and talked until noon or later. She must have shoved the participants out at 11:30 on the dot. It was only 11:35 now.

Dr. Clayborn stood. Gloria introduced them.

"We were just talking about you," Dr. Clayborn said. "Miss Holmes said you went to school with my grandfather."

"Oh, I could tell you stories about those days."

He lifted his eyebrows in mock chagrin. "You mean he wasn't the model student he claims to be?"

"Oh, he was that. He was senior class president and very smart. He played piano for the chorus and could he sing! We all knew he'd go places with his music." Tess began to shake her head, remembering the past. "It was his jokes that kept us in stitches. You never knew when they'd come. Usually in biology class. We'd be bored stiff and about to fall asleep. He'd raise his hand. The teacher would say, 'Yes, Billy Bob?' "

"Billy Bob?" Dr. Clayborn questioned, surprise in his voice. "He was called Billy Bob?"

"Why, yes," Tess said. "We didn't even know his name was William Robert until many years later after he became famous."

The doctor grinned, apparently pleased he'd learned something about his grandpa that he hadn't known. "Sorry I interrupted you. Please continue."

"Well," Tess said dramatically. "This one incident I remember in particular. I've told it many times. Billy Bob asked, 'You know why Noah never went fishing?' The teacher stared at him over his glasses, and we students did what we'd become accustomed to doing and said in unison while Billy Bob conducted, 'Tell us, Billy Bob, why Noah never went fishing.' Then Billy Bob would get a silly grin on his face and say, 'He only had two worms.' "

After laughing with her, Dr. Clayborn asked, "The teachers let him get away with that?"

"Oh, sure. He was a straight-A student, and everybody liked him. Nothing smart-alecky about him. I think the teachers looked forward to a break in the boredom as much as the rest of us."

"You should come up and visit with him sometime," Dr. Clayborn invited. "I think he'd enjoy talking over old times."

"Oh, he probably wouldn't even remember me," Tess said, brushing away the remark with her hand. Then she lifted her chin, and a smile touched her lips as if she just that moment thought of something. "Gloria and I planned to have lunch in the cafeteria. Would you join us?"

Gloria saw his moment of hesitation before he apologized. "I'm sorry. I would like to, but I have another commitment."

"Perhaps another time," Tess said cordially. "Maybe at my house. I make a mean chocolate cake with double-fudge icing."

"Now that, I need to stay away from. But it is very tempting."

Did he really have another commitment, Gloria wondered, or was it because he felt it improper to fraternize with an employee? Or had he decided not to hire her? After all, who wants to work with a woman so clumsy she runs into something as big as a desk? Then she talks his ear off about Indonesia. Would he think she was nervous about. . .him? Oh boy!

"We're about finished here, aren't we, Miss Holmes?"

"Oh, yes. You're the boss. That is, if you hire me."

Tess lifted a hand. "You two work that out. I'll be in the cafeteria, Gloria."

❄

William said good-bye and stood looking at the doorway a moment, thinking about Tess. He really would enjoy talking with someone who had known his grandfather when he was a boy. He wouldn't mind at all sitting at her table and eating chocolate cake. But that would mean Gloria would be there too.

Gloria. He'd never known a woman who touched his heart and mind quite like she had done. President Hunt had presented him with a woman whose credentials were so high he couldn't argue with them.

He could think of no reason for not hiring her as his assistant. He could not ignore the fact that she was a remarkably attractive woman. That too, was an asset. Making a good appearance was important to the position.

He faced Gloria. "Well, Miss Holmes, as far as I'm concerned, we'll be working together if that suits you."

Gloria extended her hand in agreement and smiled. She lifted her face to his, but her eyes did not quite meet his. "Thank you," she said. "I assume you want to work out of my office."

"Yes, if that meets with your approval. I understand it's another month before students arrive for the fall semester. Most of our work should be done by then, except for fulfilling the obligations. So, might we begin tomorrow morning?"

"Perfect," she said, smiling.

"And," he added congenially, "might we be on a first name basis for our informal settings?"

"Certainly," she said.

Their business settled, William said good-bye and headed for his BMW in the parking lot. An idea came to him as he drove from the campus, through the mountainous community of Highland, up and around the curves where only a few private homes were scattered along the mountainside. His grandpa's weathered log cabin was now a haven to him. In a sense, he felt like he'd come home. Life for so long had been lived in big cities, in his parents' apartment in New York that he had inherited, and in their country home in southern Italy.

He parked on the rough gravel at the side of the cabin and took the side steps onto the porch, past the swing where he and his grandpa had sat last night looking down upon lights that flicked on at dusk like fireflies lighting up the mountainside. It was a peaceful place, yet full of memories of his beloved family that he missed so much.

He stepped on the welcome mat and opened the screen door. Grandpa never locked the doors. He said the only things of value were the grand piano in the music room and his violins. He also said he wasn't any good at playing the violin anymore and if a crook wanted the piano badly enough to get it out of the cabin, he was welcome to it. If a hunter or hiker decided to take refuge in it, then he too was welcome.

Not seeing his grandpa anywhere, William walked through the paneled living room, past the fireplace and the bedrooms, into the kitchen, and out the back door where he heard a thudding sound.

He worried at the sight of the chain saw, a felled tree, and his grandpa splitting wood with an ax. He'd learned long ago, however, not to even try and tell his grandpa how to live his life.

"Getting ready for winter, I see," William said, walking up.

Grandpa glanced up, put the ax down, and walked

over to the back step and sat down in the shade. "It'll be here before you know it. My bones are telling me cold weather's on the way. And look up there in the tops of those maples. Leaves turning already."

William looked. He took a deep breath and tried to smell autumn as his grandpa said he could. William wasn't that adept yet.

"Okay, son," his grandpa said. "How's your new assistant?"

William sat down beside him and bent his head. "Before I get into that, I want to ask you a question."

"Fire away," Grandpa urged.

William pretended to be serious. "Who is this guy called Billy Bob?"

Grandpa stood, his tall frame slightly bent. "I think we'd better go inside and have a bite of lunch while you tell me who you've been talking to."

After he washed up, Grandpa returned to the kitchen where William was making sandwiches from last night's leftover roast beef.

"A lovely lady named Tess Brooks said she went to high school with you."

Grandpa shook his head as he mulled over the name. "Tess Brooks?"

"I don't suppose she was a Brooks then."

"I knew a Tess," Grandpa said, smiling as he remembered. "She was vice president of the senior class. Real nice girl. Pretty too. Everybody liked her, but the guys were kind of scared of her too. She was real strong in her views. Her dad was a preacher. Back then, we had religious emphasis weeks, and her dad always came and preached to us."

"You seem to remember a lot about her," William said.

"Well, sure. I don't have any trouble remembering what happened over sixty years ago. It's where I put my reading glasses two minutes ago that slips my mind." He nodded, going to the refrigerator and taking out the milk. "I thought about asking that little lady out a time or two but never did."

"Why not? Tess gave me the impression you were quite a character."

"Oh no," he said, pouring the milk. "I was considered a brain because I studied and made good grades. And I knew that a fellow who played the piano and sang was called a sissy behind his back. That didn't bother me too much, but it did make me a little self-conscious. That's why I studied jokes and told them to try and be one of the crowd."

William set his grandpa's plate in front of him at the table. As soon as his grandpa said, "Amen," following the blessing, he jumped right in. "I have an idea, Grandpa. Now, I want you to listen carefully before you jump down my throat."

Grandpa looked innocent. "Would I do that?"

William simply snorted at the irony of such a question. "Okay," he began, "you remember how you used to joke about your violin playing when your arthritis began to stiffen your fingers?"

Grandpa gave a slight nod. "There's a saying, son. 'Anyone who can laugh at himself, never ceases to be amused.' And there's another saying, 'There's no sense crying over spilt milk.' Anyway, I've been greatly blessed. I've had it all. I can't complain."

William smiled affectionately, watching his grandpa bite into his sandwich. He knew his grandpa had favored the piano, but his fingers hadn't had the dexterity necessary for concert playing. Being a lover of music, however, and refusing to let his spirit be daunted, he switched to the violin and became one of the world's most acclaimed violinists.

"You might not go for this, but hear me out." Despite his fame, William's grandpa often reverted to some of the old-time sayings like, 'You can't make a silk purse out of a sow's ear.' William considered his grandpa already to be a silk purse. He hoped his idea would not sound like he was trying to make a sow's ear out of him. With fear and trepidation, he plunged in. "Here's my idea."

three

Surprise covered Gloria's face when she opened the door of her office at ten minutes of nine and found William already waiting. "Good morning," she said. "Am I late?"

"Not at all, Gloria," he replied. "I'm early."

She had dressed in a cream-colored pants suit which made her feel comfortably casual. William must have had a similar idea, she thought as she noted his casual slacks and knit shirt. Perhaps he was as eager as she to get the schedule set up so he could prepare accordingly.

"Excuse me," he said abruptly and left Gloria standing in her tracks. She was still standing in the middle of the room when he returned with two foam cups of coffee.

He grinned. "I thought you might like coffee before we get down to business. Cathy says you take yours black."

Surprised and pleased, Gloria managed to say, "Yes. How thoughtful." This was quite a gesture for a world-acclaimed concert pianist. Apparently fame hadn't harmed his ego. He'd even taken the time to learn the secretary's name. He really seemed to be a down-to-earth guy, and he even looked it this morning, dressed in casual attire.

William gestured for her to sit behind the desk, and

Gloria didn't protest this time. Successfully avoiding the corner of the desk, she sat in the swivel chair and placed her briefcase in front of her.

She took a sip of the coffee William had brought for her, carefully returned it to the desk, and unlatched the briefcase. She took out the top folder and opened it. "I made a list of all the civic centers, large auditoriums, and conference centers in the surrounding area. Here—"

He took the folder from her hands and laid it on the desk. She swallowed hard when he scooted his chair closer, but then she turned her chair to face him. His dark eyes danced with a strange expression. "There's been a change in plans," he said.

He's going to fire me, was her first thought. Then she stared at him in disbelief when he said, "You have inspired me to do this. What we can do is set up concerts at local libraries and churches—probably on Sunday nights. We can advertise that the concerts are given to bring attention to the devastation in Indonesia." He grew increasingly animated as he laid out his plans. "We won't charge a fee, but it will be announced that any voluntary donations will be given to help alleviate the pain and suffering of the needy in Indonesia."

"You're serious," she said in awe.

"Absolutely. You say there is a dire need. We will do our best to meet that need."

"You're world renowned," she protested, "yet you would play in small churches to raise money for Indonesia?"

"I would be delighted to do so," he replied, as if it were strange of her to question it.

"I'm. . .speechless," Gloria said.

"Why, Gloria?"

"That's so generous of you."

"Not really. I am not giving more than you. You will give your salary. I will give a small amount of my time."

"Oh, I'm sure you would make much, much more for one concert than I might make in a year."

"That depends upon where the concert is held, who the sponsors are, how many people are in the audience, and the price of the tickets. But we both know that money is not the most fulfilling of things in life, don't we? We cannot buy our loved ones back once they have departed this life. We cannot buy our health."

Gloria detected the concern that clouded his eyes and felt he was thinking of his own loved ones. She could sympathize to a certain extent since she had lost both her maternal and paternal grandparents. Before she could decide whether or not to mention that, he quickly changed the subject.

He pulled his chair closer to the desk. "Grandpa and I have performed together seriously, but we've never done a program together like what I have in mind. I've talked it over with Grandpa, and I think he's considering it. I'd like your opinion of whether or not we should add this to the schedule."

As William outlined his plans, Gloria wondered if Jane would also be added to the schedule or if she was simply the motivating influence behind this wonderful man. Gloria hadn't the nerve to ask about her yet.

four

"Oh, I wouldn't miss seeing Billy Bob again for anything," Tess said when Gloria asked if she'd like to go to the performance with her. William and his grandfather would go in William's car. This was not the type of performance for which William required a driver.

Three weeks had passed since Gloria and William had begun working together each Monday, Wednesday, and Friday. This would be the first program they had planned. The schedule had been set up the way William had suggested. Gloria had taken notices to schools. Articles had appeared in the newspapers. William Clayborn I and III would present a whimsical and serious performance on the piano and violin for children in kindergarten through third grade at the library. The following Saturday would be for students in fourth through sixth grades. The week after would be for sixth through eighth.

The fee was one dollar for adults and a minimum of a coin of their choice for each child. The money would be donated to help get fresh water to children in areas of Indonesia devastated by drought.

The hour program was to begin at 10:00 A.M. Gloria and Tess arrived at 9:30. Only a few other cars were in the parking lot. "I wonder how many children will come out to a musical program," Gloria commented, for the first time concerned about an audience.

"Oh, parents will bring them," Tess said. "Don't worry."

By a quarter to ten, Gloria and Tess sat at a table placed at the entrance to the meeting room. A library assistant and a local newspaper reporter with his video camera were set up at the back of the room. Gloria ceased worrying. Parents and children began to file in. Parents dropped their dollars in the white-covered shoe box marked "Indonesia," and bright-eyed children dropped their coins.

"This is for the children in 'Donesia," said one perky, blue-eyed little girl who carefully placed a bulging envelope in the box.

"Her entire life-savings since Easter," her mother said proudly. "She saves up for projects like this." The mother and child looked at each other with great affection.

A little boy pulled a small wallet from his back pocket and opened it up. Gloria saw he had a five and a one. He pulled out the five. "Is it okay to give money instead of coins?"

"That would be perfectly all right," Gloria answered, her big smile matching that of the eager little boy.

One father whispered, "He actually worked for this money."

At a slight lull, Gloria turned to Tess. "William was absolutely right in suggesting that we ask the children to give a coin." Her light laugh was ironic. "But I don't think anyone gave only one coin."

Tess was not at all surprised. "We could all take a

lesson from the giving spirit of children."

Gloria nodded her agreement and delightedly accepted a couple coins from another child.

The room was filled. Some parents stood at the back so the children could sit in the chairs and see.

Ten o'clock came. Gloria and Tess turned their chairs around toward the two-foot-high stage on which sat a piano with a bench and two chairs at the back wall.

Gloria worried that the children would never be quiet enough for a musical presentation. They were eager to give, but was their attention span long enough? When William had talked the idea over with her, she had thought it fabulous. Now, she wondered if she'd faced the reality of small, active children sitting still for a musical concert.

In the midst of the scuffling, laughing, and loud excited talking, a louder sound like a long extended laugh permeated the room. Some of the children looked around, surprised. The laugh came again, slightly lower, and the children became quieter, some whispering, wondering about the sound. The lower the sound, the quieter the children. By the time William I appeared from a side door, moving slowly across the floor, the laugh from the violin was so soft, the children stared in rapt attention, scarcely breathing in order to hear the sound.

"Good morning," said the tall, lean, gray-haired man with a smile that would win anyone's heart.

"Good morning," the children responded.

"How many of you have a grandpa?"

Hands went up all over.

"I'm Grandpa Clayborn," he said, "and this is my grandson, William." William came from the side door, waving at the children while he quickly crossed over to the piano. Everyone applauded.

Tess nudged Gloria. "Why, he's the same ol' cut-up he was back in school," she said with a pleased expression.

Grandpa moved closer to the piano. "Sometimes the piano argues with the violin."

William hit a note. Grandpa Clayborn played the same note on the violin. Before long, the musical instruments were like competitors trying to make the best argument, and soon they were full-fledged dueling instruments with the children laughing every time Grandpa made weird facial expressions and body motions. Grandpa was the comedian, and William the straight man. The children obviously understood it as if the piano and violin were speaking. Grandpa's facial expressions of struggling to keep up with that piano was as entertaining as the music. The two interrupted each other with the music.

"And sometimes we work together." The two instruments stopped competing and blended their music in a beautiful crescendo. The children sat in rapt attention.

The two men talked about how musical instruments are used in the background of TV programs, movies, and videos. William played base notes on the piano depicting fear. Grandpa produced lighter sounds suggesting flight and dancing.

The children identified with the sounds, understanding background music that accompanied programs they watched on TV.

In between the entertaining segments, both William and his grandpa gave brief examples of playing simply, such as William playing a melody with one finger, then one hand, then both hands, then the two instruments blending their notes.

The two performers played and sang, "Jesus Loves the Little Children," and then had the children join in the song.

The grand finale was a rousing rendition of the children standing and acting out "If You're Happy and You Know It." They clapped their hands, stomped their feet, shook their heads, and turned around enthusiastically to the exciting sound of music.

Gloria was pleased with the program. Despite Grandpa's being the star of the show, she saw a playful side of William that she hadn't seen before seen. The two men were obviously energized by their receptive young audience, many of whom stood around the stage asking questions, particularly of Grandpa and his seemingly magic talking violin.

After others had left, William reintroduced Grandpa and Tess, who immediately began to discuss high school days like old friends. William helped the library attendant who was putting away the video equipment.

Gloria picked up the box of money. She'd take it home, count it, and get it to the bank first thing Monday morning.

"Let's all stop somewhere for lunch," Grandpa suggested.

"I made a big chicken pot pie this morning," Tess said, "just in case somebody might stop in for lunch. All we have to do is heat it up in the microwave. How does that sound?"

Grandpa was delighted, and when Gloria said she would share with them a letter she'd received from her sponsored Indonesian girl, William appeared eager to accept.

"Billy Bob's still down-to-earth like he always was," Tess said as Gloria drove them home. "You'd think a world-famous person like that would have gotten uppity. And that grandson of his is a doll, don't you think?"

Watching the traffic, Gloria replied, "He's very nice."

❄

Since Tess had already seen the letter, she insisted upon putting lunch on the table while Gloria showed William and Grandpa her letter from Yuliati. The three of them stood in the living room as Gloria read the letter to them.

"Dear Mama Gloria," Gloria read. "Yuliati calls me mama," she explained and laughed delightedly, glancing from William to Grandpa, who smiled warmly at her enthusiasm.

> *With this letter I inform you that I and my grandma and grandfa are fine. I hope you and Tess are too. Our family prays everytime for your health and your successful.*
>
> *I received birthday gift from you amount US$ 20.00 (Rp. 129.500). I spent it for buying a dress and three mother hens. And I also saving of the rest. In my village we still have no rain. Is it snow in your country? Is it cold?*
>
> *O ya mama.*

Gloria stopped reading long enough to say, "Isn't that darling. I mean, can't you just hear her saying, 'O ya mama'?"

Yes, William could imagine it. Gloria had a warm, loving spirit. He could very well imagine her as a wonderful mama.

Gloria continued.

> *O ya mama, I am learning English too here, writing and reading. But I cannot speak English very well yet, it's quite difficult for me, but someday, I hope I can be able to master it and be number one in my family. Please pray to God for me.*
>
> *My grandfa and grandma send you're a sweet regards. That's all my news. See you in the next letter."*
>
> *Love,*
> *Yuliati*

Gloria folded the letter and returned it to the envelope, then stepped over to a side table and picked up a small picture in a frame. "This is Yuliati and her grandparents," she said.

"She sounds precious," Grandpa said solemnly, looking at the photograph for a long moment before handing it to William.

What could he say? The child looked thin and haggard. So did her grandparents. Their ill-fitting clothing seemed to hang on their gaunt frames. The photo was black and white. The three of them stood, barefooted, in front of what appeared to be a one- or two-room, flat-roofed structure that looked as if it could be made of boards. There was a door but no window on the front. The picture revealed no trees or foliage of any kind—not even grass.

"She's one of the fortunate ones," Gloria said. "She

has a sponsor. Many children couldn't begin to get a new dress, or buy hens, or put away money for an emergency." She pointed to the box of money on the coffee table. "This will save lives," she said.

William stared a while longer at the "fortunate" little girl, and for an instant he thought his heart would break. He and his family had always given to the church and donated to charities. That was the least they could do. But he was beginning to understand the difference between giving out of a sense of duty and giving out of a caring heart.

❄

During lunch, Tess and Grandpa dominated the conversation, talking about olden days and how the area had changed during the years. Afterward, Tess took Grandpa out to the garden to gather some tomatoes for him to take home.

William asked if he could help with the dishes, and Gloria told him no. "Tess would be upset if a guest in her house washed the dishes."

William took a sip of coffee, then leaned comfortably back in the kitchen chair. "It's good to see Grandpa out and about," he said. "He hasn't given a concert in years because of the arthritis in his hands. He's felt rather washed up as a musician. But this has revived him. Although he is a man of strong faith and good humor, he'd sort of given up on performing. I think he sees now he doesn't have to give a concert in order to be effective."

"It was wonderful," Gloria said. "He related to the children so well."

"He's always done that sort of thing on a smaller scale around children and even in groups of adults."

Gloria could tell William loved his grandfather very much. "It's amazing," she said, "how two grown men could keep a roomful of little kids entertained for an hour."

William smiled warmly and stood. "Come into the living room and I'll show you. That is, if you think Tess won't mind if I use her piano."

"You use that piano, and she'll have it bronzed," Gloria jested, leading the way into the living room.

She hovered at his shoulder while William sat on the piano bench and positioned his hands. He played a simple, light airy tune and abruptly switched to a dramatic bass. Gloria gave a light laugh at the difference.

"Ah!" he exclaimed triumphantly, looking up at her, "It worked. You laughed. You see, music has a language of its own, a mood you can feel."

She began to understand his meaning. "You and your grandfather did a lot of that abrupt change."

"Exactly," he said. "It's the same principal as when one falls down. Another laughs because it's unexpected. It's the sudden change that causes the reaction. Abruptness is funny."

"I see," she said. "So you and your grandfather used that principle to plan your program. The dueling instruments act on that same principle."

"Yes," he said. "And we combined the difference or the contrast of my being serious and Grandpa being funny. It makes for good entertainment."

"Makes sense," she said, "and it worked. As you can tell, I'm no student of music or performing."

William glanced up. "I'm glad," he said. "Otherwise what would we talk about?"

"Hmmm, good point," she said and laughed.

He turned his attention back to the piano. "But for adults or for a serious concert," he said quickly, "there must be a bridge between a change in tones." He played the same notes he'd done before, but this time he moved gradually from the high notes to the low.

Gloria could readily see what he meant by the bridge. "Well, I learned something today," she said.

William laughed and stood. Gloria stepped aside. For an instant his gaze lingered on her face. "Well," he said formally, "thanks again for the lunch. I think I'll walk outside a little. I'll be waiting in the car."

Gloria wondered what she'd done to chase him away. Had he noticed that she had difficulty tearing her eyes away from his? Did he sense that when she was near him her pulse accelerated? Could he see the warmth she felt in her cheeks when he was close? And when he'd risen from the piano bench, had he been aware that she stood so close to him? Oh, why was her brain so befuddled around him? She dared not answer.

One thing she did know. He had left abruptly.

But it wasn't funny.

❄

"I asked Billy Bob about Jane," Tess said later that afternoon after the two women had settled in the living room to read.

Gloria's mouth opened and her book closed. "What did he say?"

Tess simply shook her head. "Billy Bob wouldn't tell me. He said he didn't think William would approve. The situation involves William's faith, career, and daily living."

Tess lifted her eyebrows as if there were plenty of room for speculation there. Gloria didn't want to do too much of that. She must simply accept that Jane, judging by William's dedications and by his own grandfather's admission, was the most important person in his life.

Gloria found her place in the book, but after a long time realized she wasn't reading. She glanced at Tess, who quickly looked at her own magazine as if she had not been watching Gloria. She forced herself to read the words before her. However, in the back of her mind was the knowledge that she could admire and like William Robert Clayborn III but must keep in strict abeyance any stronger emotions.

five

In September, students returned to campus. The noise of excited young people filled the air, bringing back Gloria's memories of her own school days when she had been earning her bachelor's degree. She'd thought that was tough until she went to graduate school to earn her master's and realized how carefree the college days really were.

Two weeks into the semester, her Tuesday night adult education class started, which meant she'd get in bed around midnight and soon have original and revised essays to grade, as well as lessons to prepare.

The work for William was a welcome respite. Most of the concert dates were set. He continued to stop in on Mondays, Wednesdays, and Fridays to confirm schedules and have her respond to letters.

One day after they'd finished working, his eyes filled with mischief, and with a rather silly looking grin on his face, he said, "O ya mama, how is our little Yuliati?"

Gloria threw back her head and laughed. It wasn't often William let her see his playful side. She loved it! From then on, she shared every letter with him. She knew that Yuliati had come to symbolize to him the difference that even small donations could make to needy children in a devastated country.

It was a good feeling. She felt it every month when

she wrote the sponsor check for Yuliati and when she sent her weekly salary. She knew William felt it every time he signed a check for the amount his and Grandpa's library performances brought in.

Then October was upon them, bringing with it cool days, marked by brisk winds, cold nights, and gradual changes from a lush green world to the deep red leaves of dogwood and heralding the beginning of fall along with the beginning of William's Sunday night concerts at churches.

Gloria had expected to drive William to the local church concerts, but he decided that he would drive himself, the trips ranging from only ten to thirty minutes. William was pleased that his grandpa would attend the concerts. As he told Gloria, "He had planned to keep a low profile, but has decided to join the human race again."

Since Gloria would not be driving William, Tess decided to go too. Billy Bob sat with them at each concert. Children and parents came up to him, saying how much they enjoyed his performances at the library. Many adults would ask about the conditions in Indonesia, while children with big, inquisitive expressions in their eyes looked on. Gloria knew that they, too, cared.

The Sunday night concerts were more serious and were videotaped. Before he began, William looked toward the camera and said, "This concert is dedicated to Jane." Then he would launch right into saying what a pleasure it was to be asked to perform. He told about his grandfather having been raised in the area, going to area schools, and working his way through music school. Between pieces, he talked about his education and his parents and told stories about various places in the world where he'd played and what he'd seen.

He played hymns such as "My Jesus I Love Thee," "Great Is Thy Faithfulness," and others the audience could readily recognize. He asked them to sing "Amazing Grace" with him. Then he played some of his own compositions. With the world a riot of color and the leaves at their peak the third week in October, his rendition of "Autumn Leaves" was particularly well received.

The audience loves him, Gloria thought. She stared at him, long and hard, the sentence lodged in her heart and mind. She refused to allow the thought to go further but felt a fear take root in her heart as her mind continued to echo, *The audience loves him.*

It had rained all week. William hoped it would stop before the concert scheduled for Greenland, South Carolina, two hours away. However, the day of the concert brought flash flood watches in the low-lying areas and near creeks. November winds roared through the trees and shook the tops as if trying to make the last brown leaf fall to the ground.

Grandpa came down with a bad cold, and the rainy weather made his arthritis and his foul humor act up. "I'm not stepping a foot out of this house till it clears up," he asserted.

William called to tell Gloria and Tess that Grandpa wouldn't be going. Tess answered the phone. Upon hearing the reasons that Grandpa couldn't make it, Tess said, "Oh, good. Not that I want him to be ailing, mind you, but I have not looked forward to going all the way to South Carolina in this storm."

William could identify with that!

"I know what," she said cheerily. "I'll take Billy Bob some chicken soup and red raspberry cobbler I made this morning from the berries growing on my vines in the backyard. That'll cure anything."

"In that case," William said, laughing, "I might cancel the concert and sit here in a rocking chair with an afghan over my legs and wait for you."

The rain had let up some by the time William arrived at Tess's to pick Gloria up, which he had insisted upon doing. He would let her drive down the mountain since he needed to keep his fingers limber and didn't need the pressure of watching traffic in the rain. As soon as he pulled into the driveway at Tess's, the front door opened and Gloria stepped out on the porch. She hesitated at the edge, looked out at the steady rain, then raised her umbrella and hurried to the car.

Not until she appeared at the driver's side did he realize he needed to slide over into the passenger seat. *She's an employee and this is her job*, he reminded himself.

He'd never had to remind himself of such a thing before hiring Gloria. It had been a given. And too, he'd always ridden in the back of a limo, and the driver had always been male. Of course, those concerts had been on a larger scale. This was different.

Yes, very different. It had been easier remembering that he and Gloria worked together when they were setting up schedules and attending to business. Once they'd begun going to concerts together, he'd grown accustomed to her sitting in a seat near the front. Invariably, his eyes would search for her, and he would remind himself how good it was to see a familiar face in the audience, someone in rapt attention, as if spurring him on, believing in him, appreciating him. The audience always appreciated his work, but concerts were extra special since he'd begun to rely on someone he knew being there. Gloria brought a special warmth to his heart. He'd come to depend on her. And of course, he needed her.

She opened the door and jumped in. "Whoa, it's raining gorillas out there," she said and shivered. Little raindrops had splashed on her face, and a few wet spots were on her hair.

As if reading his thoughts, she pushed at her locks. "This kind of weather makes my hair curl."

Before he could tell her that her hair was perfectly acceptable, quite pretty in fact, and the faint odor of her perfume was delightful, she looked over her shoulder toward the backseat where the tux was in plain view. "You have your shoes, socks, and hair-grooming kit with you, I suppose?" she asked.

He assured her that he did. She was doing her job, making sure he had everything. She dug into her raincoat pocket. "Here's a copy of the program," she said. "They're printed and waiting at the auditorium."

"Very good," he said and scanned the program while she became familiar with the car's controls. They engaged in light conversation, with her asking about Grandpa and talking about the weather.

"Is Tess really going out in this downpour?" he asked.

"Oh, yes. She calls it liquid sunshine." Gloria laughed. It was a nice laugh. "Besides, she says she knows these roads like the back of her hand, so she'll be fine."

He smiled, watching as Gloria became more relaxed

driving the BMW for the first time.

"The forecast for Greenland is the same as here," she said.

William noted her hesitation, as if she wanted to say more. "You're wondering if people will come to a concert in this storm," he guessed.

Her laugh was light. "It crossed my mind."

He gave a short laugh. "Do you really think people will stay home because of rain, when the concert is given to raise money because of a drought?"

"Since you put it that way. . ." She grinned, watching the entrance ramp as she pulled up to the interstate.

Once she was on the interstate, mingling with traffic, and appeared relaxed with the car, William glanced over the program again, although he knew the schedule by heart. Then he switched on the CD he'd recorded of the music he would play at the concert. He rested his head back against the seat and let the sound penetrate his consciousness. He must concentrate on the concert.

❄

Tess didn't bother to call Billy Bob. He might say, "Don't come, I don't feel like having company." She'd made up her mind. There were a few things she had to get off her mind.

Billy Bob must have seen the car lights against the window. He met her at the door, looking like he was really glad to see her. "Here, let me help you with that," he said, taking the plastic-covered basket from her cold hands.

He set it on the floor, then helped her off with her coat and hung it on a hook near the fireplace. "Warm yourself," he said, nodding toward the brightly burning fire. "I'll just put this in the kitchen."

"Go ahead and pour the soup, if you'd like. It's probably still hot. I'll be right there."

"You're not going to make me eat alone, are you?" he asked, stopping at the doorway to look at her over his shoulder.

"Food tastes better when it's shared," she said.

"Spoken like a true Christian," he replied.

Tess looked into the fire and smiled and rubbed her hands together. They felt plenty warm enough. She went into the kitchen where Billy Bob had set the basket on the table. He got two bowls from the cupboard. Tess took the thermos, hot rolls, and cobbler from the basket.

Billy Bob's eyes grew big with wonder when she began to pour the soup into a bowl. "I see carrots, chunks of chicken, and big noodles. This can't be homemade, now, can it, Tess?"

"Why, you don't think I'd bring you canned soup, do you?"

"Oh, I hoped not. My Cora never gave me canned soup."

Tess smiled. "I was a nurse, you know. Nothing like homemade chicken soup to cure what ails you. And being on the mission field for so long, there were a lot of things that ailed a lot of people."

"You've done a good life's work, Tess," he said.

"You haven't done too badly yourself, Billy Bob—getting yourself all world-famous." She pulled out a chair and sat at the table.

He snorted as if that were nothing and took his seat across from her. Being accustomed to holding hands with William when they prayed, he reached across the table.

Tess detected that moment of uncertainty in his eyes. She smiled. "Gloria and I pray this way too," she said. "You do the honors?"

Billy Bob prayed for the safety of William and Gloria, for the success of the concert, and for travelers in the rain and gave thanks for the rain, for the food, and for Tess.

After the "Amen," he uncovered the bread basket. "Homemade rolls too," he said. "Did I tell you Cora was a good cook?"

"You did," she said. "It's good to hear a man compliment his wife like that. My Bertram always appreciated my cooking. He was a man with a great faith in God. Cooking for him was the least I could do."

"Sounds like you two complemented each other," Billy Bob said.

During supper and later in front of the cozy fire, they exchanged talk about their spouses. It was good remembering, sharing about loved ones who had gone on before them.

"I'd looked forward to coming back up here and being a recluse," Billy Bob said after a while. "But after William talked me into giving that little program for the children at the library and seeing how much they liked it, and then getting reports of how much good that money does for Indonesia, I wonder if maybe the Lord's not through with me yet."

"Well, the way I feel," Tess said, "as long as we're here on earth, there's plenty for us to do. There's plenty that needs to be done."

"I've had it all, done it all," Billy Bob said. "There were times when I went off track some, but the Lord and Cora always brought me back." He smiled reminiscently. "I think I'm ready to get back into living—on a small scale. Get involved at church or something. Make a few friends."

"I hope you include me among them," Tess said.

"Either that or hire you as a cook," he answered.

"I'm not for hire!"

"Oh, I'm kidding you. We have a woman come in and clean twice a week. She does some cooking for us, but William and I enjoy preparing our own meals for the most part. I think you and I might be friends. I'm not afraid of you anymore. At least, not too much."

"Afraid?" What was he talking about?

"Oh, in high school all us fellows were afraid of your dad. We thought you were real pretty but couldn't bear going up to your house and having him open the front door and ask what we were doing there. We were sure he'd tell us where to go, and being a man of God, he had pull with the Creator."

They both laughed. "And too," he added. "We thought Bertram had an inside track with you."

"That he did," Tess agreed. "From the time when I was fourteen and I first saw Bertram when he and his family joined our church, I never had eyes for any other fellow." She smiled, remembering. "Both of us felt God had a special mission for us, together."

"And so He did," Billy Bob said. "And He gave me a wonderful woman. Now that I'm rejoining the human race, I think I can enjoy the memories of happy times."

Tess agreed. "It takes a while. Sometimes you have to go on living and doing, and eventually the feeling comes back."

Billy Bob nodded, looking into the fire. "I think you and I can be friends, Tess."

Now, that was settled. She supposed she could lead up to the question she'd wanted to ask for a long time.

Slowly, softly, she said, "Billy Bob. . .what do you think of my Gloria?"

"Oh," he said immediately. "Lovely girl. William has been pleased with her work from the beginning."

She leaned forward toward him. "What about personally, Billy Bob?" she asked, pointedly.

William was right. It appeared no one had stayed away because of rain. Gloria always felt anxiety before a performance, as if she were the featured performer. However, judging by the applause before intermission, no spirits were dampened by the weather.

She relaxed more after the intermission, her eyes fastened on William, absorbed in his music. Without consciously thinking about it, she was aware that William was a man she respected and admired. He fit the pattern, like her dad did, of everything she could hope for in a Christian man.

Except. . .she had doubts about his private life. Was he involved? But that was not for her to judge—she must remember that he was off-limits. Before she knew it, the concert had ended. William had given another standing ovation performance for an appreciative packed house.

Gloria was making her way backstage to wait while William changed into his casual clothes for the drive up the mountain. Someone pecked her on the shoulder and she turned.

"Pardon me," an elderly woman said. "I'm the mother of the director. I came in through the private entrance too and saw you enter with the pianist. I wonder, I mean, are you Jane?"

"Oh, no. No, I'm. . .not."

"Forgive me for being so forward. I just thought—"

"It's quite alright," Gloria said and hurried away from the embarrassed woman, unable to think of anything to say that might make either of them feel any better.

The incident was still occupying Gloria's mind a few minutes later as she and William were being escorted by a security guard to the private entrance where the BMW was waiting.

"I'll drive," William said. The guard opened the passenger door for Gloria and gave William the keys.

As William walked around the car, Gloria took the opportunity to reprimand herself for being upset by the older woman's words. William had a right to his private life, and she was an employee. Just because he'd decided to drive didn't change anything. Forcing herself into the employee mode as he slid into the driver's seat, she quipped, "Does this mean I'll get a cut in pay? Or don't you trust my driving up the mountain in the rain?"

"Maybe 'no comment' would be in order here," he returned. "I might get myself in trouble." Then he laughed and looked at Gloria with mischief in his eyes. She could tell he wasn't exhausted, as he had said he often was after a performance. Rather, he seemed exhilarated. He turned the key in the ignition, switched on the lights, and looked ahead, following the directions of the guard who motioned him toward the exit.

"To be truthful, Gloria," he said, going up the exit

ramp, "if anything, you deserve a raise. I think you know how pleased I am with your work."

Yes, she thought as he pulled out into the rain, *it had been a good night. A successful night.*

Despite the weather, the first big concert they'd planned together had been a huge success. But it wasn't over yet. Her job was still to get him safely home, even though he was driving.

"You don't mind a backseat driver, do you?" she asked.

"On a night like this, I'll take all the help I can get," he replied seriously, leaning forward slightly to peer through the heavy rain drenching the windshield despite the wipers running on high.

Gloria brought to mind the map that the director had sent her weeks ago and his words of direction before they left the civic center. She watched the black asphalt roads that looked like mirrors, reflecting the glare of car, street, and store lights. Hard, blowing rain battered the vehicles. "The interstate should be coming up soon on your left," she said.

Once they were on the interstate, she breathed more easily. There was less traffic and less glare. William seemed more relaxed too as the BMW smoothly made its way toward the mountains.

They conversed easily. William talked about his grandfather and the great influence the man had always been on him. As a young child, he'd spent more time with his grandparents than with his parents, whose careers took them traveling around the world. He talked about the opera and how his parents loved it. "But they worked hard at it," he said. "The Italian word for *work* is *opera. Operio* is a laborer."

Gloria hadn't known that but smiled at how William rolled the *r* when saying *operio*.

"But it's always been fun too," William added. "There was always friendly competition and loving bantering when we were together as a family." He laughed, remembering. "But it was Grandpa who would always remind us that it is the music of the violin that calmed the soul of Mary Shelly's Frankenstein."

"I have experienced that calming effect," Gloria said, then quickly added, "not that I'm anything like Frankenstein."

He laughed with her. She explained. "I never thought I could sit for hours listening to classical music. But I'm beginning to understand music a little. It touches my heart and soul."

"I grew up with Bach, Beethoven, Mozart, Liszt," he said. "And I wanted to play their music, sing, write my own, and enjoy it. I wanted to be world-famous, like my Grandpa and my parents." After a pause, he added, "But what I've done these past few months has been just as fulfilling. Maybe more, because I can relate on a personal level with children and adults in church who have the same kind of faith I have."

He glanced over, and Gloria smiled. Such a tender expression was on his face, such warmth in his eyes. She loved this, being in the car with William, the two of them apart from the rest of the world, in the darkness of the car, the rain keeping out anything that might intrude. Her pulse raced. Could he be thinking of staying in the area? Would they continue working together? Going to concerts together? Talking like this?

"But do you know what's the best part of these local concerts?" he asked.

Gloria held her breath, wondering what he might say. Would it be something akin to what she had been thinking?

His words brought her back to reality. "It's donating the proceeds to the children in Indonesia. I have my charities, and they are very special to me. But in these past months, the Indonesian project is close to my heart. I pray for Yuliati and those children in Indonesia. I picture clean water being piped in, another child starting to school, families planting and harvesting their crops. I like the picture."

"It's happening that way, William," she said. "Relief organizations and my parents report that crops are being planted. Social workers, local school teachers, and community leaders are joining together to improve both education and diet."

He smiled. "And Yuliati is thriving?"

"Under the circumstances," Gloria replied. "The sponsorship enables her to stay in school and be eligible for low-cost medical treatment. My parents stay in touch with her family and keep me informed."

The conversation soon turned to Tess and the years she had spent on the mission field in Korea. "We have wonderful talks about the mission work she did and that my parents have done."

"Speaking of Tess," he said, "Grandpa said she invited him and me to have Thanksgiving dinner at her house."

"Yes, she mentioned that," Gloria said, trying not to sound too excited.

"Grandpa says he might take her up on it. But I have another engagement."

Yes, Gloria reminded herself. *He has a private life that I know nothing about.*

She also told herself the reason the conversation dwindled after his remark of "another engagement" was because they'd reached Highland and he had to concentrate more on oncoming traffic.

The rain had slackened to a steady downpour by the time they pulled into Tess's driveway. William switched off the engine and turned toward Gloria while she attempted to put her hood over her head. He reached out to help, and she felt the brush of his velvet touch against her cheek.

He quickly moved his hand to the back of the seat, while she looked at her purse in her hands and grasped it firmly.

"Thank you for a wonderful evening, Gloria," he said, and she turned her face toward him in wonder. There had been something special in his words, or in the tone of them—as if they had just returned from a date. It took all her strength to remind herself this had not been a date. It was a job. And at times when she thought there was a special look in his eyes, it was probably either her own reflection or her own longing. From somewhere deep within her being, she understood how someone could be tempted to care too much for a person who belonged to another.

God forgive me, she whispered silently. Smiling, she said to William, "Good night. Be careful going up the mountain."

She opened the car door, held the coat at her neck

to prevent its falling from her shoulders, and hurried up the walk, across the lighted porch, and into the house.

Leaning against the door, she closed her eyes, hearing the engine start. He was driving away. Her errant thoughts must go away too.

"Gloria?" Tess called.

Her eyes flew open, and she saw Tess reading by lamplight. Gloria turned quickly and threw the bolt on the door. "It. . .it's raining," she said needlessly, hoping Tess would think the flush in her cheeks was because she'd run in out of the weather. She shucked out of her coat, noting that it really wasn't wet except for a few drops on the shoulders.

She hung it in the foyer closet then walked into the living room as Tess asked about the road conditions.

"He drove back," Gloria said and began describing the concert.

"I'm sure the audience loved him, as usual," Tess said.

Gloria agreed and gave Tess the details. "How was Grandpa?"

"He's going to make it," Tess reported. "He said he'd come for Thanksgiving dinner. In fact, he said neither hail nor high water would keep him from it."

Gloria smiled. "William can't come. Well, I'd better get to bed."

"Me, too," Tess said and stood. Her heart went out to Gloria, trying so hard not to be in love with William. But it was in her tender voice, in her wistful eyes when she spoke of him. Tess didn't dare mention and didn't even know how to pray about the situation—about William and Jane, the situation Billy Bob had revealed to her and about which he had sworn her to secrecy.

Later in bed that night, Gloria kept staring into the darkness toward the ceiling as the rain slapped against the window in frustrated drops. The wind sometimes whispered quietly, “The audience loved him.” Then again it picked up, howling loudly, “No, I’m not Jane.”

But I’m going to find out just who she is. I think it’s time I asked.

six

William was driving along at a pretty good clip, pleased that Thanksgiving Day was clear with only a few fluffy white clouds in the bright blue sky. The air was windy and cold but invigorating. He'd left home shortly after Grandpa had left for Tess's. They'd be having a tasty meal, he was sure. But what William had to do was far more important than observing a traditional Thanksgiving.

He was humming along with a CD of Handel, reminding him of the mood he wanted in the composition he was writing for Jane. Suddenly he felt a difference in the BMW. It seemed to be veering to the right. By the time he recognized the problem, the car was definitely leaning to the right. He pulled off to the side of the interstate, got out, and sure enough, the right front tire was flat.

Although he had the equipment in the trunk, he'd never changed a tire in his life. He didn't have time to practice. Jane was expecting him. Returning to the car, he reached into the glove compartment for the road service number and dialed it on his cell phone. After coming close to arguing with the person on the other end of the line, he accepted the fact that it would be an hour or more before road service could reach him.

He gave them instructions and, after a moment's

deliberation with himself, knew he had no choice but to call his grandfather. This was Thanksgiving Day. He'd made a few friends he felt he could count on in times of trouble, but it wouldn't be fair to take them away from a family dinner on a holiday.

Besides, he didn't know any of their phone numbers. He dialed Tess's. Gloria answered and in response to his questions said that they hadn't eaten yet but were about ready to sit down. He asked to speak to his grandfather.

Grandpa listened to William's problem and his description of where he was located on the interstate. "Be there as soon as possible."

After hanging up, Grandpa related the situation to Gloria and Tess. "So, I'd better go and see what I can do."

"I'll go," Gloria offered. "You stay and enjoy your dinner. After all, I am William's employee."

"Well," Grandpa said, "what's an old man to do when challenged by an insistent young woman?"

After Gloria grabbed a jacket and left the house, Grandpa's eyes met Tess's questioning ones.

"Do you think that's a good idea?" Tess asked.

"I don't know," he said. "Could be I've just invited the wrath of God." He reached for the sweet potatoes. "Or worse, the wrath of William."

As soon as Gloria pulled up in front of his BMW and parked the little green bug, William opened the passenger door and forced himself into the cramped space. "I expected Grandpa," he said. He laid his cell phone on the dashboard, shifted to put his briefcase on the back seat, fastened the seat belt, and looked quite uncomfortable. He took up a lot more space than Tess. Gloria would have to be careful that they didn't rub shoulders!

"But I do appreciate this," he said as Gloria pulled out onto the interstate at the first opportunity. William gave directions, then punched in a number on the cell phone. When someone answered he said, "William Clayborn here. Please tell Jane that I've been delayed, but I'm on my way and should be there in about twenty minutes."

There really is a Jane, Gloria thought but was soon distracted by the need to follow William's directions.

"Take the next exit to the right," he said. After the turn, he gave instructions for other turns. She had been in this area before when she'd taken Tess to visit a friend who had a house on several acres of pasture on which cattle grazed.

Yes, I'll ask William about Jane, Gloria resolved as the flow of directions momentarily stopped. "Beautiful countryside," she found herself saying.

"Yes it is," William said absently. "Not many level stretches of land in these mountains." He again looked at his watch. "By the way, road service will fix the flat and deliver my car here, so I won't need to impose on you further."

"I don't mind," she said.

"Thanks," he replied. He was saying the right things, but Gloria knew his mind was elsewhere. He gazed out the window. "Turn left at the next road."

It was a long, winding road. She'd never been this far out but soon came to chain link fencing enclosing land, apparently as well kept and immaculate as a golf course green.

Following his directions, she turned onto the land at

the open gate and drove a long distance up a paved drive until she came to a wrought-iron fence with a one-room building beside it. After she stopped and William identified himself, the gate opened and she drove through. Bordering the drive and immaculate lawn was an evergreen hedge as far as the eye could see. Several evergreen trees dotted the landscape.

Soon, perched on a slope, a long, modern, one-story building came into view, gleaming white in the bright afternoon sunshine. Flanking the building were oaks, maples, and lush magnolias.

"Park in front," William directed, and she turned onto a curved flagstone drive, wide enough for two cars. In front of the porch and along the walkway was a myriad of shrubs, orange and yellow marigolds, and red and yellow asters.

Then she noticed the white sign ahead of her at the edge of the flower bed. "Faith Hospital" stood out in black letters. Hospital? It was small for a hospital. It must be private. William's beloved Jane must be a nurse or a doctor.

"I really appreciate this, Gloria," he said as he opened the car door. "I'm sorry to have inconvenienced you."

"It's all right," she said, before he closed the door. *Well, don't just sit here*, she told herself and put her hands on the keys in the ignition. She didn't want to see the woman who had stolen William's heart. Yet, another part of her wanted to see—to know beyond a doubt that William belonged to someone else.

Just as William walked in front of the car, Gloria remembered the briefcase. At that same moment she saw an expression of joy transform his face. His eyes shone with emotion. His lips turned into a tremulous smile. Who could cause such a transformation in him?

Like a magnet, her eyes were drawn to the open door of the hospital. Then she saw her. A tall, elegant woman in dark slacks and a cream-colored blouse. She had a classic face and black hair smoothed back into a bun. A young girl, who looked to be about fourteen, stood beside her.

As William strode up the wide concrete walk, Gloria wondered if Jane had a daughter. William reached the entry and opened his arms. The girl rushed into them. William lifted her as if she were a little child, and the girl put her arms around his neck. Her eyes closed, and her fair face was a picture of pure love.

Gloria got the briefcase and stood at the car door, waiting until the right moment to call to him. She should do it before he embraced Jane.

"Dr. Clayborn," she called.

William turned. Gloria stood rooted to the ground and held out the briefcase. The young girl looked over her shoulder. She tugged on William's arm and said something, prompting him to beckon. "Miss Holmes, do you have a minute?"

A minute? Gloria felt she'd just lived a lifetime. What was a minute more? Slowly, her feet came unglued while her brain remained in limbo. She was about to meet Jane, the mystery woman in William's life.

"Jane," he said. "This is Miss Gloria Holmes, my efficient assistant who I told you about."

Gloria was about to lift her hand to the woman, but the woman had walked away toward someone inside who had summoned her just as William was saying,

"Miss Holmes, meet my sister, Jane."

Sister? Jane? His sister? This young girl with flawless complexion, white like milk. A thin face surrounded by black curly hair. Eyes, large, brilliant blue. This was Jane?

"Will you stay, Miss Holmes?" Jane asked, her eyes bright with expectation. "I'd like for her to, Willy-wum, pretty please with sugar on it?"

He shook his head and smiled wryly, as if to say he could refuse her nothing. "If it's not an imposition. . . ," William began.

"Please, Miss Holmes," Jane pleaded.

"Only if you call me Gloria," she answered, smiling, trying not to reveal that it just dawned upon her that there was a reason this young girl was at Faith Hospital. Was she an aide? A volunteer? But when Jane walked over to her, Gloria felt the bony arm against hers, covered by the long-sleeved loose sweater. The girl was thin. Her skin translucent. Suddenly Gloria understood. Jane was ill.

The tall woman returned to them after Gloria, William, and Jane entered a spacious elegant room with several living room groupings. Lighted Christmas trees seemed rather out of place on a sunny Thanksgiving Day. But if this was a children's hospital, it seemed likely decorations would be put up early for them to enjoy. Gloria assumed it was a visitor's waiting room.

Jane excitedly talked about the decorations. "We just put them up yesterday. Well, not we," she corrected. "They put them up. But I helped decorate the one in the parlor."

"Sorry I had to leave so abruptly," the woman said. "I'm Ana Kesin."

"Gloria Holmes," William said before Gloria could introduce herself.

"Nice to meet you," Ana Kesin said with a friendly smile, then glanced at William. "Go into the parlor if you like," she said. She shared a secretive smile with Jane.

"I'll say good-bye," Gloria began, not wanting to intrude.

"Oh, please stay. Make her stay, Willy-wum."

William looked helplessly at Gloria. "Could you?"

"I would like that," Gloria could honestly say. She was drawn to this beautiful girl, so open with her wishes, so delighted with Christmas decorations, so loving of her brother.

William looked apologetically at Gloria. "I can't refuse her anything."

"Then neither will I," Gloria said and followed Jane to the parlor.

The parlor looked like a living room that might be in many homes. A comfortable couch faced a fireplace, obviously gas-burning, since no wood was in evidence. That gave a cozy glow to the carpeted room, with its long windows flanked by lined drapes.

But it was to the piano set out from a corner that Jane rushed. "Ta daaa," she said, gesturing with her hand, facing William, who had stopped at the doorway.

"It came," he said.

"Yes," Jane exclaimed. "Thank you very much, William."

"It was your suggestion and your money," William countered, coming over to touch the shiny baby grand.

"Oh, but I wouldn't have known what to get. You know everything. Well," she tilted her head and wrinkled her small nose. "Maybe not *everything.*"

"Just what is it that I don't know?" he asked, feigning chagrin.

She shrugged one shoulder and grinned impishly. "It's a secret."

"Do you play, Jane?" Gloria asked.

"Not much," she said. "My mind knows what it wants to do, but my fingers just won't obey."

Seeing a painful look cross William's eyes, Gloria apologized. "I'm sorry. I shouldn't have—"

Jane reached out and grasped her hands. "Oh, no. You don't need to be sorry. I'll even be glad to tell you all about my sorrows." She screwed up her face as if she had no sorrows at all. Then she turned accusing eyes toward William. "He's the one who doesn't want to face the facts. He won't open his mouth about it." She looked back at Gloria with wide eyes. "But everybody knows I can't keep my mouth shut."

Gloria returned her smile, not knowing what to think or how to respond. William stepped over and mussed Jane's soft curly hair. "You're right about that."

She playfully hit him on the arm, then turned to Gloria again, as if the two of them had become conspirators against William. "You made him bring the video of his last concert, didn't you?"

William answered for her. "It's in the briefcase."

"Great! But now, I want you to be the first to play the piano. I haven't let anyone touch it."

William lifted his eyebrows and grinned before sitting on the bench. He cleared his throat, lifted his hands, then played a rousing rendition of parallel scales from one end of the keyboard to the other. He looked over his shoulder. "It's in tune."

"Don't get up," Jane commanded. "I want you to play something for me." She slid onto the bench beside him and snuggled close, with her arms around him.

"Little imp," he said and kissed her forehead.

Gloria's heart was filled with tenderness at the sight of brother and sister, so obviously affectionate toward each other. She couldn't begin to know what problem existed, but for the moment, she sat in a chair, softly smiling at the display of love between the two siblings.

Jane looked over. "Come over and sing with us, Gloria."

"I would sound like a frog compared with you two."

"Don't worry about it," Jane said. "My voice is very weak now, and I'll probably have a coughing fit right in the middle of it. But I'm going to try anyway."

Faced with that kind of determination from a young girl in a hospital, Gloria couldn't very well refuse. Frankly, she didn't want to. Her voice was not the greatest, but at this moment she, like William, didn't want to refuse this delightful girl anything. She went over to the piano.

"Wait," William said. "I need to make one quick phone call."

While he was gone, Jane showed Gloria the Christmas tree near the fireplace, saying that several of the residents made some of the decorations. Jane had helped with the delicate white snowflakes. Then Jane glanced toward the doorway and back at Gloria. She spoke quietly. "You don't know about me, do you?"

"No," Gloria admitted, feeling Jane must be referring to her physical condition. "Only that William dedicates his concerts to you."

"He doesn't want to talk about it," Jane said. "And he doesn't want me to talk about it, as if ignoring it will make it go away. But I want to talk about it. Maybe you could come to see me."

"I would like to, Jane. But I work for your brother. I couldn't do that without his permission. I wouldn't be here tonight if it weren't for the flat tire."

Jane nodded. "I know. He called about that. But I made him tell me about you. He thinks you're efficient." She giggled. "Now that's an understatement."

Gloria smiled. "Are you complimenting me?"

"Yes," she said sweetly. "I like you."

That almost brought tears to Gloria's eyes, but she forced them back. This girl was so forthcoming, so full of life. What could be wrong? "Oh, honey," she said sincerely, "I like you too."

"When I was little, I couldn't say William, so I said 'Willy-wum.' " She giggled. "I think he likes it."

"I think so too," Gloria returned with a smile. "How old are you, Jane?"

"Seventeen," she said. She looked younger.

William returned to the room. "Okay," he said. "You name it, I'll play it." He sat down on the piano bench, and Jane perched beside him. Gloria leaned on the piano.

"Let's see," Jane said, tapping her jaw with her finger. Suddenly she brightened and said, "'When We All Get to Heaven.'"

Gloria had known that hymn all her life and smiled broadly until she looked at William, whose face clouded as if he wasn't too pleased with that selection. Without comment, he played an introduction and then nodded for them to begin.

Jane's voice was soft, but the tone was beautiful. Gloria knew how to sing only the melody, but William and Jane added beautiful harmonies, and Gloria thought their voices were as good as any she'd ever heard. Then she reminded herself that William sang professionally and that his parents had been famous opera stars. She tried to quit and let them sing alone but neither would hear of it.

"We need your melody," William insisted, "so that the other parts are effective."

Gloria doubted that but obliged, wanting to please Jane.

They sang several songs, all of them at Jane's suggestion, including "Angels we have heard on high, sweetly singing o'er the plains. Glo—o-o-o-o—o-o-o-o—o-o-o-o—ri-a, in excelsis deo." They laughed and sang until Jane put her hand to her chest. "My voice is giving out."

"Then we have sung enough," William said and abruptly rose from the bench.

Jane followed. "I'd like to show you my room, Gloria."

Jane held Gloria's hand, and William walked behind them down the corridor. They turned the corner to another wing. At first glance they might have entered the bedroom of a very privileged child. The furniture was polished cherry. The wallpaper was a delicate floral pattern, with subtle shades of pink, rose, and green against a cream background. The bedspread was cream-colored, the drapes a soft rose. Green rugs adorned the floor. There were paintings on the wall that Gloria recognized as Monet or Manet—she could never tell them apart.

"These are my parents," Jane said, taking a picture from a long, narrow table on which sat a beautiful arrangement of silk flowers. They were a handsome couple: the man in a tux, the woman in a striking sequined turquoise gown.

There were other pictures, informal ones of the family, including her two sets of grandparents. "These are in Italy. They came to see me a few months ago. And this is my grandpapa Clayborn. William said you've met him."

"Oh, he's wonderful."

Jane smiled and picked up a piece of wood into which was inscribed: *Insilvis viva silui jam mortua cano.* "It's classical Latin," she said. "It means, 'In the forest I lived silently. Now that I am dead, I sing.' "

Knowing nothing about what was going on here, Gloria dared not show surprise nor ask questions. William must have known her mind was full of questions because he explained, "Jane loved the forested hills where Grandpa lived. She protested when a logging company began cutting on another mountainside. Grandpa explained to her that musical instruments were made of wood. Trees had a great purpose after being cut."

Jane put the plaque back on the table and turned toward the two of them. She spoke to her brother. "When I think of trees being cut to make musical instruments, I think of that," she said. "The trees sing when you play the piano. I know you've given up your career for me. Oh, I'm glad you're nearby. It increases my joy. But what I want is for you to go on dates, hold hands with a girl, kiss, slide down a snow-covered hill.

I want you to enjoy life for me. I'm not going to, Willy-wum. I'm going to be with the Lord. . .soon."

As if ignoring some of her words, William scoffed. "I'm a little old to be sliding down snow-covered hills."

Jane turned twinkling mischievous eyes toward Gloria. Gloria blushed, knowing the young girl was thinking William hadn't said he was too old to kiss or go out on dates.

Before they left, Gloria could see that Jane was considerably weaker than when they'd come in. A lot of her enthusiasm had gone and at one point she stumbled and had to reach out to the bed to keep from falling. William reached out to prevent her fall, as if he had expected her to lose her balance.

It was then that the rest of the room registered with Gloria. There were side rails on the bed. On the rails were several buttons, most likely to summon needed help. A crank was at the bottom of the bed to raise or lower it. A television was mounted high on the wall facing the bed, where one could lie down and watch it. A panel above the bed had several electrical outlets for various kinds of equipment. A private bath was located near the door, like in hospital rooms. Regardless of how modern or private, this still was a hospital.

Before they left, William asked if they could pray. Jane sat on the bed, while William and Gloria stood near her, all holding hands. "Dear God," he prayed. "Keep Your loving arms around Jane. Keep her in Your care. You are the Great Physician, Lord, and we pray for Your divine healing. Amen."

"Thy will be done," Jane added quickly. "Amen."

seven

Unless God gives her a miracle, Jane is dying," William said on the way home. The phone call he'd made earlier was to road service, asking them to deliver his car to Tess's home.

"It seemed easier not to talk about it," he said. "We've done so much of that through the years."

Now, it seemed, he couldn't say enough. Gloria tried to quell her tears and keep her eyes on the road as he told of the downhill journey that Jane had taken. She'd been a beautiful girl, with the most musical potential in the family. Her voice had a range and tone greater than that of her famous parents.

She'd begun to be sick. She would awaken in the mornings with headaches and nausea. She began having difficulties with speech and balance. She'd been an active, inquisitive, but well-behaved child, who accepted her extraordinary talent and understood that her destiny was in music. Then she began to experience behavior problems. After Jane visited her grandparents, Grandpa told her parents that there was something wrong with the child.

Then came a battery of tests. Finally Jane was diagnosed with glioblastoma, a tumor on the brain stem. Immediately, she underwent surgery, followed by radiation and chemotherapy. Her long black hair had been shaved off for surgery. Then the hair that began growing back fell out during radiation and chemo. The surgeons were unable to get all the tumor.

"The radiation and chemo reduced the symptoms and slowed the growth," William said. "But the diagnosis devastated my parents. Jane was the unexpected child of my mother's middle-age and such a joy for us all. I've always thought Jane's condition had something to do with my dad's pulling out in front of that truck the night my parents were killed. They'd just gotten the news that the tumor would recur, and he probably wasn't able to concentrate on his driving."

Oh, Lord, keep my attention on the road and traffic, Gloria prayed. As badly as she felt, she knew her emotions couldn't begin to compare with what William was experiencing.

"After surgery and radiation," William explained, "she had a team of medical care specialists. Ms. Kesin is a neuropsychologist who has been with her from the time she had her surgery. Jane is now in what is called remission."

"Then there's hope," Gloria said.

"Not medically," William replied. "We were never told that she was cured. We've known all along there might be a recurrence. That is happening." He took a deep breath. "But I'm hoping, praying, living for a miracle. I've vowed before God not to have a personal life of my own as long as Jane is not able to have one. I cannot bear to think of making plans for my life or career, the way I have in the past, after seeing the way Jane has suffered and how she might have to suffer again. My life and work is dedicated to her and to the Lord."

Gloria felt she had begun to understand William. He was doing remarkably well, considering the circumstances. "Miracles do happen," she managed to say over the lump in her throat.

"Yes," he agreed. "But Jane is intent upon dying."

❄

Grandpa's car was nowhere in sight, but William's car was parked in Tess's driveway when he and Gloria got back. She parked on the street in front of the house.

"I'm sorry to have burdened you with this," William said. "It was never my intention."

"We all need friends in times like these, William," she said softly. "If you'll let me, I would like to be a friend to you and to Jane."

He grasped her hands. Her face was so close to his in that little car. William realized he had found great release by having confided in someone.

"Jane would like that," he said. "And so would I." His gaze dropped to their hands and he stiffened slightly. "But you can't expect—"

"I know," she said immediately.

He gave her hands a squeeze, then turned from his cramped position in the car and climbed out, stretching as if trying to get the kinks out of his legs and shoulders.

Tess came out and stood on the lighted porch. "William, Gloria. Could you come in for a moment? Something has happened."

They followed her into the living room. "Your dad called," Tess said to Gloria. "Yuliati is ill. She fell down some steps at school. She has a broken arm."

Broken arm? William wondered. Any other time that might seem important.

"It's not healing properly," Tess added. "Infection has set in and is spreading through her little body."

William glanced at the picture of Yuliati, aware of how thin she looked. "Surely," he said, "medication will clear up the infection."

Gloria turned to William, her face bleak. "There's no hospital near where she lives. There would be no money for treatment anyway. Maybe not even any medication." She took a deep breath before adding shakily, "It's serious."

Serious? William questioned. *This was incredible! Could it be possible any person in this world could die from a broken arm?*

"Can't we get medication to her?" William asked. "Fly an antibiotic to her?"

Gloria shook her head. "We're doing about all we can by sending money for the people there to work with. But they have so little and need so much." She walked over and picked up the picture of Yuliati. "These children just don't have enough strength to fight disease and infection."

William left, feeling as helpless about Yuliati as he was about Jane. His sister had the best doctors the world could provide. She had the best care, and no expense had been spared. In another part of the world, a little girl might be dying of a broken arm. That was hard to fathom.

"William told me about Jane," Gloria said after he left. "He has vowed not to have a personal life of his own as long as Jane is sick."

"I know," Tess answered. "Billy Bob told me. Neither

of us feel that is necessary. The Scripture tells us that God doesn't require sacrifice, but a broken spirit and a contrite heart."

"Oh, William has that."

"Yes," Tess said. "And he has imposed his own restrictions upon himself. However, when one makes a vow to God, he must be careful to keep it."

"He can't bear going about life thinking of himself while his sister is dying. He will dedicate all his life to her. His life is music and Jane. It's very hard to know how to pray, Tess," Gloria confessed. "I must, like William, put myself and my feelings aside and concentrate only on Jane. I love that young girl. As much as I love Yuliati, who is like a little sister to me. Is that possible, Tess, when I've only just met Jane?"

"Nothing strange about that. I loved you the moment I saw you."

"Oh, Tess, and I love you." She got up and went over to Tess. They embraced, and Gloria let the tears come. She needed this wonderful woman so much.

eight

The opportunity didn't present itself in the next three weeks for Jane to have many visitors. She had an unexpected seizure the first week in December—the first one since her surgery. She had been playing the piano and singing weakly. When she got up to go to her room, she fell against the side of the fireplace before Ana Kesin could reach her. The result was a bad bruise on the side of her face.

A decision needed to be made about medications. Steroids were discussed. "It's hard to know what to do," William said to Gloria. "Steroids can reduce symptoms temporarily, but then there can be side effects both from the tumor and the steroids."

"Does Jane know about all this?" Gloria asked.

"That's the problem," he said. "She reviewed all the information available before her surgery. She knows the risks and she knows her chances are slim. Since she's only seventeen and I'm her legal guardian, I can make the decision." He raked his hair with his fingers. "I'm inclined to try anything. But she's asking that Grandpa and I hear her out. She says you may come too. She thinks you would understand what she's doing."

"Oh, I wouldn't attempt to influence any decision like that," Gloria said. "I can only imagine what a burden that is. But I'll be more than glad to visit with her."

"Thank you. She'd like Tess to come along as well."

❄

After church on a cold December Sunday, William drove Grandpa, Gloria, and Tess to Faith Hospital. He'd been informed this was one of Jane's good days. According to Ana Kesin, Jane hadn't had another seizure. Only a sliver of bruise remained under her eye.

Jane did not meet them at the door this time, but she was curled up in a chair near the blazing fire in the parlor, an afghan draped over her legs. Gloria thought Jane looked even thinner and weaker than when she'd seen her two weeks before. However, her spirits were high, and she was obviously delighted that she had several guests. She reached up to hug each of them and kissed her grandpa on both cheeks. She even asked Tess if she would be her proxy-grandmother, a request that thrilled the older woman. No one could be around Jane and not fall completely in love with her.

"Before we discuss grievous matters," Jane said with a slight roll of her gaze toward the ceiling, "you should play for me, Willy-wum. Maybe that will help you stay calm."

They all laughed with Jane, agreeing that William could be unreasonable. The glance the brother and sister shared, however, spoke of the love they felt for each other. Jane stayed in her chair, rather than sitting next to her brother on the piano bench. She looked tired.

Jane wanted to hear about Tess and her mission work in Korea and about Gloria and her parents' work in Indonesia. Jane and Grandpa talked about old times, including the good times they'd had when her grandmother was alive. She wanted to hear all about the mountaintop home and how they'd decorated for Christmas.

"We haven't done that yet," Grandpa admitted.

"Promise me you will. I want you to celebrate."

"I'm writing a composition for you, Jane," William said, coming over to the couch and sitting in the corner near her sister. "I'll play it for you on Christmas Eve."

"Can you do it sooner?" she asked with a sweet smile. "I don't know if I can wait that long."

William lowered his eyes, but not before Gloria saw the glimmer of pain in them. "No," he said. "Not until Christmas. It's your present."

"We need to celebrate early," Jane said softly and reached over to touch his arm. William reached over and enclosed her hand. Gloria felt her heart would break.

"We need to have a long talk," Jane said.

He shook his head.

Jane was determined. "You have to listen. That's why I wanted you to bring the others. Maybe they can convince you that I'm right."

"Right?" he questioned. "How can it be right when you refuse further treatment?"

"It's futile," she said. "I accepted the fact that I might die before I went into surgery. It's settled between me and God. I am going to die young, and I am honored that God is glorified through my experiences. I believe that God has chosen me to minister to those here in the hospital who fear death and pain. With each painful moment, I know I am one second closer to God and to eternity, and I can hardly wait."

"Please, Jane, don't talk of these things."

"You have to hear it, William. I know you are sad

and that you will grieve when I go to heaven, but I truly believe this is what God wants for me right now and that He has His reasons. I don't want you to be always lost in grief. I want your life to sing." The glow of the fire gave color to her face and warmth to the white dress. She looked up at her brother, who stared into the fire and looked as if his eyes were burning.

"Willy-wum," she said softly, "the Lord Jesus Christ is in my heart. My great joy is looking forward to seeing Him. I know God has made a beautiful world. Lots of my friends here want so desperately to get well and live on this earth. I wake up every morning and thank God that I am one day closer to seeing Him—that with every breath I am that much closer to my eternal home."

He held her hand. "I love you more than anything, Jane. If I could change places with you, I would."

"I know," she said. "And this is selfish of me, but I'm so glad you can't. I want to go. The Lord has put that desire in me. I don't know why and I know it's different from most people. Their great hope is to get well. Mine is not."

"If it were, Jane, then you could perhaps conquer this disease."

"No, Willy-wum. If the Lord wanted me to conquer this disease, He would put that desire in me. I do not have it. This doesn't make me sad. It fills me with joy and expectation."

Jane looked around at the others. Gloria and Tess lowered their gazes, feeling it was not their place to comment.

"My Cora felt similar, Jane," Grandpa said. "She wasn't eager to leave me, but she'd lived a full life, and in those last months she wanted to go to her eternal home."

"I've lived a full life too, Grandpa," Jane replied. "Wasn't it you who told me it's not how long a person lives, but how well?"

"I believe I did, honey."

"There isn't one person in this hospital who has had the opportunities I have. They never will. I've had a full life, and I've told many about Jesus, and it has made a difference. What more could I want? Are marriage and children better than heaven?"

When no one answered, not even William, she added softly, "I love the Christmas season, when the birth of Jesus is celebrated, and I want to be in heaven to celebrate with Him. That's what I want for Christmas."

She moved her hand away from William. "Oh, don't be morbid, guys. William, play for us, and we'll sing."

William looked as if he couldn't speak, but he obeyed his sister. She asked that they sing "My Jesus I Love Thee." Her sweet, small voice was little more than a whisper, words like honey on her tongue, the sound of birds and wind and joy and peace:

I'll love Thee in life,
I will love Thee in death,
And praise Thee as long as
Thou lendest me breath;
And say, when the death-dew
lies cold on my brow;
If ever I loved Thee, my Jesus 'tis now.

Then Grandpa joined in. So did Tess and Gloria, then

William. Who could deny that Jane was a touch of heaven on earth?

A week later, Jane got her wish. William had agreed she would not take steroids, although she would continue with anticonvulsants and pain medication. She became weaker, lost her appetite. Her vision blurred.

Jane's death was not the slow, agonizing one it might have been. She died quickly after a grand mal seizure when a blood clot rapidly made its way to her brain.

William, Grandpa, Tess, Gloria, and President Hunt attended the private memorial service held in the chapel at the hospital. The hospital chaplain told about the extraordinary young girl named Jane, who had donated her good organs to help others and her brain to medical research. He explained the plan of salvation through Jesus Christ. Grandpa talked about her incredible faith and how now she was in heaven with her parents and grandmother. William spoke through his music. He played some of Jane's favorite hymns and led the residents, staff, and guests in the singing.

William and his grandfather flew to Italy the next day where a funeral service would be held at a site where Jane's parents and grandmother were buried. A memorial stone would be placed in Jane's memory.

"Yuliati died early this morning," Gloria's mom called to say. "They did everything possible with such limited facilities. For a few days her temperature fluctuated. She fought hard, but finally the fever and infection took over. She just wasn't strong enough to overcome it."

Gloria had held onto hope but had known from the

moment she heard the word *infection* that the prognosis wasn't good. Yuliati's condition had been as serious as Jane's.

There was one major difference: Jane's condition had been incurable. Yuliati's infection could have been cured with proper facilities and medication, something taken for granted every day in the United States.

"Just remember," her mother said. "Many lives are being saved every day because of the funds you're sending our way."

❄

After William returned from Italy, he was scheduled to give a Christmas Eve concert. He was subdued when he came to the office and outlined the program for the concert and where his composition for Jane would be inserted.

When he finished, Gloria said quietly, "Yuliati didn't make it."

William blinked. He cleared his throat and stood, moving away from the papers they were working on. He walked to the window, his back to her. It was a cold, gloomy day and Gloria felt as if the chill of it had entered the office. "I'm so sorry," he said.

"Oh, William," Gloria said, going over to him. He turned his head away but not before she saw the tears on his face. Hers began to fall, unrestrained. He started to move away, but she touched his arm.

He saw her tears and, with a heart-wrenching sob, enfolded her in his arms. "I don't normally do this," he said after a moment. "But this news about Yuliati just brought it all to the surface."

"It's all right, William," she said, lifting her face to

his. "You have to find release for your grief."

William agreed. "And I feel joy when I think of her and how her suffering is over. But I miss her so. . . ."

Gloria reached up and tenderly touched his wet cheek with her fingers. William closed his eyes for an instant, then took her hand in his and gently pressed his lips to her fingers. "Thank you," he said softly, "for letting me cry on your shoulder."

"I understand," she said tenderly.

He nodded, gazing into her moist blue-green eyes. "I know you do," he said. "I learned a long time ago that you're a very compassionate person."

William stepped away. He took a handkerchief from his back pocket and wiped his face. "My relatives and I have decided not to give personal gifts to each other this Christmas, out of respect for Jane."

His voice wavered on Jane's name. "We will be donating to the cancer fund specializing in brain tumors. I thought you and Tess might—"

"Oh, yes," Gloria responded before he could finish the sentence. She wouldn't even mention that she couldn't give much, knowing how even a few coins added up. "I want to donate. I know Tess will too. Thank you for including us."

"You both have been included for a while now, Gloria. You've been good friends to Grandpa, me, and Jane. We appreciate that."

Gloria didn't know if she could look away from him. And yet, now that his arms no longer enfolded her, she could feel the cold of the gray, dismal day creep into the office. Their embrace was not personal, she reminded herself. She must be grateful that she had been there for him in his moment of grief.

Gloria and Tess saved a seat for Billy Bob on the second row. William had decided he wouldn't need Gloria to drive him since the concert was only about fifteen minutes away from the cabin. Gloria had felt a stab of disappointment but reminded herself that she would see him at least one more time. Tess had invited William, Billy Bob, President Hunt, and his wife, Ellen, to her house for Christmas Eve refreshments after the concert.

It marked an end to the most inspiring time of Gloria's life. She would always remember William, as he did Jane, with a feeling of painful joy.

"Brrrr," Billy Bob blustered, taking his seat beside Tess. "Cold out there." He rubbed his hands together. "Wouldn't be surprised if it snowed."

"Snow on Christmas Eve would be perfect," Tess said, smiling at her friend. "But this cold weather sure didn't keep anybody away."

Billy Bob looked around at the packed auditorium and up at the full balcony.

The lights went down. The roar of voices quieted. The curtain opened. Red poinsettias lined the edge of the stage. Men and women in green robes with white collars stood behind the orchestra. The organist and pianist entered from opposite sides of the stage, amid applause.

Gloria expected William's usual dedication to Jane when he leaned toward the microphone on the piano. "This concert is dedicated to my sister Jane, who has gone to be with the Lord," he said. He paused, then added, "Many of you in the audience have been valued friends during this difficult period in my life. Therefore, I dedicate this not only to Jane, but also to you, to God, and particularly to my friend and assistant, Miss Gloria Holmes."

Tess gently nudged Gloria with her elbow, causing Gloria to glance her way with a smile. Then she remembered the first concert of William's that she had attended when she had thought it was so romantic that he dedicated his concert to Jane. Now she understood that instead the dedication had been a sort of farewell to his sister. And that's what this dedication meant too—a farewell. A good-bye. Their work together had ended. Their relationship had ended. *Lord*, she prayed, *help me accept what you have in store for me with the same grace that Jane had. Keep me from wanting more.*

With that, Gloria put her thoughts to the side. She wanted to enjoy every moment of this concert dedicated to her. She concentrated as the conductor, his back to the audience, faced the choir, raised his arms, and the concert began.

The theme of the concert centered around the presentation of the life, death, and resurrection of Jesus. The recurring musical themes made the musical successful as a dramatic presentation rather than as simply a collection of beautiful songs. At the finale, which was the composition written for Jane, the audience was ready to accept the repeated "celebration" theme of the introduction not just as a declaration, but as an affirmation and confirmation that the man Jesus was indeed the risen Savior and Messiah. The concert came to a unifying conclusion with a majestic rendering of the "Hallelujah Chorus" from Handel's *Messiah.*

The audience stood as the instruments played the introduction, and when the words "King of Kings, and Lord of Lords" reverberated throughout the auditorium, Gloria doubted there was a dry eye in the place.

That, she thought in wonder, *was dedicated to Jane, God, and me? Wow! What company!* The music would live in her heart for a lifetime.

nine

President Hunt and Ellen arrived shortly after Tess and Gloria. Sending Tess in to talk with her guests, Gloria stuck the meatballs into the microwave to heat. She took the cheeseball out of the refrigerator and set it on the table along with the crackers, cookies, and candies they'd put out before going to the concert. She needed only to remove the plastic wrap from them.

Her heart thudded expectantly when she heard William and Grandpa come in. Again, Grandpa complained about the cold weather. The Hunts began to compliment William on the concert.

The dedication was particularly impressive, Gloria said to herself. She nodded approvingly as she poured the fruit juice into the punch bowl, then added ginger ale. Tess's best china plates and cups along with red paper napkins were the perfect touch. Yes, they'd done all right, making these refreshments. Gloria popped a butter fudge candy into her mouth.

"Uh uh, I saw that!" said a deep voice she'd know anywhere. Gloria thought she'd choke. There stood William in his tux, leaning against the doorframe, smiling at her with a look of mischief in his eyes.

"I'll share," she said, picking up a piece and holding it out to him.

He walked over. Gloria swallowed hard while his teeth took the candy from her fingers and he ate. It was disconcerting, his standing so close.

He pretended thoughtfulness. "I may have to have another before expressing my opinion."

They smiled at each other. Then he looked serious. "You are particularly beautiful tonight, Gloria," he said softly.

"Well, thanks," she said. "Um, you look the same."

He tilted his head slightly and laughed. "Same ol' monkey suit."

"I think we could invite the others in now," she said.

"I'll tell them," he said.

Gloria took a deep breath and exhaled slowly. He was so different tonight. But, she realized, there were good reasons. The past months had been filled with concern about Jane and the stress of William's self-imposed restrictions upon himself. Although he would always remember Jane, he could begin to live for himself.

And he had just said she was beautiful. She had tried. It was Christmas, and she needed to feel attractive. This was her and William's last night together. She was wearing a new dress, a soft deep-green silk with a thin rhinestone belt, and she wore rhinestone earrings. She stepped over to the small mirror hanging on the wall near the table. The woman looking back at her had a smile on her face, color in her cheeks, and a sparkle in her blue-green eyes. The light brought out a golden sheen in her light brown curls. But she knew that after William left this magic would leave her, like a clock striking midnight, turning Cinderella back into a char maiden.

❄

After the Hunts left, William asked Gloria to ride up to the cabin with him. "I have a present for you."

"Oh, but you said no presents." She hadn't bought him a thing.

"It's not from me," he said, smiling at her chagrin. "It's something Jane wanted me to share with you."

"Oh," Gloria said and got her coat. Well, of course she shouldn't have jumped to the conclusion he had bought her something. Their good-bye would simply be his reiterating that she had been a valued employee, and then he would thank her. How in the world was she going to casually tell him good-bye?

Both Gloria and William were relatively quiet on the drive up the mountain, making only light conversation about Christmas lights and the weather. Low-hanging clouds, burdened with moisture, hovered about the treetops and obscured some of the mountain peaks. A few flakes of snow struck the windshield. The wind had picked up.

He turned into the driveway and parked on the gravel next to the steps. Gloria got out and held her coat closer. It was always colder the higher up on the mountain one went. A lamp was on in the living room. Once inside, William flipped a switch, and the Christmas lights glowed softly on a tree in a corner near the fireplace. He reached up on the mantle for a match and lit the already laid fire. Flames leaped through the paper and caught the kindling.

"If you don't mind, I'd like to change," he said.

"Go ahead." Gloria sat on the couch facing the fire. She glanced around the cozy room with its paneled walls, hardwood floor, dark-colored rugs, and heavy furniture. It looked like a man's place but comfortable and cozy. Soon the chill had dispelled, and she took off her coat and laid it across the back of the couch.

William returned, dressed in casual tan slacks and a black cashmere turtleneck sweater, with the sleeves pushed up, revealing the soft dark hair on his arms. The color of the sweater and orange glow of the fire combined to make him even more handsome than ever.

He walked over to the stereo system in a corner. "Jane wanted you to hear this on Christmas Eve." He turned on the speakers and pushed a button on the tape deck.

"When you play this," came Jane's sweet voice on the cassette, "remember our good times together and how happy I am to be singing and shouting the victory in heaven, along with Mom, Dad, and Grandmother. I'll save a place for you William, and you Gloria, at the Lord's table."

William crossed the room and sat on the edge of the couch, facing Gloria while the songs played. He reached for her hand. She watched the changing emotions in William's dark eyes, ranging from sadness to joy, as they listened to the recording of the songs the three of them had sung the day Gloria met Jane, including "Gloria in excelsis deo."

The cassette ended, but he still held her hand. He spoke softly. "I will always miss Jane, but I think I've come to terms with her death. When she asked me, about a week before she died, why I couldn't accept it, I told her I wanted her to live, grow up, marry, have children, have a career." He grinned wryly. "You know what she told me? She said I was trying to impose that on her because that's what I wanted for myself."

"Most people do," Gloria admitted.

He smiled. "My precocious sister had a wry sense of humor and an uncanny insight into other people's true feelings. She thought God brought you and me together for a purpose." He paused and looked at her for a long, long moment. Was that longing in his eyes—or just a reflection of what she was feeling?

"I refused to allow myself to consider anything personal between you and me," he said, "not after the vow I'd made to the Lord." He drew in a breath. "But in spite of the fact I dared not act upon them, my feelings for you grew. You have been special to me from the time we met."

Special? How special? What could she say without assuming too much? "And I," she said, "knew you were. . . special. . .too, but at first I thought you were involved with Jane. I didn't know she was your sister."

He shook his head. "I'm not involved with anyone. I broke all personal ties when I made that vow." He paused, then added, "I've never been in love. . .before."

Before? "Before wh–what?"

"Before you, Gloria," he said, concern in his voice.

"You. . .you love me?"

"Yes. You're everything a man could want. How could I not fall in love with you?"

If he didn't know, she wasn't about to offer any reasons why he shouldn't. Her eyes began to burn with unshed tears of joy. "I was just scared to death you might be asking me to be your friend forever and that we'd have to go back to Tess's and eat meatballs."

He laughed. "That's not a bad idea. But first things first."

"Oh, I do love you, William. I had to fight it too, believing you were involved with a woman named Jane. When I found out about Jane being your sister and about the vow you made, I tried to be only a friend to you."

"Besides being beautiful, you're incredible. I want to make a vow to you, before God, to love and cherish, to have and to hold, in sickness and health—"

"William," she interrupted, "could we start the holding process now?"

"With pleasure," he said softly. The velvet touch of his fingers touched her cheek, caressed her face, moved to the back of her neck, and entwined itself in her hair, keeping her close to him. He was the musician, playing a concert of lovely music on her heartstrings.

The kiss was sweet, tender, loving, and then more demanding. If she were dreaming, she never wanted to awaken. She reveled in their words of love, spoken between kisses.

Reluctantly, William moved away and took her hands in his, seemingly overwhelmed. "To think," he murmured, "a few months ago I thought this would possibly be the saddest Christmas of my life." He paused. "In a way, it is. And yet, God has been present with me through it all. Working in me, showing me what is most important in life, and best of all, sending you into my life."

"Oh, William," she whispered, "I couldn't begin to hope for a wonderful man like you."

She moved toward him, but he held up his hand. "There's something I need to know."

"I don't have a past," she said quickly, then added

reluctantly, "at least, not worth mentioning."

He stopped her words with his lips.

Breaking the kiss, he murmured, "I'm not concerned about your past. It's the future we need to discuss. When we first met, you said you didn't know if you would go to the mission field or remain here and teach, or just what you would do. Have you decided?"

"I've discussed this with my parents and Tess. They have all said the same thing. It takes a special kind of person with a special calling to spend years on the mission field. I haven't felt that calling. I have applied to sponsor another child. But I think, like you, in these past months, I have an even stronger feeling about the needs right around me, wherever I am."

She saw his nod and the serious look on his face. "What I'd like to do, Gloria, is fund the building of a hospital in the area of Indonesia where Yuliati lived. Medical treatment helped Jane, but it couldn't prevent her death. But Yuliati could have survived a minor illness if there had been a hospital. I would like it to be in memory of both Jane and Yuliati."

"Oh, William. That's wonderful. What I'd like to do is go and see if she has a little grave, put a bunch of flowers there in her memory."

"While we're there," he said, "I could ask your Mom and Dad for their blessing on our marriage."

"Marriage?" she squeaked.

He nodded. "That usually follows love. Don't you see? You have become everything to me. You are the unexpected change from my well-planned, well-structured life. You are the bridge that connects all the disjointed sections of my life. I love you, Gloria, and love and marriage. . ."

"Oh, William, are you asking me to marry you?"

"If you're not sure, I could get on my knees."

"I'm sure," she said and melted into his arms as they came around her.

"We'd better get back down the mountain before Grandpa eats all the meatballs," he said.

"Is food all you men think about?" she asked, moving away.

"No, I had to force myself," he answered, reaching for her coat. He grinned as she stood and slipped into it, then he shrugged into his jacket.

William switched off the Christmas tree lights and opened the door. "Look," he said.

"Oh, it's snowing." Gloria gasped at the beauty of it as they walked out into the huge flakes falling from the sky like confetti, resting gently on the trees, adorning the mountainsides with soft white lace. "This reminds me of the snowflakes Jane cut from paper to decorate the tree in the parlor."

William smiled, put his arm around her waist, and held Gloria possessively at his side. He looked up, letting the cold moist flakes fall on his face. "Now she's spending Christmas the way she wanted," he said contemplatively, "celebrating Jesus' birthday in heaven. It's almost as if I can hear her laughter."

Yes, Gloria thought in the silence the falling snow brought to their surroundings, *the soft wind had the sound of light, happy laughter.* "I hear it too," Gloria said. "And now she's throwing confetti at us."

William looked down at her quickly, then he laughed lightly. "Exactly," he said. "Jane is just the sort to have led the snow angels into doing this."

"Heaven's confetti," Gloria mused.

They both looked up into the sky, respecting the bittersweet memory of dear, dear Jane.

"This is the season of miracles," William said. "God did not answer my prayers for Jane the way I wanted, but he gave me a most unexpected, welcome gift." His smile was beautiful. "He gave me someone I need, and want, and love. He gave me you. And if you allow it, I will dedicate the rest of my life to you."

"I'm all for it," she said, smiling warmly.

Persons wishing to receive information about brain tumors are urged to contact

National Brain Tumor Foundation
785 Market Street, Suite 1600
San Francisco, CA 94103-2003
1-800-934-CURE
Web site: www.braintumor.org
Email: nbt@braintumor.org

Yvonne Lehman

As an award-winning author from Black Mountain, North Carolina, in the heart of the Smoky Mountains, Yvonne Lehman has written several novels for Barbour Publishing's **Heartsong Presents** line. Her titles include *Southern Gentlemen, Mountain Man,* which won a National Reader's Choice Award sponsored by a chapter of the Romance Writers of America, *After the Storm,* and *Call of the Mountain*. Yvonne has published more than two dozen novels, including books in the Bethany House "White Dove" series for young adults. Her novel *Gomer,* a reprint of *In Shady Grove,* is being published by Guideposts. In addition to her writing, Yvonne teaches an occasional adult class at Montreat College.

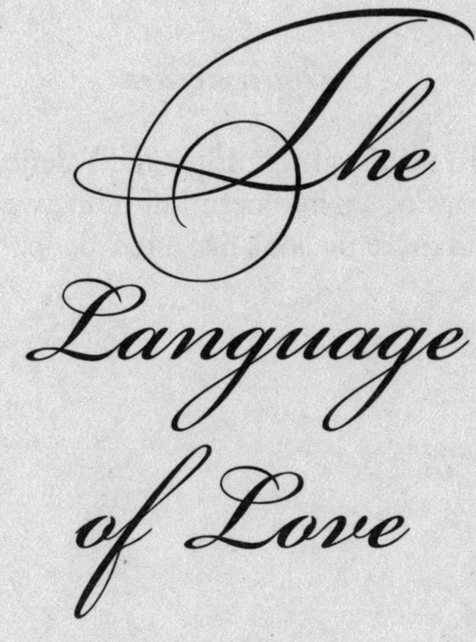

Loree Lough

Dedication

To my daughters, Elice and Valerie,
for growing up into beautiful young women
who make me look like a terrific mom!

one

Shannen opened one eye to see what all the commotion was about and sat up in time to see the conductor rubbing his thumb across his fingertips. "*Prezzo*," he demanded of a man up front. "*Prezzo!*"

The dark-haired, handsome fellow responded hesitantly, "*Quanto. . .ah. . .trattiene di. . .uh. . .di commissionie?*" Surely he didn't really believe the Eurail employee earned a commission on the fares he collected. . . .

"*Commissionie?*" Smacking a heel to his forehead, the conductor growled under his breath. Then, drawing a spiral in the air beside his temple, he said to himself, "*Chiami un polizia. . .un medico. . .qualcosa!*"

Call the police. . .*or* a doctor?

Suddenly it began to make sense: The handsome passenger had obviously not paid the full fare, which made the conductor believe he was either a deadbeat. . . or a certifiable nut!

"*Quanto trattiene. . .um. . .di commissionie?*" Handsome repeated.

Another sigh escaped the conductor's lungs as he searched his memory for a word this *touristo* might understand. "*Liere, si? Piú. . . . Ah–h–h–h. . .dinero. . .* okay?" He'd used nearly every word in the Italian-American handbook that meant "money," and *still* the visitor didn't understand. His pained, lost expression reminded Shannen of a lost child.

Shortly after boarding the Eurail in Rome, she'd seen the tall, good-looking guy get on the train. He hadn't seemed to notice her as he glanced around and took the seat nearest the car's entrance. Five minutes into their trip to Florence, he'd yawned expansively and folded his magazine. Ten minutes into the ride, he'd leaned back and closed his eyes. It was as good a way as any to pass the time until they arrived in Florence, she'd thought. If it hadn't been for the commotion, she might still be asleep.

Shannen took a look around at her fellow passengers, who appeared only mildly interested in the ruckus or were paying no attention at all. She sighed heavily, wondering why things like this were always happening around *her*.

Two weeks ago, for example, she witnessed a traffic accident at the corner of Old Annapolis and Columbia Road. The teenaged girl had clearly been at fault, but the middle-aged man had no cause to shake his fist and shout obscenities at the poor kid. And so Shannen had marched up to the stranger and, hands on her hips, said, "I certainly hope you don't kiss your mother with that mouth!" It had been enough to quiet him until the policeman arrived to write up a report.

In the grocery store a few weeks before that, a customer lambasted an elderly lady for getting into the "Ten Items or Less" line. . .with twelve cans of cat food. The old dear's eyes had filled with tears, and not even her trembly apology seemed to satisfy the lady in the purple suit. Shannen tapped the businesswoman on the shoulder. "I wonder how you'd feel if someone talked to *your* grandmother that way." Red-faced, the woman began explaining her long and harried day. . .and apologized.

And what about what happened on her way to the airport, when she ducked into the mall to grab a few pairs of cotton socks? As she searched for an open cashier stand in the midst of the start of the pre-Christmas frenzy, a pitiful little voice had captured her attention. Following the sound, Shannen located a boy—no more than four—cowering near the register. Between sobs and sniffles, he'd explained, "M–my m–mother is *l–l–lost!*" Knowing it might make her miss the plane to Italy, Shannen had led the child to the mall office. . .and sat with him until his grateful mother showed up.

Handsome's expression reminded her of that little boy's face. Surely the conductor knew as well as she did that the man spoke little or no Italian; why wasn't he being more understanding? Shannen walked purposefully up to the conductor and opened her purse. "*Quanto le devo?*" she asked, gesturing to the passenger who hadn't paid his fare.

Why would *you* want to pay his way? was the silent question written on the conductor's face. He tucked his black-billed cap under his arm and, eyes narrowed with suspicion, pursed his lips. "*Cinquantatre*. . . ."

She'd expected him to say five dollars more. Ten, perhaps. But fifty-two dollars? "Why, that's highway robbery!"

Handsome stood, grasped her wrist and grinned with gratitude. "You're. . .you're *American!*"

From a distance, thanks to his swarthy good looks, he'd looked like an Italian movie star; up close and personal, Shannen observed, he was even more attractive.

There were bronze highlights in his dark hair, and the slight growth of whiskers accented his powerful jaw.

"Maryland born and bred," she said meeting his dark gaze. "And you?"

"I live in Annapolis."

"The state capitol? You're kidding."

The conductor cleared his throat, loudly, as if to remind them he still hadn't been paid. Hand extended, he pointed at his empty palm.

"How much does he want?" Handsome asked.

Shannen tucked in one corner of her mouth. "Fifty-two dollars."

"Hoo–*ha!*" he sputtered, brow furrowing as he opened his wallet. "That *is* highway robbery!" He fished several bills from his wallet and handed them to the conductor, who jammed his cap back onto his head, nodded smugly, and headed for the next car.

"I feel sorry for the folks up there," Handsome said under his breath. Smiling, he put the wallet back into his jacket pocket. "Mind if I join you?"

"Not at all. I'm right—"

"—across the aisle. I know."

So he'd seen her after all!

Shannen felt the beginnings of a blush coloring her cheeks, and to hide it, turned toward her seat.

"Name's Joe," he said, sitting beside her. "Joe Malone." He extended a big hand.

She put hers into it. "Shannen Flynn."

"This must be my lucky day."

"Why?"

"Gorgeous li'l Italian-speaking gal comes to my rescue, and it turns out she's Irish." He winked. "Like me."

She tucked in one corner of her mouth and kept silent about his seemingly obvious flirtations. "I'm only half Irish. My mom's Italian."

"Go figure."

She raised her eyebrows, determined to ignore his glibness. Something didn't ring true, though: If he *was* all that suave and sophisticated, why the slight tremor in his voice? And why the quirk in his devilishly handsome smile?

"*My* mother is Italian, too." Joe settled back, smoothing the newspaper across his knees. "So tell me, Shannen Flynn, what're you doing in sunny Italy?"

"Sightseeing."

"All by yourself?"

She nodded. "I've been here twice before."

"Alone?"

She chose to ignore the question. "It's perfectly safe," she said instead, "if you practice common sense."

"Then I hope what the sages say is true. . . ."

"About what?"

"That practice makes perfect, because a pretty little thing like you could get into some dangerous situations traveling alone."

She'd gotten an identical lecture at her parents' house on Thanksgiving, the day before her departure. "Shannen," her big brother Sean had said, "what makes you think you'll be safe, all by yourself, in Italy of all places!"

"Yeah," Liam had agreed. "The guys over there are famous for their pinchers." He'd turned his hand so that the thumb pressed against the side of his forefinger.

"Well," her dad had said, "you know how I feel

about this trip."

Her mother's sigh had punctuated her father's statement. "And I *still* think you should see if Bonnie can go with you," she'd suggested.

"I think she's just trying to prove something to Toady Todd," Cody put in. "Ever since he called off the engagement, she's been determined to prove how independent she is."

Cody, in fact, had come closest to the truth. Shannen *did* feel she had a lot to prove. As the youngest —and the only girl—she needed to show them, once and for all, that she could meet life head-on, without their help!

"I know you're only saying these things because you love me," she'd admitted, "and I love you all right back! But I'm twenty-five years old," she'd reminded her three older brothers, their wives, and her parents. "It's high time you started treating me like an adult; the only way that's going to happen is if I start *acting* like one."

So now, Shannen told Joe exactly what she'd told them: "No need to worry about me getting into dangerous situations, because I can scream *police* in four languages."

Her eldest brother's response had been a terse. "That's not funny, Shannen." It amazed Shannen how like Sean Joe sounded when he said, "Is that supposed to be a joke?"

Changing the subject usually worked with her brothers. She tried it with Joe. "I teach Italian back home, so being here gives me a great opportunity to speak the language."

He gave her a look that said, "You're not foolin' me,"

then said, "Where's 'home'?"

"Ellicott City."

"You mean to tell me we live less than thirty minutes apart, and I had to come all the way to Italy to meet you?" He shook his head. "Go figure."

Grinning, they shared a moment of compatible silence.

"So, you're an Italian teacher, eh?"

"Well, only part-time. . .at Howard Community College. Full time, I teach French and Spanish at Centennial High School."

"Yep," he said again, "must be my lucky day." Joe began counting on his fingers. "You're cute, Irish *and* Italian, a natural-born caretaker, and you're smart, too." A chuckle punctuated his comment. "Seriously, you have to let me do something to repay you." He held up a hand to forestall her protestations. "If you hadn't stepped up when you did, that conductor would have tossed me off the train. So. . .how 'bout dinner?"

"I was happy to help. Really. Repayment isn't nec—"

"Are you kidding? I saw you open your little knapsack there; you were all set to pay my fare, so yes, it *is* necessary."

"But I'm staying in Florence and you're—"

"—staying in Florence."

"If you tell me you're registered at The Hotel Baglioni, I'll. . ." She grinned. "The coincidences are mounting up so fast, we're going to need a shovel to dig our way off this train!"

Joe laughed nervously. "You think Someone is trying to tell us something?"

For the third time since meeting him, Shannen got

the distinct feeling Joe wasn't accustomed to flirting with strange women. Not that he wasn't good at it, she mused, grinning as she recalled his clumsy compliments, but the tension was written all over his fascinating face. She couldn't help but wonder *why* he seemed to be such a curious mix of cosmopolitan and uncomfortable.

Curiosity killed the cat, she reminded herself. "So tell me, when did you arrive in Italy?"

"Just over a week ago. But mine isn't a pleasure trip." He shrugged one shoulder. "I own an import-export company, see, and every now and then I like to choose the goods myself instead of sending a buyer to do it for me."

Her eyes widened. "Ooooh-la-lah," she said in a thick French accent, "a reeeech Americahn beeez-nessman."

Joe chuckled. "My shop is barely more than a hole in the wall, down on the Annapolis docks."

He had a delightful, masculine laugh that under-scored her presumption that he was the genuine article, rather than a fast-lane playboy. "Will you be visiting other countries in Europe. . .to find, ah, *finds* for your shop?"

"Already made stops in London and Paris," he told her matter-of-factly. "Another week here, and it's back to Annapolis for me."

"And you really haven't done *any* sightseeing?"

"Not unless you call scrounging around in the shops 'sightseeing'."

She narrowed her eyes. *I was right*, she told herself; *he's one of those 'all work and no play' kind of guys*. "How do you bargain with the shopkeepers when you don't even speak the language?"

"I brought my secretary along for that very reason. She's second generation Italian. Most efficient assistant I've ever had. Speaks six languages fluently. Keeps the books, makes my appointments. . . She's one of those 'place for everything, everything in its place' kind of people, y'know? My office has never been more organized, and you should see my warehouse. She runs that place like she's a Marine drill sergeant!"

"Is she married?" Shannen teased.

"Matter of fact, she isn't."

It didn't make any sense that she felt jealous of a woman she'd never met. . .over a man she'd known less than ten minutes. "Maybe you oughta snap her up, before somebody else does. She sounds like quite a woman—"

"Too late," he said on a sigh. "She met someone in Rome. Fell in love like that." He snapped his fingers. "I told her to take her time in Rome getting to know the guy."

Shannen smirked. "*Ah–ha!* So having a chaperon *isn't* a surefire guarantee a woman will be safe in a foreign land."

"Helen? In danger?" Joe laughed and slapped his knee. "For one thing, if the guy ever got out of line with her—"

"Is she a big woman?"

He gave his comment a moment's thought. "Let's just say she's not petite. . .," he gave her a quick once-over, "like you."

Again, the compliment seemed strained, a trait that only endeared him to her. "Is this your first trip to Italy?"

"Matter of fact, it is."

"Then I hope you at least got a chance to see the Colosseum while you were in Rome."

"From my hotel room."

"The Vatican?"

"Saw that from a taxi."

She frowned. "Do you *want* to see it?"

"Rome? Sure. I guess." He regarded her from the corner of his eye. "Why. . .you volunteering to go back? . . .be my tour guide?"

She patted her knapsack. "If you have the time, I have the tour book."

"It's a date. But first. . .dinner at the Baglioni. I hear they have a roof-garden restaurant with a view like you wouldn't believe."

"Really? Last time I was in Florence, I stayed at the Ra-pallo. No restaurant, no rooftop view, but it was affordable."

"That settles it, then."

"But. . .I'll be leaving Florence day after tomorrow, for—"

"If you say Siena, *I'm* gonna explode."

"I want to see where the *Palio* festival is held. I missed it last time I was here, too, but I've seen pictures. It's medieval and colorful, with parades and races and processions—"

"When is it?"

"July second. I'm afraid I'm going to miss it again."

"Say. . .this isn't the thingamajig where they bring out banners and get into these ritzy costumes and—"

"And trumpets and mace-bearers, and standard-bearers, too."

"Hmmm. I'm going to have to look into this. I might be able to get my hands on some flags for the shop. . . ."

"So how long will you be in Siena?"

"Hadn't made any definite plans."

Shannen sighed. "Small world."

"Real small."

They sat quietly for a moment, listening to the *click-ida-clackida, clickida-clackida* of the train's wheels, chugging over the polished steel tracks. Anytime in Italy was beautiful. Shannen wished she could open the window to inhale the fresh smell of fields of grapevines and apple trees along the tracks.

Joe broke the silence to say, "Tell you what. . .let's skip the hotel restaurant." He impulsively grabbed her hand. "Helen told me about a place right around the corner, where the locals go. . . ."

Biting her lower lip, Shannen hesitated.

Only then did he seem to notice that he'd taken her hand. Flushing slightly, Joe let go suddenly. "But Shannen," he pressed, "you *have* to go. What if I order 'Jail Sentence Al Fresco' from the menu? It'll be all your fault."

He has a point, Shannen thought, remembering the trouble he'd had with the conductor. *And he has gorgeous eyes, too.* She was mesmerized by flecks of gold and green that glimmered in his dark brown eyes. His words were definitely brash and confident, but something in those eyes made her more certain than ever that it was all a facade. "Okay. I'll go," she said, feeling strangely safe and secure. "But only to save you from yourself. And only if you promise to try and mix a *little* pleasure with the business while you're in Italy. Because who knows? You may never have another chance to see it!"

Joe sat back, leaned against the headrest, and closed his eyes. "Mixing business with pleasure, Shannen Flynn, is exactly why I invited you to dinner." And in minutes, it seemed, he was asleep—leaving Shannon wishing he hadn't let go of her hand.

❄

Shannen sent a prayer of thanks heavenward for the warmer than usual early December morning. Temperate breezes set leaves to bouncing on the tree branches that shrouded the Bridge of Santa Trinita—an ancient structure that was daytime home to Florentine artists—and cooled the sketch artists and painters gathered under its graceful arches. Joe insisted that Shannen pose while a young prodigy sketched her in brown charcoal on cream-colored paper.

In *Il Battistero*, they oohed and aahed at the detail in each panel of the gigantic bronze doors carved by masters like Ghiberti, Pisano, and Michelangelo.

At the Straw Market, they rubbed the nose of *Il Porcellino*, the bronze boar. "Now throw a coin into the fountain," shouted a merchant from a nearby stall, "and you will someday return to *Firenze!*"

And in the echoing interior of *Galleria del'-Academia*, they stood in silent awe, admiring Michelangelo's *David*. "He has a chipped toenail," Shannen observed. "Why didn't I notice it last time I was here?" Joe pointed upward. "And there's even a stone in the leather strap of his slingshot."

Too tired from their long day of sightseeing, Shannen and Joe agreed to skip the local eatery and decided on a quiet dinner in the hotel's restaurant instead. From their table near the wrought-iron railing, they saw miles of red clay rooftops, illuminated by a bright half-moon. In the street below, mopeds and tiny cars zipped around pedestrians, their drivers honking and shouting greetings to one another.

Their affable waiter, who spoke fluent English, insisted they try some gnocchi. "You can-a *manja* the spagett' when you go back-a to America." Squinting, he'd looked toward the star-studded Italian sky. "What is it you say in you' country. . .'when-a in Roma. . .?' " Two bites of the airy potato dumplings in pesto sauce had them comparing it to the same dish served in the restaurants in Baltimore's Little Italy. "It's right tasty at Sabatino's," Joe said. "And at Chiaparelli's," Shannen agreed, "but for some reason it's *better* here," they said in unison.

The next day, after boarding a train in Florence, they'd headed east, to Pisa, where Shannen's curiosity earned her a stern lecture from a machine gun-brandishing soldier. "I can't believe you climbed over that rope!" Joe scolded as they walked away from the Leaning Tower.

"How else was I going to find out if it's made of granite or marble?" she'd asked.

"So. . .what's it made of?"

They both doubled over with laughter when she admitted, "I have no idea!"

They traveled south, then, to Siena, to tour the *Piazza Del Campo*, the *Palazzo Di Guistizia* Cathedral, and stand on the cobbled streets where, in a few months, people from around the world would revel in the elaborate and picturesque *Palio*.

Next, they went further south and returned to the ancient city of Rome.

"I don't know if I'm reacting to the tour guide's speech or if it's my imagination," Joe whispered as they walked the brick path that separated two rows of lions' dens, "but does it smell like wild animals in here?"

She grinned. "Do wild animals smell different from other animals?"

"Absolutely!" Joe insisted. "There's the 'barn scent' and the aroma of the zoo. . .this is definitely not Old MacDonald's farm."

Shannen knew what he meant. She'd been to the Colosseum before; both times, she'd experienced a similarly strange and eerie sensation. She hadn't been able to put a name on the feeling that enveloped her standing amid the bleachers and staring into the huge circular arena that had been "center stage" to Roman audiences. But this time, with Joe at her side—giving commentary to every brick, every board, every metal bar—she could almost picture pagan throngs, cheering wildly as the beasts devoured Christians.

Despite his claims that this trip was "business only," Joe had gotten caught up in the historic splendor of it, just as he'd been entranced by Florentine art, the planned festival in Siena, the quaint little town of Pisa. "It's probably just the cats," she said in a not-so-veiled attempt to be the voice of reason.

Joe squatted to scratch the ears of a scraggly feline that had been following him for five minutes or so—one of hundreds that roamed the interior of the ancient place. "I guess you're right."

"Chester," an elderly woman hissed to her husband.

"Will you take a look at that! Didn't the tour guide say these cats never allow themselves to be petted. . .and that we shouldn't try, because they're feral?"

"Young folks," her husband said, shaking his head.

"*You're* the reason Europeans call the rest of us 'Ugly Americans!' " the woman snapped at Joe. "Leave that mangy animal alone before you get fleas or lice. . . or *arrested!*"

Shannen's heart ached when she saw Joe's brows raise in response to the woman's hurtful words. "Excuse me, ma'am," Shannen said to the woman, "but it really isn't your concern if my friend gets scratched by one of the Colosseum cats, and I fail to see how his behavior makes all Americans look—"

Joe stood and, smiling patronizingly at the lady, said, "I apologize, madam. Thank the Good Lord there are busloads of New York tourists in the parking lot to counteract my lady friend's outspokenness."

"It just so happens *I'm* from New York," she huffed.

Joe shrugged and grinned. "Well, then. . .I'm *really* sorry."

Biting back a giggle, Shannen tugged at his hand. "And I thought *I* was the master of putting people in their places! C'mon," she said, "I see a gelato stand on the other side of the piazza."

Joe smacked his lips. "I hope they have chocolate. How 'bout you?"

"You're not going to believe this, but chocolate's my favorite flavor."

He stepped into line at the ice cream stand. "Go figure," Joe said, slipping an arm around her waist. "Go figure."

two

They stood side by side at the baggage claim watching an assortment of luggage crank by like odd-shaped horses on a silent, slow-motion merry-go-round. When Joe hoisted an elderly lady's suitcase onto a rented cart, Shannen was reminded of the many similar acts of kindness he'd performed all over Italy—small things, like giving up seats for ladies with children and senior citizens. . .and more generous gestures, such as the time he dropped a L.10,000 bank note into a raggedy gypsy's mandolin case. On the flight from Milan to New York, he'd slipped his dessert to the little boy across the aisle, and when they boarded the two-propeller plane headed from Kennedy to BWI, he helped a white-haired gentleman store his weighty carry-on in the overhead bin.

Joe is a good man, she told herself as he wheeled the old woman's cart toward the pick-up stand outside, *a kindhearted, decent human being. Surely he's a Christian.* She bit her lower lip. *Please God, let him be a Christian.* When Shannen broke off her engagement to Todd a year earlier, she'd promised herself never to get involved with a non-believer again. *One close call is one too many!*

Joe was beside her again, smiling and happy, but then, there was nothing unusual about that. In the seven days they'd spent together, visiting museums and art galleries, walking through topiary gardens and over cobbled streets, taking meals in charming sidewalk cafes and the diner cars of fast-moving trains, she had seen Joe lose his temper once. They'd been in Milan when a swarthy fellow on a moped nearly ran her down as she attempted to cross the street. Angry as he was at the driver's inattentiveness, the moment Joe saw how shaken she was by the near miss, he'd stopped shouting and shaking his fist at the offender and pulled her into a comforting embrace, right there on the busy street corner.

"You know," he said, rousing her from her reverie as he hefted a bag for a woman with stair-step toddlers in a stroller made for twins, "I'm really going to miss you."

Shannen's heartbeat doubled as the heat of a blush colored her cheeks.

Pocketing both hands, he faced her, head-on. "I don't suppose you'd want to. . .ah. . .see me for dinner or lunch sometime, once we get home. . . ."

One of the prayers she'd been praying off and on the entire time they were in Italy had been that the Lord would provide her with a ladylike, sensible excuse to suggest a get-together, soon. The other was that God would give her strength—lots of it—if Joe turned out to be a non-Christian. "I'd like that."

He seemed pleased by her response, and smiling, Joe straightened to his full six-foot height and squared his broad shoulders. "If I ever find *our* suitcases, what do you say to lunch and a ride home?"

"I, um, I left my car here. . .in the Blue Lot."

Joe shook his head. "You're never going to believe this. . . ."

She held one hand up. "Let me guess: *Your* car is

in the Blue Lot."

He nodded as she grabbed one of her two big gray suitcases. "I don't mind telling you, I'm disappointed," he said. "I was hoping to have an excuse to stretch out these last few minutes together."

That's what he'd said when he found out what flight she'd booked out of the Milan airport. It had taken three phone calls and nearly an hour, and cost him nearly a hundred American dollars, but Joe managed to change his reservation so that he could fly home on Shannen's plane. Since he'd been a last-minute addition to the passenger list, the airline had assigned him a seat near the flight attendants' compartment. Shannen doubted she'd ever learn how Joe had convinced the gentleman who'd been seated beside her at the start of the flight to switch seats with him, but if the winks and nods that passed between her former seatmate and Joe were any measure, it was probably better that way.

Shannen wanted to stretch these last moments, too. "I always keep a supply of TV dinners in the freezer," she told him. "You could follow me to my place. . .let me thaw you a meal. . ."

"You mean it?"

"Sure." She grabbed her second big bag. *If only you knew how* much *I mean it!*

Somehow, Joe had managed to pack two weeks' worth of clothes into one midsized bag. He tucked it under one arm, lifted her suitcases in each hand and, with a nod of his head, gestured toward the shuttle parked outside. "Let's blow this pop stand," he said with a grin and a wink.

They rode in companionable silence as the vehicle

lurched and bounced over potholed roads outside BWI's newly constructed international wing, leaning into one another as the driver made wide, unwieldy turns. When the traffic light at the end of the airport entrance ramp went from yellow to red, the driver brought the vehicle to a jerky stop that nearly unseated Shannen. If not for Joe's quick thinking—and strong arm around her shoulders—she might have landed on her tailbone in the middle of the aisle. Long after the near mishap, his arm still rested protectively across her shoulders, his hand still gently but firmly gripped her bicep.

They located his car first, loaded the bags into his trunk, and drove to Section B. As Joe transferred her suitcases into the backseat of her tiny sports car, Shannen scribbled hasty directions to her place on the back of one of Joe's business cards. As she pulled into traffic, she wondered whether or not she'd remembered to run the dishwasher before she'd left, if she'd tidied the living room and straightened the guest bathroom. Despite the bright sunlight, Shannen shivered and flicked on the heat. *Well,* she told herself, *it is mid-December after all, and you're not in sunny Italy any more, either. . . .*

She checked the mirror every other blink, it seemed, to make sure Joe was still behind her. *Thank goodness for sunglasses,* she thought, *because if he knew how often you were checking on him, he'd think. . .*

What *would* he think? Surely he wouldn't be able to tell that she'd dreamed of him nearly every night since they'd met on that Florence-bound Eurail train, or that what had begun as a chance acquaintanceship had—for Shannen, at least—turned into full-blown infatuation.

And surely it was nothing more than that, because

it had only been seven days, after all.

Still. . .he was drop-dead gorgeous, with a smile that would charm the leaves from the trees. And he had a voice deeper and more resonant than any radio disc jockey she'd ever heard. Add the fact that he was one of the sweetest, most thoughtful men she'd ever known, and Shannen believed she'd need a heart of steel to keep from feeling *something* more than friendship for Joe Malone.

She nosed her car into the driveway beside her townhouse as Joe pulled in beside her. In a heartbeat, it seemed, he opened the passenger door and began pulling her suitcases from the car. "Nice place," he said, nodding toward the house. "Live here long?"

"Almost two years," she said, climbing the long white staircase leading to the front door.

"You have one of those condo deals where somebody mows the lawn and stuff, don't you?" he asked as she unlocked the door.

Shannen stepped into the foyer, held the door open as Joe passed through with her suitcases. "There's a gardener available. . .for a fee," she said as he put them at the foot of the stairs, "but I prefer the luxury of traveling to the extravagance of a gardener."

He grinned. "Smart girl." Then, "But how do you keep it looking so neat, with your job and traveling and all?"

"Easy-care perennials and lots of bark mulch," she said, laughing as she closed the door.

"I live in a small apartment above my shop, but I've been thinking about settling into a house. This is a great area."

"Would you like the nickel tour?"

Bowing from the waist, he extended his arm. "Lead the way, m'lady."

As she showed him around, Shannen said a silent prayer of thanks that she had, indeed, remembered to clean up before leaving for Italy. Except for the box of Christmas decorations in the middle of the living room, the place looked fine. Joe nodded his approval and said things like "Clean as a whistle" and "Neat as a pin" in every single room. "My 'Reasons to Like Shannen' list is getting so long, pretty soon I'm gonna need a hand truck to cart it around."

Stomach fluttering, she headed for the kitchen. "I have some diet sodas in the fridge," she said, hoping to distract him from her flushed cheeks. "Or I can brew up some iced tea."

"Iced tea. . .that isn't from a jar?"

She wrinkled her nose. "I'm a fussbudget. Just ask my brothers. Instant iced tea and coffee from a jar just doesn't suit my taste buds."

Smiling, Joe shook his head. "Mmmm-mmmm-mmmm. Where have you been all my life, Shannen Flynn?"

The question nearly caused her to slam her fingers in the cupboard door. She filled a small saucepan with water, then proceeded to de-tag the tea bags. "So when am I going to see this infamous shop of yours?" she asked to change the subject.

Joe helped himself to a stool at the snack bar. "You pick a time, I'll be there." Peering into the cookie jar on the counter, he said, "Hey. Chocolate chip." He met her eyes. "Homemade?"

Wincing, she nodded. "But they're nearly three weeks old. They'll be stale."

He bit into a cookie. "Turn off that stove," he said, on his feet again. "You're coming with me."

"Where are we going?"

Joe led her to the front door. "You'll see. Do you have a grill?"

She locked the door. "You mean. . .as in barbecue? But it's the middle of December!"

Joe nodded, opening the passenger door of his four-wheeler.

"Well, sure, but I'm our of—"

"Charcoal. And milk." He held out his hand. "Can't enjoy a homemade chocolate chip cookie without milk." He fired up the car. "Which way to the nearest grocery store?"

Blinking, she buckled her seat belt. "Left out of the driveway, through the stop sign, right at the first traffic light."

He blended smoothly into traffic. "We can't have frozen TV dinners, not on our first night home from a place like Italy. We need a couple of thick steaks. Some salad fixin's. And a. . .a—"

"A juicy apple pie for dessert?" she finished, smiling.

Reaching across the console, he took her hand and gave it a gentle squeeze. "And a great big bag of charcoal."

❄

Joe stood on Shannen's deck, poking the New York strip steaks with a long-handled fork. "How do you like yours?" he hollered through the slightly opened kitchen window.

"Medium rare," she yelled back. "And I *really* like it when my steak is nicely charred on the outside."

"Hey. Is my name Dominick?" he called, reminding her of the waiter at Baglioni's.

"I should be so lucky," she retorted, laughing. "I've been craving gnocchi all day long!"

"Yeah, well, you're gonna have to make do with me and my steaks."

That is definitely not *a problem*, Shannen thought, grinning as she put the items he'd asked for on a tray.

"I do things plain and simple," he was saying when she stepped onto the deck.

The screen door banged shut behind her and she put the tray on the end of the picnic table nearest the grill. "Do you want me to set the table out here?" she kidded.

"There's a chill in the air," he said, painting sauce onto the steaks. "I don't want you to catch a cold, so maybe we'd better eat inside."

She gave him a playful jab to the ribs with her elbow. "Hey. I live here, remember. If I get cold, I can put on a coat. A winter picnic might be fun. . . ."

"Yeah," he teased, "well what about me?"

Shannen couldn't say she hadn't noticed that he'd worn a short-sleeved polo shirt with his blue jeans, because she'd been ogling the bulging muscles of his biceps since they boarded that plane in Milan. The sun had set and she could see the puffs from each breath. *Todd's sweater is still on the shelf in the front hall closet*, she remembered. It was the one she'd knitted for his thirtieth birthday, and since he'd broken off their engagement a week before the big three-oh, it had never been out of the gift-wrapped box.

Todd stood five-feet, ten-inches tall. . .a full three inches shorter than Joe, by Shannen's estimation. But Todd had been a vain man who'd spent hours in front of the mirror working with free weights. His "work" required her to add several inches to the pattern so the sweater would fit over his exercise-thickened shoulders. It was the last "Todd thing" in her house. . .in her *life*. Once she tossed the multicolored wrapping paper and ribbon, she'd be rid of him, for good.

"I have a sweater that might fit you," she said, heading inside.

He held the steak fork in one hand, the salt shaker in the other. "One of your brothers'?"

She stopped just outside the closed door and shook her head.

"Your dad's?"

"No."

The well-arched, dark brows rose high on his forehead as understanding dawned. "Ahh," he said, "it belonged to an old boyfriend, didn't it?"

"Fiancé," she said, pulling open the door. "But that ended ages ago. Seems a shame to waste a perfectly good—"

"He had an excuse to come back and didn't take advantage of it?"

It was her turn to raise her eyebrows. "Sorry. I don't get it."

"He left his sweater here, right," he said more to himself than to Shannen, "so he could have called, said he was stopping by to pick up his sweater, y'know? And apologized for whatever idiotic thing he did that—"

She stood in the doorway, a half-grin on her face.

"What makes you think it was his fault?"

Joe chuckled. "Gimme a break. You couldn't do anything to rile a guy. Not on your worst day." He paused, tilting his head slightly. "Am I right?"

She nodded, remembering how Todd had called her naive. Innocent. A babe in the woods. Todd had political aspirations and felt he needed a sophisticated woman by his side to help coerce the bigwigs into voting for him.

"He's a jerk," Joe grated out. "I don't want to wear his sweater; some of his 'stupid' might rub off on me."

That inspired a smile. "The sweater isn't really his. I mean, I made it for Todd, but he. . .he broke things off before I got a chance to give it to him."

"What was. . .what was this *Toad* guy like?"

Shannen grinned mischievously, because ever since the breakup, Cody had only referred to her ex-fiancé as Toady. "He was a 'todd' much," she said, laughing softly, "pun intended."

Chuckling, Joe put down the steak fork and crossed the deck in three long strides. "Whoa. Lemme get this straight. You mean to tell me you *made* the guy a sweater, and he. . .and he left you anyway?"

"It was supposed to be a surprise. He never knew I'd—"

Joe tucked an auburn curl behind her ear. "Does he have any idea how few women these days even know how to knit?"

She smiled. "I'm afraid I'm not up on the latest statistics."

He assumed a pompous, all-knowing expression. "It just so happens that only twenty-four percent of females between the ages of twenty and sixty even know how to thread a needle."

She feigned surprise. "I had no idea I was in such a minority!"

"All I can say is, good riddance to bad rubbish."

Shannen sent a silent prayer heavenward for the dusky light that hid her blush. "I'll just. . .I'll just go and get the sweater. . .so that whenever. . .if you feel like using it, it'll be here for you."

His knuckle gently grazed her cheek, and he slowly shook his head. "Like I said, the guy's a jerk." And with no warning whatsoever, Joe leaned forward and kissed her.

She closed her eyes when a quiet murmur escaped his lips as he ended the delicious moment.

"I've been wanting to do that since I laid eyes on you," he said softly. "I knew it'd be like that."

"Like what?" she managed to say.

"Soft, gentle, sweet. . ."

He made a move as if to do it again when Shannen's heartbeat doubled. Afraid Joe might hear it, she took a deep breath and a big step backward. "Well, I'd better get the plates and napkins," she said over her shoulder as the screen door closed quietly behind her, "and silverware, glasses. . .and candles so we'll be able to see what we're doing."

Chuckling under his breath, Joe returned to the grill. "And the sweater," he said through the open kitchen window. "Don't forget the sweater."

three

Joe carried the dishes to the counter as Shannen put the leftovers into the refrigerator. She'd turned on the tiny black-and-white TV on the counter so they could catch up on the news. "If my mother wasn't a happily married Christian woman," Shannen said in response to the anchorman's story about Ian Cole's most recent Hollywood divorce, "she'd be on the next flight to L.A."

"But from what you've told me, she seems so level-headed. How could she be an Ian Cole fan?"

"She says it's something in his eyes," Shannen explained, shrugging.

He harumphed and stuffed a dirty fork into the dishwasher. "I suppose you'd like me better if I looked more like that," he said, pointing at the TV with a steak knife, "if I were rich and famous and—"

"If you were rich and famous, we wouldn't have a thing in common," she said matter-of-factly. "Don't get me wrong, Ian Cole is handsome enough, but he isn't my type."

"What's your 'type'?"

Another shrug. *You're my type*, she thought. But it was way too soon to admit such things to Joe; too many compliments too soon was precisely what had gotten her in over her head with Todd. "Well," she answered hesitantly, "certainly not a guy whose biggest claim to fame is the number of wives he's had."

Joe nodded thoughtfully. "I've been wondering when to ask you this. . . ." Joe closed the dishwasher and leaned back against the counter. Crossing both arms over his chest, he said, "I'd like you to go to a wedding with me."

A wedding was a joyous, uplifting occasion, so why the somber expression? Shannen wondered. Was it marriage in general that had turned his mouth down at the corners, or just *this* wedding? Perhaps an old girlfriend was tying the knot, or an archenemy. . . .

"When?"

"Next weekend, just before Christmas."

She opened the pantry door and checked the calendar hanging inside it. "I don't have any plans."

He'd pulled up the sleeves of the sweater to rinse the plates. Now, Joe tugged them back down to his wrists. He looked wonderful in the fisherman's knit. She'd more or less expected the fit to be a bit baggy—especially around the chest and shoulders, since Todd had bulked up with strenuous exercise—but it skimmed Joe's torso as if she'd made it for *him*.

"Good," he said, " 'cause I'd look pretty silly if I went to my own mother's wedding without a date."

"Your. . .your *mother's* wedding?"

Joe's expression intensified to grim as he focused on the window overlooking the deck. He exhaled a long sigh. "It's her fifth. She expects this one to last," he said without looking at Shannen, "because he's 'one of her own kind.' "

The subject was obviously a distressing one for him,

so Shannen poured them each a cup of coffee. She carried both mugs into the adjoining family room and sat cross-legged on the far end of the overstuffed sectional near the gas-powered fireplace. "Take a load off," she said, smiling as she patted the cushion beside her.

Joe sat, draped an arm across the back of the couch, his fingertips playing in her hair. "Before you circle Saturday in red pen, I'd better fill you in on some of the details. You might want to change your mind."

"Why?"

Another sigh. "Well, for one thing, the wedding is in L.A."

Her eyes widened. "Los Angeles. . .*California*?"

He nodded. "And there's likely to be a crowd of TV and magazine reporters there."

Shannen laughed softly. "Reporters! Good grief. Who's your mother. . .the Queen of England?"

"Close. She's the Queen of Hollywood."

Shannen glanced at the out-of-date TV listings booklet on the coffee table. Beneath the color photo of a longtime movie star, the caption said "The 'Queen' Celebrates Twenty-Five Years in Tinsel Town." Martha Malone had played the leading lady in some of Shannen's favorite movies.

She met his eyes and pointed at the TV book. "*That's* your *mother*?"

Joe tucked in one corner of his mouth. " 'Fraid so," he said dully.

She'd read that article on the morning she'd packed for Italy. *Funny*, Shannen thought, *I don't remember reading anything about an upcoming marriage. . .or a son.* She gathered from Joe's demeanor that growing up in the shadow of a star hadn't been all glitz and glamour. "You don't approve of the marriage?" she asked.

He shrugged. "It isn't that, exactly." His knuckles skimmed her cheek as he said, "Ever since my dad died, she's been like a little bird, flitting from one relationship to another. She'd never admit it, of course, but she's trying to replace him." He paused. "And it ain't a-gonna happen."

"Was your father in show business, too?"

"Ever hear of a guy by the name of Joe Malone?"

Shannen linked her fingers with his and smiled. "As a matter of fact, I believe I have." Squinting one eye, she pretended to be deep in thought. "If my memory serves me correctly, he's a very successful businessman. . .and boy-oh-boy, can he grill a steak."

That inspired a grin. "Dad was a director and producer." The grin faded when Joe added, "He gave Mom her first break. He built her career, made her a star."

"How long ago did you lose him?"

"I was ten when he had the heart attack. I found him on the bathroom floor."

She gave his fingers a gentle squeeze. "Oh, Joe, that must have been awful for you. I'm so sorry."

He shrugged one shoulder. "Ancient history."

But his nonchalant attitude did little to hide his true feelings; Shannen read the pain and misery on his face, in his eyes, and knew that Joe still missed his father very much.

"He'd only been gone a year when she married her co-star. Stefan Erickson."

Shannen knew that name, too; like every other teenaged girl in America, she'd dreamed of growing up and marrying Stefan some day. *But wait*, she thought, *Stefan would have been fifteen years younger than Martha. . . wouldn't he?*

"That's right," Joe nodded. "She replaced my dad with a husband young enough to be my big brother." A bitter laugh escaped his lips. " 'It was the best of times, it was the worst of times,' " he quoted. "He taught me how to field a grounder. . .but he hogged the remote, too. She stayed single for nearly two years that time. And then she brought Jennings Richardson home."

"The anchorman?"

"Uh–huh. He looked pretty good, sitting there under his pompadour on the evening news and when we were out in public, but he was a mean, crotchety old man around the house."

Joe leaned forward and grabbed his cup of coffee. Sitting back, he took a drink of it and shook his head. "Jennings had a close buddy. He didn't introduce Mom to his liquor cabinet till they'd been married a couple weeks. . . ."

"He was an alcoholic?"

"Still is."

"I never would have guessed. He seems so poised, so sophisticated on TV."

"Stand a man on the lens side of a camera, and he'll act," Joe said bitterly. "It's human nature."

Not knowing what to say, Shannen sipped her coffee.

"We had four years of peace and quiet—if you can call life in the fast lane peaceful or quiet—before Bob Harris took the title of Mister Martha Malone. I think I could actually have grown to love Bob. He moved his office into the house, so he was there when I left for school, and he was there when I got home. Taught me how to figure square roots, how to play chess, how to balance my checkbook—"

"You had a checkbook? At sixteen?"

"Seventeen," he said as he gave her a look that said, "Didn't *every* Hollywood kid?"

While she was sitting there wondering how long *that* marriage had lasted—and what ended it—Joe said, "Bob was Mom's financial advisor. He wasn't pretty—paunchy, balding, thick glasses—but he had a good heart. He wouldn't have hurt her for anything." Another bitter laugh escaped his lungs. "Want to hear something funny?"

She had a feeling that whatever Joe was about to say would be anything *but* humorous.

"Mom got rid of Bob because he didn't photograph well. 'He makes me look old and frumpy.' That was her reason for giving Bob the boot."

He took a deep, grating breath, putting his mug back on the coffee table. "So it's been a while since my very-married mother has taken a husband. Ought to be quite an extravaganza." He met her eyes. "You still interested? Could be a media feeding frenzy."

Truthfully? Shannen wanted no part of Martha Malone. . .or any of the Hollywood types who had hurt Joe. Besides, she lived on a carefully planned budget. The money she'd set aside for travel had been spent. . .all over sunny Italy. If she booked a flight to California and a hotel room in L.A., she'd have to dip into her savings. What if the water heater sprung a leak? Or the furnace broke down? Most important of all, her brothers would likely explode if she got on a

California-bound plane with the son of Martha Malone!

She chose her words carefully. "Joe, I'm afraid I don't—"

"Didn't I tell you? This trip's on me. I couldn't ask you to pay your way. Not to a wedding like that. . .in California."

Shannen gasped. "I couldn't let you do that. How would it look?"

"What do you mean, 'how would it look?' "

"W–well, well," she began, blinking and stammering, "People would think. . .naturally they'd assume. . . they'd say we're—"

"Frankly, nobody out there is gonna notice. . .or *care* how you got there."

"I'm talking about people *here*, Joe; my family, my friends. . . I don't want them thinking I'm some kind of—"

"Martha Malone?"

She felt the hot flush creep into her cheeks. "No. No, of course not. I didn't mean that at all," she rambled. "It's just. . .it's that I'm part of a very big, very traditional family. My father and brothers watch over me like I'm made of spun glass or something. And my mother!" Shannen rolled her eyes. "She's the most devout Christian I'll know in my lifetime. She'd probably melt if I announced I was going to a Hollywood wedding, all expenses paid by the son of the bride—"

Joe took her hand, giving it a soft pat. "Shannen, you've got to believe me, things will be completely aboveboard." He rolled his eyes and gave a disgusted chortle. "Trust me, with a background like mine, I have no intention of getting involved with a nice girl like you."

She frowned. "What does *that* mean?"

Lips taut and brow furrowed, he let go of her hand. "Nothing." He brightened then and said on the heels of a wide, seemingly practiced smile, "How 'bout if I talk to your folks? If I can convince them that you'll be absolutely safe, that my intentions are completely honorable, will you go?"

"Wouldn't it be easier to ask someone else?"

"Someone more like me, you mean?"

She looked into his eyes, reading the hurt and disappointment there. *Lord Jesus*, she prayed, *why is he so determined to take* me *to his mother's wedding?*

"Look, Shannen," he said, taking her hand again, "it might come as a surprise to you, since I'm not one to jump and shout about it, but I'm a Christian, too. Have been for nearly two years now. I don't want to go out there and fall right back into step with that crowd. I want them to see that I've changed—from where I live, to what I do for a living, to the kind of women I choose to associate with."

Frustration made her blurt, "But. . .but you said you have no intention of getting involved with a girl like me. If a nice, Christian girl is what you want, why draw the line at. . .at. . .at romantic involvement?"

He raised one dark eyebrow and tilted his head slightly. "Why Shannen Flynn," he said, grinning, "I had no idea you had designs on me."

She got to her feet in a heartbeat and walked to the French doors leading to the deck. "Of all the arrogant, self-important things to say," she huffed. Whirling around, she said through clenched teeth, "I don't have 'designs' on you, *Joe Malone*. What I have is a head full of questions."

He stood, pocketing both hands. "What kind of questions?"

Why did you follow me all over Italy? And why did you rearrange your plans so you could fly home on the same plane as I did? Why did you say you'd miss me, that you didn't want this to end? Why buy dinner, and cook it, and invite me to your mother's wedding unless—

She pressed her fingertips to her temples. "Never mind," she said. "I must have a serious case of jet lag."

Joe glanced at his watch. "Wow. It's after ten." He met her eyes and sent her a sheepish grin. "Time sure flies. . . ."

The cliche was supposed to end with "when you're having fun." Cupping her elbows, she stared at the toes of her shoes and completed it her own way: ". . .When you're surrounded by mixed messages," she said under her breath.

"What?"

"Nothing."

Joe crossed the room and put both hands on her shoulders. "It's been a long day. We're both tired." He pressed a kiss to her forehead. "I'll call you tomorrow, after we've had a chance to catch up on our sleep. We'll talk about the wedding then, okay?"

She heaved a sigh. Far better to agree with him now and set him straight tomorrow, because, as he'd so astutely put it, they were both tired. "Okay," she agreed.

He kissed her cheek, then bracketed her face with both hands. "I want you to know," Joe said softly, slowly, "that I had a terrific time in Italy. . .because of you." Lifting her chin, he forced her to meet his eyes. "If I was in the market for a. . .for romance," he said, quoting himself, "I can't think of a better candidate."

She tucked in one corner of her mouth. "Thanks," she replied dryly. "That's high praise. . .coming from the son of Martha Malone."

He pursed his lips. "Touché," he said. "I guess I did sound a bit arrogant and self-important, didn't I?"

It's not how you sound that worries me, Joe, she told herself, *it's all these mixed signals you're sending. . .kissing me like you mean it. . .then saying you don't want it to mean anything. . . .* Shannen broke free of his almost-embrace and headed for the front door. One hand on the knob, she turned to thank him for supper, but stopped when she saw him start to remove the sweater. "What're you doing?"

"Returning the loan," he said, handing it to her, "what else?"

Heart pounding, she held it at arm's length. "I have no use for it. It's yours, if you want it."

"But you made it for. . ." The well-arched left brow rose high on his forehead again. "What was his name again?"

"Todd. Todd Hudson."

"Sounds like a movie star."

Shannen couldn't suppress a laugh. "Don't let *him* hear you say that; he'll be on the next plane west!"

"Stuck on himself, was he?"

"All Todd needs to be happy is a mirror." She held the sweater out to Joe. "I know it seems a bit weird, since I made it for him and all, but honest, he never knew. He took a hike long before I had a chance to even buy a birthday card to go with the gift."

He reached out, touching a sleeve. "Well, it is nice, and it fits like a glove. . . ."

"Then it's yours." She shoved it into his hands. "Please. I want you to have it. Consider it a 'thank-you'."

He pulled it over his head, mussing his brown, wavy hair. "For what?"

Instinctively, Shannen reached up and brushed the dark locks back from his forehead. "For making Italy more enjoyable than it was the first two times." She smiled. "For buying dinner. . .for cooking it. . . ."

She'd always been pretty good at reading between the lines; he'd told her more by what he *hadn't* said than with stories of his mother's rocky marital past. Joe believed the only reason anyone would want to get close to him was because he could put them in touch with Martha Malone, and that belief, she suspected, is what had inspired him to say he couldn't get romantically involved with a "nice" girl.

She wanted to prove to Joe he was worthy of love and affection, for no reason other than that he was a child of God. *Help me show him, Lord,* she prayed, *that he's the wonderful, lovable man I think he is. . .or could be. And if I'm getting in over my head. . .show me that, too.*

Something happened during that instant of intense eye contact, something that changed his expression, his posture, his breathing. Joe drew her close, his dark eyes glinting with longing, as if it had been a very long time since he'd felt the warmth of true affection.

If he had his way, Shannen knew, Joe was going to kiss her again, right here, right now, in her tiny foyer.

Should she let him?

Guide me, Lord, she prayed. *Don't allow me to begin a relationship that isn't Your Will for me.*

As his handsome face drew nearer and his arms pulled her closer, she closed her eyes and licked her lips. Heart pounding and pulse racing, she waited.

The kiss was surprisingly gentle as his lips brushed hers, and burying his face in the crook of her neck, he whispered her name. "Shannen. . . ."

His touch was almost unbearably tender as he pressed his big hands against her cheeks, his breath warm and moist against her skin. "Ah, Shannen, you're so lovely, so sweet. . . ." He proceeded to shower kisses around her mouth, along her jaw, and then, with a brush as light and soft as a spring breeze, he drew her face to his, caressing her mouth more than kissing it.

It surprised her. . .how completely she'd surrendered to the gentleness of his touch, his voice, his kisses. But was the reaction what God intended for her?

Until she knew for certain, she would do her best to resist Joe's charms. Lifting her chin, she squared her shoulders. "Thanks again for dinner," she said.

"My pleasure."

She had a feeling his response had little or nothing to do with the meal.

Drawing a deep breath, she forced herself to open the door. "I rarely sleep past eight," she said, reminding him of his promise to call. . .hoping he wouldn't see her struggle to recapture her composure.

His voice was a mix of gentleness and resignation as his dark eyes probed hers. "Can I buy you lunch?"

She took a frank and admiring look at him and studied his face, feature by handsome feature. "Absolutely not. I'll fix us something, right here."

They exchanged a subtle look of amusement before he said, "Okay. Noon, straight up?"

She nodded.

"Then I won't call. . .unless something comes up."

Another nod.

Joe stepped outside. "Ever seen San Francisco?"

"Only in postcards."

"This porch of yours reminds me of the houses out there. . .lots of steps, white railings. . ."

"It's the main reason I bought the place," she admitted, smiling.

He started down the stairs. "Maybe we'll get there one day."

She watched as he slung himself behind the wheel. *We?* she thought. But what she said was, "Maybe."

He started the car's motor. "See you tomorrow, then. Twelve o'clock."

Shannen waved from the door as he backed down the drive and, when he was gone, closed the door behind her and looked around at the living room and dining room, at the arched entry to the kitchen, and finally the cozy family room beyond. She'd lived here, by herself, for nearly two years and had never felt alone in the house before. *Why does the place seem so* empty *all of a sudden?* she wondered.

But she knew.

Except for the hours they'd spent sleeping in separate hotel rooms throughout Italy, they'd been together nearly every second, from the moment they'd met on that Eurail train until he drove away just now.

He'd been gone less than two minutes—and already, she missed him like crazy.

four

Joe punched his pillow, then punched it again, but no matter how hard he tried, he couldn't seem to get comfortable. Was it because his European travels had kept him away from his own bed for three weeks? Or was it jet lag?

He needn't search his mind for answers, because Joe already knew what had him tossing and turning, and his restlessness had a name: Shannen Flynn. She'd slipped into his head, his blood, his heart, almost from that first moment in Italy, simply by being herself.

Rolling onto his back, Joe clasped both hands under his head and stared at the night-darkened ceiling. He could see her in his mind's eye. . .short and sweet, more beautiful than anything Michelangelo had created. Her eyes, big and round and long-lashed, they were the color of cinnamon and warmer than an Italian sunset. And her hair, soft as velvet, reminded him of the chestnuts his grandmother used to roast at Christmastime. But it hadn't been her eyes or her curls or even her curvy little figure that had first caught his attention on that train. Her wide, winning smile was what had captured his notice.

They say the eyes are the windows to the soul, he thought, grinning to himself, *but that* smile *is what took me straight to her heart*. Or, more accurately, took *her* straight into *his* heart. He'd traveled a fair amount in his lifetime—to Asia and Africa and numerous other countries when his mother was "on location"—to Europe and South America in search of products for his company.

But he'd never appreciated the jaunts as much as the time spent in Italy—because *Shannen* hadn't been a part of those trips. If she had, he might have brought home memories of greater value than the collectibles he'd sell in his shop. He hadn't yet developed the film of photos shot in Florence, or Milan, or Pisa, but Joe didn't need to see pictorial evidence of his enjoyment. He had the images in his mind for that.

Like the time in the city of Forte dei Marmi, when Shannen had stood on the Tirrenic coast and looked up at the snowcapped Apennines Mountains, then turned her big-eyed gaze to the aquamarine Ligurian Sea. She'd grabbed his hand and, smiling past the tears in her eyes, said, "Oh, Joe, it's positively breathtaking! Michelangelo must have loved it here." Her comment hadn't been inspired by the artist's quest for marble, harvested there in Mount Altissiomo's La Mossa Quarry. Instead, she seemed to have shared the craftsman's enthusiasm for the land that had held those boulders captive until he could rescue them with pick and ax and, by way of chisel and hammer and keen artist's eye, turn rock into realistic renditions of Christ, the Holy Mother, David. . .

And what about that day in Florence, as they walked beneath a canopy of olive trees and cypresses, following the cobbles of Torre del Gallo, the street that led them to the Arcetri Astrophysical Observatory. They had a bird's-eye view of Florence from that high perch, and Shannen, elbows leaning on a gnarled stone wall, pointed out churches and castles and fortresses that housed famous paintings and statues and stained glass. "This *view* is a masterpiece," she'd proclaimed breathily.

Her enthusiasm was contagious, and for the first time in his life, Joe thanked God for having caught something from a fellow human being!

Turning onto his side, Joe glanced at the red numerals of the alarm clock on his nightstand. Twelve forty-four. In less than twelve hours, he'd be with her again, and the realization put an immediate smile on his face.

Just as suddenly, his exuberance faded. *Careful*, he warned, *Shannen is different from other women you've known. She's so good, too good for the likes of you.*

God may have forgiven him for the wrongs of his past, but Joe hadn't yet absolved *himself*. In his mind—and in his heart—those transgressions could only be vindicated if he lived life as the apostle Paul had lived it: devoid of romantic involvement, dedicated completely and only to Christ.

And so Joe had volunteered at area hospitals, putting what he considered to be his mediocre artistic talents to use by painting doggies and kitties and sailing ships on the pale cheeks of terminally ill children. It was why he put in a full day every weekend doling out dinners to the hungry, and why he worked one evening a week at a homeless shelter sorting donations of blankets and clothing into boxes earmarked for those in need. *For if I do this thing willingly, I will have a reward.* Another Scripture that called him to action had been James, 4:17 (NIV): "Anyone, then, who knows the good he ought to do and doesn't do it, sins."

Joe believed it would take more, far more than "doing good deeds" to cleanse him of his sins. Oh, he'd felt the power of the Lord's mercy and compassion all right, and he'd felt it for no reason other than that he'd said, "I believe." The Bible had taught him that the Father's love was so all-encompassing, so far-reaching that the simple proclamation was all He required of His children.

With those two simple words, Joe had put himself in the Creator's loving hands and felt the soul-stirring strength they'd awakened in every fiber of his being.

But he didn't believe he deserved such joy, because in his mind, he hadn't earned it. And he wouldn't feel worthy; not until he found a way to make right all that terrible wrong he'd committed. . . .

Shannen's angelic face hovered in his mind. *Too bad you didn't find a way to "fix" your miserable self before you met her*, he thought, frowning.

The fact that he didn't have a loving woman in his life had never bothered him before, mainly because he believed there was a lot of truth in the age-old cliche "What you don't know won't hurt you"; how could a man miss something he'd never known?

Well, he knew it now! He'd just had a weeklong blissful taste of it. Holding Shannen in his arms tonight had felt so good, had felt so *right*. Looking into her trusting, innocent eyes had shown him exactly what had been missing in his life: to care for another more than he cared for himself.

And oh, how he cared for Shannen!

Trouble was, he believed he didn't deserve *her*, either —might never deserve her—and the knowledge aroused an ache inside him like none Joe had known to date.

Teeth clenched, Joe sat up abruptly and tossed the covers aside. "There has to be a way," he prayed aloud, throwing his legs over the edge of the bed. As he stomped toward the stairs he said it again. "There has to be a way. Please, God, show me the way."

❄

Shannen didn't know how he'd accomplished it, but as they watched the football game on TV, Joe had managed to convince her father and all three overprotective big brothers that she would be completely safe with him in California. When they came out of the family room, laughing heartily, arms slung over one another's shoulders as they bickered good-naturedly about the referee's decision on a call, Shannen knew that Joe had become one of them, that they'd invited him into their tight circle.

Last night, as the Flynn men and their wives and children gathered around her parents' dining room table, Shannen's father passed a twenty-dollar bill down to Joe. "Buy me a baseball hat," he'd instructed, grinning mischievously. Joe sent the money back to its owner with a promise to accept payment—if he managed to acquire the cap. Hearing this, Sean and Liam and Cody immediately (and enthusiastically) put in orders for memorabilia of their own and received the same promise.

He'd charmed her sisters-in-law and captivated every one of Shannen's nieces and nephews. The biggest surprise of all came when they were leaving and her mother kissed Joe's cheek. "You drive safely now, y'hear?" she'd said, patting his shoulder.

The whole Flynn clan had gotten up early, piled

into Sean's van, and followed Joe and Shannen to the airport. Since they'd never endured the crowded parking lot or the time-consuming metal detector process to see her off before, Shannen could only surmise they'd shown up to say good-bye to *Joe*. The concept left her grinning and shaking her head.

Joe insisted that she sit near the window. "I've seen the view too many times to count," he'd said, settling into the aisle seat. "This way, I get to stick my leg out when the food cart's not in the way."

That had been hours ago, before the snack, before the movie, before the light meal served up by the flight attendants. Now, the crackling baritone of the pilot broke through the high-pitched whine of the 747's engines: "Ladies and gentlemen, this is Captain Turner. Please take your seats and fasten your seat belts, as we're about to begin our approach to Los Angeles International Airport. . . ."

Through the oval portal, beneath a cover of opalescent nimbus clouds, Shannen saw the multicolored patchwork of farmers' fields, housing developments, and industrial parks. Here, neighborhood pools sparkled up from the ground; there, the many-hued rooftops of vehicles gleamed in dealership parking lots. Inside the plane, she saw her fellow passengers scurrying around to prepare for the landing.

But she couldn't see Joe, because soon after the flight attendant picked up the last of their meal, he'd fallen asleep—with his head resting on her shoulder.

He'd been dozing for nearly an hour now, his hushed breaths puffing into the crook of her neck, soft hair pressed against her cheek, big hand resting almost possessively on her forearm. She'd half expected a man of his size to snore like a chain saw. Instead, Joe's steady, quiet breathing had lulled her into a near sleep state, too.

The grinding whir of the lowering landing gear told her they'd be on the ground soon. Much as she hated to disturb Joe's peaceful slumber, she gave his hand a gentle pat. "Hey, sleepyhead," she whispered, "time to wake up. We're almost there."

His thick, dark lashes fluttered, and then his big brown eyes met hers. After an exaggerated yawn and a luxurious stretch, he smiled. "How long have I been out?"

He looked so much like an innocent boy roused from a nap that she wanted to take him in her arms and hug him, tousle his hair, and kiss his sleep-wrinkled cheek. "Not long," she said, acknowledging how cold her left side felt now that he'd sat up.

Knuckling his eyes, Joe ran both hands through his hair and leaned across her to peer through the window. "Landing gear is down," he said, nodding as he checked his watch. "We're right on time."

"I suppose your mother is pretty tense about now," Shannen said. "There must be a million last-minute details to tie up, what with the wedding being tomorrow and all."

"She has 'people' for that."

She ignored the sarcasm in his voice. "Still," she persisted, "I'm sure she's nervous."

"With all the practice she's had, she could do it in her sleep."

"But. . .but I thought you said that this time, your mother was hoping it would last forever."

His bitter chuckle grated in her ears. "I did say

something along those lines, didn't I?" Joe wiggled his brows and gave her a grin that never quite reached his eyes. "Newsflash: She says that *every* time."

Shannen tucked in one corner of her mouth as the uniformed flight attendant meandered down the aisle, checking to see that every tray was up, every seat belt fastened, every overhead bin secured. "The way you talk, a person could get the idea you're not terribly fond of your mother."

He heaved a deep sigh, and shoulders slumped, Joe said, "Sorry. Guess you didn't know I'm a grouch when I wake up, did you?"

"You didn't wake up grumpy on the flight from Milan to New York," she pointed out, "or the plane trip from Kennedy to Baltimore."

He shrugged, as if to say there was no rational explanation for his grumpy mood. Maybe it was because he didn't like LAX, or Los Angeles in general, or weddings. *Or maybe*, she told herself, *he doesn't like the idea that his mother is getting married for the* fifth *time!* "Joe, do you mind if I ask you a question?"

Head back and eyes closed, he wrapped his big hand around her small one. "Shoot."

"Were you raised in. . .um. . . Did you have God in your life when you were growing up?"

He opened his eyes and turned slightly in the seat to face her. "Did you say *God?*"

She nodded. "Sunday school, church services, grace before meals. . ." Shannen glanced at the plane's ceiling, then met his eyes again. "You know, *God?*"

Chuckling, he shook his head. "Please don't take this the wrong way, but *are you nuts?*" He pointed out the small window beside her. "Take a gander out there, pretty lady and tell me what you see."

Shannen blinked, frowning slightly. "What does the view have to do with—"

"Everything," he interrupted. "It has everything to do with whether or not there was a spiritual presence in my life. What you see out there. . .it's a sham, a facade, as fake as those storefronts in B-grade Westerns. What you see is exactly what you *don't* get in Hollywood." He tucked in his chin and did a perfect W.C. Fields imitation: " 'Actually, m'dear, I'd rather be in Philadelphia.' " He spoke normally to add, "The only time the subject of *God* comes up out here is when somebody wants a part in a movie." His voice turned falsetto when he said, " 'Please, God, won't you help me become a *star?*' "

"I take it the answer is 'no'." Then she asked, "Do you realize how bitter you sound, Joe?"

He looked into her eyes for a long, silent moment before his expression softened. "Sorry," he said quietly, "it's like I said, sometimes I wake up grouchy."

"But you're a Christian now."

Another grating chuckle escaped his lungs. "Wow. What gave it away?"

"The lifestyle you just described wouldn't be upsetting to you if God wasn't a big part of who you are now." She paused, tilted her head, and smiled. "When did it happen for you?"

"About three years ago, on a movie set, believe it or not."

"A movie set?"

Joe nodded. "Mom was shooting *Soft Beats My Heart* on location at Baltimore's Inner Harbor. One of the gaffers was born again. We got to talking. . . ." He shrugged. "Compared with the stars, the director, the producer, that guy had nothing. No mansion. No chauffeur-driven car. No private jet. But he seemed so sure of himself. When I asked him why he was so happy, he told me. Straight out. Like it was something to be proud of. He dug around in his backpack and gave me his Bible. . .said the answer to every question I'd ever have, the solution to every problem, could be found in the Good Book.

"I kept hanging around the set. Let the business go to pot that week. But what he said made *sense*. I wanted to feel like that. So I got myself 'saved'." Joe shrugged. "It was no big deal."

"Don't give me that. It was a very big deal."

His brow furrowed slightly.

It was her turn to shrug. "Your problem isn't that you wake up grumpy. You're frustrated, that's what, because now that you know Jesus, you want your mother to share in that joy. Only she's lived in the shadows for so long, she can't seem to find her way to the light. You're *more* than frustrated, you're angry. . .with *yourself*, because you think if you were a better Christian, you'd be able to show her the way."

Shannen patted his hand. "Newsflash," she said, quoting him. "You can lead a horse to water. . . ."

He grinned. "Don't let my mother hear you calling her a horse. You'll spend the next half hour hearing how she works out an hour a day and eats like a bird."

"Birds, for your information, eat as much as five times their own weight every day." Her smile softened when she added, "Your example and your prayers are all you can give her, Joe. Let God do the rest."

His grin vanished. "Well, He'd better hurry up, 'cause she's fading fast."

She didn't know what inspired it, but Shannen felt an urge to hug him, and so she did. "You aren't responsible for what other people do, Joe; you're only responsible for how you *react* to what they do." She kissed his cheek. "All you have to do is keep on loving her with all your heart. She'll come around. You'll see."

He kissed the top of her head. "And what if she doesn't?"

" 'Oh ye of little faith,' " she quoted Scriptures. "I have a confession to make," she said, grinning mischievously.

Joe returned the grin. "I feel you oughta know. . .I left my white collar on my other suit."

She looked around conspiratorially. "I'm starving."

"After that belly-filling meal they just fed us?" he teased. "You're kidding."

Smacking her lips, she said, "I want a hot dog. One of those extra-large jobs, with onions and relish and catsup and mustard."

Joe laughed. "Shannen Flynn, you are one of a kind."

"What do you mean? Thousands and *thousands* of people like hot dogs."

"Yeah," he said, his grin becoming a smile, "but thousands of people aren't about to meet Martha Malone for the first time. . .with onions on their breath."

She shrugged. "I have breath mints in my purse."

He wiggled his eyebrows. "Really?"

She nodded.

Joe clapped his hands together and rubbed them

briskly. "Well, then, that's a horse of a different color. It just so happens there's a place on the way to Mom's house that sells hot dogs so big, and so greasy, you'll need a bib!"

five

Throughout Europe, Shannen had visited castles and mansions, museums and art galleries—most that had once been home to kings and queens—but Martha Malone's estate put them all to shame.

Smack dab in the middle of the Hollywood Hills, the property was surrounded by elaborate wrought-iron fencing, partially hidden behind thickly-twined rose hedges.

Joe steered his rental car up a magnolia-shaded drive that snaked from the road to the house like a concrete river. The moment he parked in the circular drive, a tuxedoed gent greeted them with a curt nod of his head and a polite smile and relieved Joe of the car keys.

While the butler carried their suitcases into the house, Shannen faced the fountain, transfixed by bubbling water that trickled from a chubby cherub's slender urn and fed fat goldfish in the pond. The scent of roses hung in the air, blending nicely with the gentle sound of cascading water.

She'd never seen a house like it—at least, not one where people actually *lived*. It was grand enough, she reckoned, to be highlighted on the TV show that featured the homes of the rich and famous. Black shuttered, multipaned windows offset the wide double doors on the first floor. A dozen tiers of bloodred brick steps led from the drive to the massive portico. Tall columns supported either side of the porch roof, which was crowned by a second, equally grand balcony that had been enclosed by a white picket rail. Four imposing chimneys were silhouetted against the blue, sun-bright sky, and two gigantic, large oaks flanked the porch. A sea of roses of every hue lined the long flagstone walk. The weather was warm and balmy as a summer day in Baltimore, and it seemed strange to see Christmas decorations draped from the many-pillared porch. Shannen could only imagine how much more majestic things would be *inside*.

Joe slipped an arm around her waist. "Impressed?"

She took a deep breath. "It's hard not to be." But looking into his handsome face, she saw that he was anything *but* impressed. "That's the point, isn't it?"

Grinning, he gave her a sideways hug. "I knew you were the right choice."

"The right choice?"

"I didn't want to bring someone here who'd get all dewy-eyed and starstruck by the place—or the people. Something told me I wouldn't have to worry that you'd leave here wishing you were one of them, because you've got both feet planted firmly on the ground." Winking, he smacked his lips. "Yup. You're quite a woman, Shannen Flynn."

She was about to deny it when an all-too-recognizable voice floated to them from the front door. "Joooo-eeeeeey!"

The sound of it seemed to cause a physical chain reaction in Joe: Back stiff and shoulders squared, his jaw tensed and his lips grew taut as he squinted both eyes shut and pinched the bridge of his nose between thumb and forefinger. Surprisingly, though, in the next instant, he was all smiles as he strode toward his mother with arms outstretched. "Hi, Mom," he said, gathering her close. "Good to see you."

She was everything Shannen had expected. . .and a whole lot more. Tall and lithe, her bleach-blond hair poured down her back like a golden waterfall. Shannen winced slightly, afraid that Martha's long, crimson-painted fingertips might gouge out Joe's eyes as she wiped the imprint of a matching crimson kiss from her son's cheek. "It's good to see you, too," she cooed. Facing Shannen, she tilted her head coquettishly. "Aren't you going to introduce me to your little friend?"

Shannen knew Joe well enough to recognize a strained smile on his face when she saw it. If his mother had been facing him, would she have known how uncomfortable he was in her presence? Shannen rather doubted it since the woman had spent decades in the spotlight. Putting someone else's needs first—noticing that someone else *had* needs—would be out of character for her.

She wanted to throw her arms around him. . .promise him things would be all right—eventually. But this was neither the time nor the place to offer him the comfort of a friendly hug. Smiling, she stepped forward and extended a hand. "It's a pleasure to meet you, Miss Malone."

Martha rolled her heavily mascara'd eyes and waved a well-lotioned hand in Shannen's direction. "Goodness, dear, *please* call me Martha," she gushed. And as the star sandwiched Shannen's hand between her own, she explained: "You make me feel like a dotty old woman, calling me 'Miss Malone' that way!"

Turning to her son, Martha added, "Are you hungry? Thirsty?" But before they could answer, she pointed a crimson talon toward the sky. "I'll just bet I know what *you* want," she singsonged to Shannen. "You want a tour of my house, don't you, dear?" Again, without waiting for a response, she faced Joe. "She's simply *adorable*, darling. Wherever did you *find* her?"

"As a matter of fact," he said, the tense smile frozen in place, "it just so happens *she* found *me*. . .on a train in Italy."

Martha's blue-shadowed eyes narrowed. "You. . .you found—*where?*"

"She rescued me from the conductor, who would probably have kicked me off the train if Shannen hadn't—"

"Shannen? Your name is Shannen? Oh, what a sweet, *sweet* name! Shannen *what*? Smith? Green?"

"Flynn," she said. Joe's tension was contagious, and tugged at the corners of her own smile.

Martha gasped, her bright blue eyes widening with admiration. "Not the *Miami* Flynns. . . ?"

Grinning, she shook her head. "No."

"The Palm Beach Flynns, then?"

"The Baltimore Flynns," she said, shooting a playful grin in Joe's direction. "And I'm afraid the only thing we're famous for is multiplication."

"Ahhh," Martha said, nodding. "The *computer* moguls."

Shannen bit back a laugh. "More like baby moguls."

A furrow creased Martha's carefully made-up brow. "Babies? I'm afraid I don't understand."

"I have three brothers, you see, and between them they have fourteen children."

Martha's well-plucked left brow rose slowly on her forehead. "Ahhh," she repeated. And then, linking arms with Shannen and Joe, she led them toward the house. "Well, now, how would you like that tour? I have half an hour to kill before my personal trainer arrives."

She chattered all the way to the porch, up the brick steps, and into the foyer as, over her head, Joe mouthed "I'm sorry." She shot him a look that said, "No problem," then she sent a silent petition heavenward: *Please, God*, she prayed, *let me be what Joe needs me to be while we're here.*

Something told Shannen she'd only seen the tip of the Martha Malone iceberg.

❄

The last time Shannen had seen this many stars, she'd been watching them accepting awards on TV. Sitting alone in the front pew, she tried her best not to stare at aging stars of the silver screen—and Hollywood's newest faces.

A quick glance at her watch told her that if Martha made her entrance on time, Joe would be seated on the aisle beside her in five minutes. Why did she get the feeling the seat would still be vacant in thirty minutes?

Never one to waste time, Shannen looked around the church decked in Christmas finery on top of classic cathedral design. Its silver-faced altar and golden relics reminded her of the Duomo, located in Florence's religious hub. The ceiling, a gold-leafed polygonal dome, featured replicas of The Last Supper, The Madonna and Child, The Crucifixion, The Creation. Each wooden bench had been hand carved by a skilled carpenter, and the proof was the elaborate scrollwork that decorated each. Lime-white walls framed in gray stone had been adorned with stucco medallions and terra cotta figures. A dozen alcoves, each featuring its own pews, mini-altar, and muted frescos, had been cut into the perimeter. And underfoot lay a floor of gleaming marble.

She took another peek at her watch. *Any time now, Lord*, she said to the dome, *any time*. . . . As if in answer to the halfhearted prayer, music began overhead.

No simple organ soloist for *this* wedding! Martha had booked a dozen musicians from the L.A. Symphony, who had been sequestered in the garland-draped balcony, awaiting their cue to begin playing. They started with Marchionda's "The Greatest Gift", and slid gracefully into Damian Lundy's "Love." Soon Gregory Norbet's "Wherever You Go" was echoing throughout the cavernous cathedral.

The groom, outfitted in a white tux, stepped into place at the altar beside his best man. Shannen recognized both men immediately, for they'd co-starred in a recent action/adventure flick set in the jungles of South America. Martha's husband-to-be stood stiff-backed and grim-faced, posing—or so it seemed—for the photographers positioned around the church. Every few seconds, he drove a sinewy hand through his honey-blond hair, ran a finger under the starched collar of his front-pleated shirt, focusing dark-lashed blue eyes on one cameraman after another.

Shannen turned slightly in her seat and immediately made eye contact with Joe. He stood arm in arm in the narthex with his famous mother, whose formfitting gown hugged her like a second skin, from its high lace-trimmed neckline to the train that skimmed the floor like a stream of off-white silk. She'd drawn her platinum hair into a French braid and secured it with baby's breath, and in her hands, she held one Christmas-red rose. The muffled oohs and aahs of appreciation for her beauty were punctuated by a new flurry of clicking camera shutters.

But Shannen only had eyes for the young man beside the bride who, in his white tuxedo, looked positively princely. . .more handsome, even, than the groom himself!

The moment the orchestra began playing "The Wedding March," Joe slowly led his mother down the aisle, his gleaming black shoes in sharp contrast to the white-sheeted floor and Martha's pale, shimmering wedding dress. His dark eyes seemed fused to Shannen's; the closer he got to the altar, the more intensely they glowed.

Finally, he stood beside her.

He looked away briefly, giving his mother a light peck on the cheek. Ever so gently, he lay her delicately gloved hand onto the palm of her intended, took a step back, and joined Shannen in the pew. All eyes were on the bride and groom when he leaned over and whispered, "Thank God *that's* over."

There was no mistaking the tremor in his voice; Joe was neither relieved nor glad about this wedding. But he was a grown man, powerless to stop his mother from taking what he believed to be another marital misstep. Later, Shannen would invite him to pray with her. . .for Martha and her new husband, for their salvation, for their future happiness. For now, she believed Joe needed nothing more than to know that as his friend, she understood his concerns. To prove it, she sent him a loving smile, wrapped her hand around his, and gave it a tiny squeeze.

"You're a godsend," he said into her ear. "I honestly don't know how I would have gotten through this without you."

What had inspired it, Shannen couldn't say, but she didn't fight the urge to rest her head on his shoulder. The gesture, she hoped, would convey what words could not: "I'm here; I care."

In the next moments, between strains of cello and violin, between the trill of flute and the trumpet of French horn, Joe and Shannen stood hand in hand, listening in somber silence as Martha Malone spoke the words that made her Missus Marcus McCarty.

"May the Lord in His goodness strengthen your consent," came the preacher's baritone drone, "and fill you with His blessings." In a louder, firmer voice, he added, "What God has joined, men must not divide."

All in attendance said, "Amen."

"Martha," said Marcus in a tremulous tenor, "take this ring as a sign of my love and fidelity, in the name of the Father, and of the Son, and of the Holy Spirit." Then, vows exchanged and wedding rings in place, the congregation stood and joined hands to recite The Lord's Prayer.

The orchestra played Omer Westendorf's "Now Joined By God" as the recessional song. Shannen wondered who had chosen the music. . .and why. . .because every melody seemed as Spirit-filled and holy as the marriage vows themselves.

Martha reached out as she headed for the back of the church, her fragile hand grazing Joe's cheek as she passed. No one seemed to notice when he blinked a tear from his eye.

But Shannen noticed.

And her heart ached for him.

❄

Joe had his own way of judging a party: If tuxedoed caterers served "finger sandwiches" and the liquid refreshments were called "beverages," the occasion was too fancy for his tastes. Like every one of Martha's galas, her wedding reception would go down in the books as an affair to remember.

If only he could forget what was expected of him. . . .

He hated glad-handing big-name celebrities and kowtowing to feed their never-ending vanity. He didn't like going from table to table, grinning like the Cheshire cat, pretending to be interested as one egocentric scriptwriter after another recited lines from their latest screenplays. He found it especially annoying when young, would-be starlets threw themselves at him, hoping that by aligning themselves with the son of the Queen of Hollywood, they might garner a part in one of Martha's upcoming movies.

If his mother had even the slightest idea how distasteful all of this was for him, she wouldn't repeatedly ask why he'd moved east and settled in Annapolis.

At the moment, Joe was trying to figure out how to break free from the latest empty-headed beauty. A heartbeat after introducing herself as Buffy Belle, the young woman in the black-sequined minidress slid an arm around Joe's waist and rested her head on his shoulder.

If not for loyalty and devotion to his mother, he would have found a way to evade her. "Joey," she'd said earlier, "our little miss Buffy has been draping herself all over my Marcus like a wet blanket." She'd kissed his cheek. "Be a dear and keep the lovely leech *occupado?*" He'd opened his mouth to say, "But Mom, Shannen doesn't know a soul," when she patted his shoulder and said, "*That's* my baby boy!" and disappeared.

He was paying the price for that loyalty now, every time Buffy combed her fingers through his hair and laughed loudly, tossing her honey-blond mane as she batted glued-on eyelashes. He could only hope that later, when he and Shannen could be alone, he'd be able to make up for all the time she'd been forced to spend without him.

"Oh, *Joey*," Buffy was cooing now, bright red lips a millimeter from his ear, "I just don't know *what* I would have done if you hadn't agreed to keep me company; I hardly know a soul here!"

But he knew better. If she wasn't somehow affiliated with one or more of the guests, Buffy wouldn't have been invited at all.

Joe had met her type before—too many times to count—and believed he could predict what she'd do if he were to point out that he hadn't agreed to "keep her company." First, her lower lip would jut out and her green eyes would fill with tears. The minute Buffy's huffing and puffing captured the attention of those within earshot, she'd blurt out how unkind and unfair he was to hurt and humiliate her that way, and go running from the room. And he'd be lucky if she didn't slap him a good one first!

Hiding a scowl as he pictured the scene, Joe told himself the scene would be good acting practice for Buffy. On the other hand, Martha would never forgive him if he allowed the girl to upstage her. It was his *mother's* big day, after all. Joe took a deep breath and assumed a "grin and bear it" attitude, and prayed that God would see fit to rescue him—soon!—from the clutches of this latest Hollywood hopeful.

A "petty girl" is like a "malady," he mused, grinning as Buffy told him about every part she'd tried out for since moving to California, or when she described the way she'd hitchhiked from Gary, Indiana, to L.A. when a customer in the diner where she'd waitressed insisted she ought to be in movies.

If you had a dollar for every time you heard a story like that, he thought, wincing inwardly, *you'd have a pocket* full *of bills!* He looked at Buffy, *really* looked at her. He doubted she was old enough to vote, and yet this naive and starry-eyed kid from the Midwest wanted nothing more than to be in the movies. She might have been a cheerleader in high school, or "first chair" in the orchestra. He wouldn't be at all surprised to learn she still had a collection of stuffed animals on her bed.

His heart ached for her, because her chances of becoming a "hit" were slim to none. Like so many who'd come west before her, leaving good families and nice homes behind in the hopes of someday seeing their names up in lights, she'd go home with a broken heart and a shattered spirit—if she went home at all.

And they call it the City of Angels, he thought dismally as Buffy rambled on, because in his opinion, there was nothing angelic about a place that, more often than not, turned dreams into nightmares.

He needed fresh air, and an arm's length distance between him and the next wanna-be who thought he had the power to help them become stars. Before accepting Jesus as his Lord and Savior, Joe had abused that power too many times to count, a fact that would have him feeling guilty and repentant, probably for the rest of his life. Which was only one of the reasons he felt undeserving of a woman like Shannen.

And speaking of Shannen, Joe hadn't seen her in a while. He hoped she hadn't gotten herself cornered by some droning has-been, the way he'd allowed himself to be trapped into spending the past half hour with a wishful wanna-be. He scanned the crowd of well-recognizable faces, hoping for a glimpse, at least, of her.

The moment he spotted her, his heart thumped wildly and he smiled involuntarily. She looked so pretty, far more beautiful, in his estimation, than the women all around her who'd shrouded themselves in spangles and satin. Her tailored dinner suit quietly bespoke class and elegance, its sea green material setting off her ivory skin and auburn hair and making her golden-brown eyes look bigger and browner—*if that was possible*, he thought.

Backlit by hundreds of tiny Christmas lights, she stood beside the gigantic, live Christmas tree chatting with some of Hollywood's heaviest hitters, most of whom had been earning an L.A. living for years. In the days before Martha's wedding, the ladies in the group—knowing Martha's wedding would provide numerous opportunities for publicity—had no doubt scoured the boutiques along Rodeo Drive in search of their gowns and spent hours (and hundreds of dollars) in their hairdressers' shops. And long before today, they'd invested small fortunes in acting classes and voice lessons to learn how to smile, how to speak, how to pose.

Shannen's education had not included such instructions. *But look at her*, Joe thought, smiling, *just* look *at her!* There she stood, laughing and talking with the "beautiful people," seemingly unaffected by their wealth and fame. In her simple suit and tasteful haircut, with her genuine smile and her honest eyes, she stood out like a beacon in the night.

She's one of a kind, he told himself as Buffy prattled on. At first, he felt sorry for the girl, but pity was no reason to be with a person, and he began looking for a way to shed this clinging vine. Joe wanted to be over there in the corner, looking out through the huge picture window at the city with Shannen, not standing here in his mother's parlor with this vapid, star-focused girl. Even an alphabetical recitation of the spices in Shannen's cupboard would be more intriguing than *anything* poor Buffy could possibly think up!

Suddenly, his jaw tensed and his heart began to beat double-time when he saw Ian Cole put a hand on Shannen's shoulder. *That old codger had better keep his mitts to himself,* Joe fumed. He watched as the aging British actor leaned in close and said something into Shannen's ear, something that made her throw back her head and laugh. The music of it apparently affected Cole exactly as it affected Joe, because the man moved in closer, sliding an arm across her shoulders.

Cole had spent decades earning his reputation as a ladies' man. Any minute now, she'd give him the old heave-ho, Joe was sure of it. Soon, she'd shove his beefy arm off her shoulder and tell him in no uncertain terms that she wasn't his type.

"Joey," Buffy said.

He barely heard her.

And so Buffy stood on tiptoe and grabbed his chin, forcing him to meet her eyes. "*Joey*," she repeated, "would you mind getting me a refill?" She held her glass aloft and gave it a little shake so that the ice cubes tinkled against the crystal.

"Sorry, Buffy," he said, trying to see around her mass of blond curls. Joe pointed toward the tree. "There's someone over there I want to—"

Her eyes narrowed as she followed his gaze. "Who? A *woman?* Where is she?" Buffy hissed.

When at last he managed to peer around her, Joe searched the room. He felt as though someone had sucker punched him, right in the gut.

Because Shannen was gone, and so was Ian Cole.

six

Shannen couldn't remember feeling more hurt and disappointed, not even when Todd called off the engagement. *Maybe the family is right—maybe you're too naive to be allowed out in public without a chaperon.*

Her parents and her brothers had warned her about Todd, and they'd been right. The lesson it taught her was to let them stamp "final approval" on anyone she was interested in.

But Joe had fooled *them*, too!

She'd made certain assumptions about Joe Malone, *and obviously, you were dead wrong on every count.* She'd made the mistake of believing all the things he'd told her, like the fact that he'd moved east because he detested the jet set, Hollywood lifestyle, that he hated big, fancy parties, that he didn't like the way girls clung to him at every function for no reason other than that he might provide them with an introduction to Martha, her agent. . .*someone* in Tinsel Town who could put them in the movies.

You missed your calling, Joe Malone, Shannen had thought as she watched him from across the room. There he'd stood, grinning and nodding, looking intrigued by every word that came out of that pretty blond's mouth. *He sure didn't* look *like he hated the "Hollywood hype!"*

When he'd made one of his half dozen apologies for leaving her alone, Shannen had laughed it off. "Nonsense!" she'd told him. "It's your job to be a good host, to visit with your mother's guests." He asked her to walk along with him as he saw to everyone's needs, but she'd insisted it would reflect better on Martha if he attended to his duties without a tagalong stuck on his arm. "I'll be just fine," she'd assured him, "and I'll be waiting right here when you're finished." The look he'd given her had said, "Thanks. You're a peach!"

It had sent a warm flutter through her—until she'd seen him give that look to every one of the beautiful women she saw him with after that—and there must have been dozens of them.

Was he aware, she'd wondered, *that he sported three lipstick prints on one cheek and two on the other?* If so, the only assumption she could have come to—when he didn't wipe them off—was that the imprints were proof to every woman in attendance of his magnetic prowess.

He's a natural at this "mingling" stuff, she thought, peeking through the lacy curtains beside the front door. Frustrated that the taxi hadn't arrived yet, she let them fall back into place and returned to her seat on the overstuffed sofa against the opposite wall. *If he loves it so much, why did he leave it behind in the first place!*

If he'd been honest with her about that, she wouldn't have come to L.A. with him.

If he'd told the truth, she wouldn't be sitting here now, sniffling and red-eyed in Martha Malone's elegantly furnished foyer, waiting for a ride to the airport. *You little ninny,* she scolded herself. *He's the son of the Queen of Hollywood; surely he inherited* some *of her acting abilities, and you're not even savvy enough to recognize a well-rehearsed "line" when you hear it!*

Pride, more than anything else, had dictated her behavior for that last hour. If he looked her way, she didn't want him to see her standing alone in some corner, pouting because she didn't fit in with his family and friends. It had been a last-ditch effort to preserve *some* semblance of dignity, at least, to mingle, to laugh and talk, so that when he saw her he wouldn't feel embarrassed that he'd brought a country bumpkin to the party.

They were wrong for one another. She had known that the moment the big-haired blond attached herself to Joe's side. . .and he'd done nothing to prevent it. Shannen had never been the jealous type, but she didn't think she'd ever develop a hide thick enough to deflect overt advances like that pushy blond's!

She'd decided to go out with a bang, leave Joe wondering if maybe *he'd* misjudged *her*. And so she made the rounds, laughing at jokes she didn't get, nodding at stories that would have put her nieces and nephews to sleep, pretending to be engrossed in "how I made it in show biz" recountings. After about thirty minutes of faking and fawning, she faced the cold hard fact: It was over between her and Joe before it actually began. She doubted *any* woman in the room had enough acting talent to pretend *that* didn't matter.

It's a good thing you went into teaching, she thought now, blowing her nose, *because you'd starve to death if you had to depend on your dramatic abilities for a paycheck!*

"What's this?" asked a deep, English-accented voice. "What's wrong, cookie?"

Shannen smiled shakily. "Just waiting for a cab."

"I was wondering where you'd disappeared to." He gave a cursory glance at her suitcases, standing beside the door. Ian Cole sat beside her on the brocade upholstered sofa, slid one arm around her shoulders, and patted her forearm with his free hand. "Tell Uncle Ian all about it."

She shrugged, stared at the ivory satin purse in her lap. "There's nothing to tell, really."

"Nonsense. A beautiful young woman doesn't get all teary-eyed over nothing. It's that cad Joe Malone, isn't it?" Ian's gray eyes narrowed with anger. "If he were my son, I would have tanned his hide *years* ago. Who does he think he is, trifling with the affection of young girls?"

Shannen looked into his handsome face and grinned slightly. "How long have *you* been in L.A.?" she asked.

"Left jolly old England when I was in my twenties. . .why?"

"Then you've been here long enough to have heard the old saying 'Look at the pot calling the kettle black.' "

Ian chuckled. "Indeed. . .and I must say, touché." Another chuckle. "But it was different with me."

She stood, looked out the window again, and with a disappointed sigh, sat beside Ian once more. "Different? How so?"

"Everyone knew I was a rake. It was expected, don't you know, for me to. . .shall we say 'sweep the ladies off their feet.' " He wiggled his dark, well-arched brows mischievously.

His look darkened when he added, "Joe's another matter entirely. It's downright offensive, I say, because he's nothing but a wolf in sheep's clothing. Let me hazard a guess: You never saw it coming, did you?"

Fighting tears, Shannen shook her head. "I feel like such a little fool; we only just met a few weeks ago, and I fell like a ton of bricks."

Ian grabbed Shannen's hand and led her to the front door. "Chin up, cookie," he said, yanking it open, "because your old Uncle Ian is going to see that you get back to your hotel safely."

"Actually," she said, nodding toward the wide, curving staircase, "mine is. . .*was*. . .the third door on the left." She nodded at the front door. "The cab—if it ever gets here—will take me to the airport."

He picked up the suitcases at the foot of the stairs. "It'll give him a boatload of satisfaction, you know, knowing he has the power to break even your heart."

Even my heart? she repeated, confused. Well, if it made Joe happy to know he had the "lines" down so pat that he could use them to hurt her, he'd sleep with a satisfied smirk on his face tonight for sure!

"Are you absolutely sure you want to leave?"

She'd thought about it during her last hour at the reception as she watched Joe flit from female to female like a hungry mosquito. Thought about it some more as she blubbered like a schoolgirl in the lavish bathroom attached to her private suite. Thought about it still more as she tearfully packed her things. "I'm sure," she said softly.

"It's all settled, then. My car is right out front." He jangled the keys at a teenaged boy in a red uniform. "It's the silver convertible, parked over there under the trees," he instructed.

When the valet returned with the sports car, Ian

tossed her suitcase into the tiny trunk and held out a crisp twenty-dollar bill. "There's a taxi on the way," he said, tucking the money into the boy's hand. "When it arrives, tell the driver the lady is terribly sorry, but she's changed her mind."

The kid smirked, as if he and Ian had just shared a dark secret.

"Now, now, I'll have none of that, young man," he scolded as he helped Shannen into the passenger seat. "My friend is a lady, through and through; a rare commodity around here. I suggest you take a good long look at her," he said sliding behind the steering wheel, "so you'll be able to recognize one—if you ever *see* a lady again." He quirked a brow and grinned, started up the car, and drove off.

"That was a very nice thing to say," Shannen told him. "Thank you."

"Goodness gracious," he huffed, "you've just proven my point, don't you see? There's no need to thank a man for stating a fact."

For the next few minutes, they rode in companionable silence through the town of glitz and glamour that had been made even brighter by the glow of Christmas decor.

"You know," Ian said, cracking the quiet, "I've never held Joe Malone in particularly high regard, but I've never felt any ill will toward him, either. . .until tonight."

She focused on the famous profile of Ian Cole and couldn't help smiling a bit.

"What's this?" he teased. "A smile? Go on, then, tell Uncle Ian what's got you tickled."

"My mother is one of your biggest fans. If she could see me now, sitting here in your Italian convertible, being escorted to the airport, she'd faint dead away."

He sighed heavily. "You 'feet on the ground' types do have a way of keeping a man's ego in check." And chuckling, he added, "But then, I guess it's true: I do appeal to the middle-aged set far more these days than to the youngsters."

She gasped. "Oh, Ian. . .I didn't mean it that way," Shannen admitted. "I only meant—"

He patted her hand. "Never mind, cookie. Now tell me, if we can get you booked on a flight out of town tonight, where will you be heading?"

"Baltimore." She slumped low in the seat and bit her lip to stanch the flow of tears that burned behind her eyelids.

"He'll follow you, you know," Ian said after a while.

"Of course he will; he only lives a few miles away."

"He'd follow you even if he still lived in Martha's mansion. I know I would. . .if I could fill his small-man shoes."

They rode in silence again until they turned onto the airport road. "No need for you to fight all the traffic; just drop me off at the terminal," Shannen said, "and I'll—"

"Out of the question," he interrupted, parking the car. "I intend to personally escort you to the ticket counter, and I'll not leave your side until your plane is Baltimore-bound." He held up a hand to forestall her objection. "And I won't hear another word about it."

They were standing at the ticket counter, side by side when the ruckus began.

Ian had volunteered to hold her ticket so that Shannen could tuck her credit card into her wallet. Just as she snapped her purse shut, they were suddenly blinded by a flurry of flashing lights. "Ian," a photographer shouted, "what's your girlfriend's name?"

"Girlfriend!" he spouted. "Are you daft, man? She's young enough to be my daughter."

"So were your last two," hollered the reporter who stood beside the cameraman. He stuck a microphone under Ian's nose. "So tell me: Where are you two lovebirds headed?"

Ian picked up her carry-on bag in one hand and grasped Shannen's elbow with the other. "Ignore them, cookie," he said, leading her through the airport. In a voice loud enough for them to hear, he added, "They're like rabid bears; the only way you're safe from them is to lie down and play dead."

Beyond the safety of the metal detectors now, Shannen and Ian sat side by side in a row of black vinyl chairs at the gate, facing the wide windows overlooking the tarmac, chatting quietly like old friends. If the people sitting around them recognized the famous movie star, they showed no sign of it.

"Flight two-forty-two is now ready for boarding passengers," came a gravelly voice from the overhead speakers.

Shannen stood and grabbed her purse and carry-on. "Thank you so much, Ian," she said, smiling gratefully. "You probably hear this all the time, but. . .you're a very sweet man."

He shrugged and blushed slightly. "Actually, I could count on one hand the number of times I've heard that." A merry chuckle punctuated his admission. "But really, it's only because I'm British, you know; helping ladies in distress is in the blood," he said, winking as he tweaked her cheek. His grin faded when he added, "Promise me something?"

"If I can."

He withdrew his wallet and pulled out a business card, scribbling a telephone number on the back of it. "Haven't the foggiest notion who this bloke is," he said, handing the card to her. "But that's my private line on the back. If you ever need me, for anything, I want you to promise you'll call. All right?"

She stared at the neat row of digits, then met his eyes.

"Now put that in a safe place. You mustn't lose it."

Why me? she wondered.

"Because you've had a strange and amazing effect on me, Shannen Flynn," Ian said as if he'd heard her silent question. "And I'm not the only one, you know. I couldn't help but notice you tonight—you're *different*, and while I couldn't say *how*, exactly, I think it's that difference that draws people to you."

He kissed her cheek. "I don't know what it is, but I feel as if we've been fast friends all our lives." He laughed. "Here's one for the books: I feel protective and brotherly. . .and have absolutely no romantic feelings toward you!"

"Boy," Shannen said, "you English chaps sure know how to flatter a girl."

"You *should* be flattered, cookie. I've never had a female friend before, not once in all my fifty-one years." He leaned close to whisper, "And if you tell anyone my true age, I'll have to cut out your tongue."

Feigning fear, she zipped her lip and imitated his English accent. "Mum's the word, hip hip, tallyho, cheerio and all that rot."

Smiling, Ian drew her into a warm and affectionate hug. "When you get home, I don't want you to give that cad Malone another thought, do you hear?"

She nodded. "Take care, Ian."

"*You* take care, Shannen," he said as she entered the tube that connected the airport to the jetliner. And settling into her window seat, she smiled, despite the events of the evening.

Because Shannen knew that tonight, she'd made a *real* friend.

He'd searched the house for half an hour before deciding to check her room. A small sheet of note paper, folded in half and leaning on the brass lamp on the night table caught his attention. Immediately, he recognized Shannen's handwriting on the front. "Mrs. Marcus McCarty" it said.

He opened it and read:

Dear Martha,

I'm sorry to have left in such a rush, but I've had something of a personal emergency and must return to Baltimore immediately. It was a genuine pleasure meeting you, and I thank you so much for your hospitality. I pray that you and Marcus will enjoy many happy years together.

All my best,
Shannen Flynn

Last time he saw Shannen, she'd been standing on the balcony, giggling at whatever that ladies' man, Ian Cole, was whispering into her ear. Had her "personal emergency" had something to do with *him*?

Joe read the postscript:

You were by far the most beautiful bride I've ever seen. If I look even half as lovely on my wedding day, I'll thank the Good Lord!

He glanced at his watch. If she'd been able to book a red-eye flight, she'd probably be snug in her own little bed by now. *Well*, he thought dismally, *at least she's protected from Ian Cole's charms.*

Although, she hadn't appeared to need protection. In fact, it seemed to Joe that Shannen had *enjoyed* hobnobbing with the rich and famous. How many people had come up to him and said, "Your little girlfriend is positively *adorable*, Joe!" or, "That sweet young thing you escorted to the wedding is so *pretty!*" and, "Where did you find *her*, Joe; she fits in like a native Californian!"

She fit in, all right. . .fit in like she'd been born to the life!

The fact had distressed him so much that the moment his mother and Marcus drove off to begin their three-week honeymoon, he packed his bags and headed for LAX.

He and Shannen had planned to stay in L.A. for a few days after the wedding, so he could show her around Tinsel Town. Though he'd seen every tourist attraction half a dozen times, Joe believed it would all look different and new. . .with Shannen at his side.

Without her, what was the point of staying even another hour in California?

He plunked down the extra eighty bucks to cancel his original airline reservation and book a seat on the next flight to BWI. On the way to the gate, Joe stopped in an airport shop to see if they had the latest mystery novel in stock.

The moment he saw it, his heart began beating like a parade drum. Unable to believe his eyes, he took the tabloid in trembling hands. "Cole's Cookie" said the bold red headline above the five-by-seven color photo of Shannen, smiling up at the aging actor, and Ian Cole, one arm possessively wrapped around her slender waist, looking longingly into her face. Beneath the picture, in inch-high black letters, the caption read, "Ian Cole's Latest Conquest. . .he calls her 'Cookie'. . .but will she crumble?"

Jaws clenched tightly, Joe wadded the newspaper into his fist and stomped out of the store, unaware that he'd left his bag near the counter. He was too busy remembering the night they'd returned from Italy, when she'd said flat out that Ian Cole was not her type.

Was this ache inside him punishment for all the hearts he'd broken? If so, he was sorrier than ever for having taken advantage of those wanna-be starlets' desires to become one of the Beautiful People.

He wished he'd remained friends with just one of them—so he could ask her how long it would hurt this way.

seven

E*nough self-pity,* Joe thought. *Just pick up that phone and ask her straight out what she was doing with Ian Cole—and while you're at it, you can explain what you were doing with Buffy.*

He wrapped his hand around the receiver and lifted it to his ear, thinking he was fully prepared to dial Shannen's number; a number he'd known by heart since the night he grilled steaks on her deck. She'd been a huge and important part of his life for four weeks now—the happiest time of his life to date.

Oh, there were other times when he'd *thought* he was happy.

Take that first month after his mother married for the second time. Stefan had played Martha's son in a movie, and she'd married him on location. Only eleven at the time, Joe felt it would have been disloyal to his father's memory if he had immediately accepted the young man into his life. It didn't take his good-natured stepfather long to break down Joe's defenses, and he began seeing Stefan more as a big brother than a stepfather, and soon, he became "friend." But all that changed on the night the newlyweds celebrated their six-month anniversary, when Joe stumbled into the library and overheard their whispered conversation:

"But darling," Martha had said, "if we go to Europe,

what'll we do with Joey?"

"Boarding school. . .better still," came Stefan's reply, "a military academy. It'll make a man of him."

A week later, they'd dropped Joe off at the Brookshire Academy in southern Virginia, where he stayed—holidays and weekends and vacations—while his mother and Stefan toured the world. Three months later, just when he'd begun to accept his fate and started finding things to like about the school, his teary-eyed mother dragged him back to California, saying she "needed" him to help her get through the divorce.

He thought he'd put the bitter taste of Stefan's betrayal and his mother's self-centeredness behind him. But seeing Shannen's picture splashed all over the tabloids had awakened the stinging sensation, and Joe felt abandoned, rejected, and resentful all over again.

But why should he feel these things, when nearly two years ago, after becoming a Christian, he'd decided to walk in the apostle Paul's footsteps? If he'd meant it when he'd made his vow of celibacy, would it matter that Shannen had chosen Ian over him? If he'd been honest about his decision never to marry, would he care that she didn't want him?

Truth was, his resolution *had* been heartfelt at the time.

But then, he hadn't counted on meeting someone like Shannen.

Joe dialed Hank Nelson's number instead of Shannen's. He'd never met a man as dedicated to God as Hank. He spent every spare minute of his free time heading up committees to help those less fortunate. Believing the inner peace that was evident on Hank's face and in his voice had been put there by a generous volunteer spirit, Joe did his best to emulate the man who'd been the closest thing to a friend Joe had ever known.

Until Shannen.

"I need more to do," Joe told him. "Doesn't matter what job or which shelter. . .put me wherever you need me."

"No can do, Joe," Hank said pointedly. "I can't in all good conscience let you use these people again."

"*Use* them. . .again?" Joe swallowed. Hard. "What're you—"

"I'll *tell* you what I'm talking about. Every time you find yourself facing temptation, you hide out at the homeless shelter or in the soup kitchen. Somewhere along the way, you got the cockeyed notion that by shutting yourself off from the real world, you can avoid 'the nearer occasion of sin.' Well, I've got news for you, Joe: You can't conquer your fears by hiding behind charity cases. You've got to face your fears head-on and stand up to them."

They'd had a similar conversation when Joe first became a Christian. Hank had warned him against doing "right" for the wrong reasons. "You've always called one mansion or another 'home'," Hank pointed out. "When you've never gone without, not once in your life, it might be harder than you think to identify with people who never even *had* a home of their own." He'd quoted Matthew 19:24, the verse where Jesus told His disciples. "It is easier for a camel to go through the eye of a needle, than for a rich man to enter the kingdom of God."

Joe remembered thinking at the time that Hank had a lot of gall, saying a thing like that, because what did he know about Joe's life? He'd gone without plenty of times—not materially, of course, because how would *that* have made the Queen of Hollywood look?—but he'd learned firsthand what neglect and betrayal and abandonment felt like. It was true that he'd lived his life in a mansion, but since it had never been a *home*, how far a stretch could it be to identify with those less fortunate?

He'd thrown himself into his volunteer work, as much to prove something to Hank as to divert his attention from what was wrong in his own life. The harder he worked, the harder he *wanted* to work, because the feeling that something was missing refused to go away. *What's wrong with me,* Joe wondered time and again, *that even with all the riches I grew up with. . .even with all the comforts I have now. . .I'm* still *not happy!*

Hank had promised that if Joe turned his life over to Christ, he'd find satisfaction and contentment. So far, the peace of spirit had eluded him.

Had he been hiding out at the shelters? *Had* he been avoiding sin by evading temptation?

In a word, yes.

He'd given up the jet set lifestyle, had stopped pretending he might be able to grant future celebrities their fondest wishes, had sold his fancy sports car and the ritzy condo, and refused to take a handout from his famous mother. He'd learned a thing or two about art and antiques over the years; would have been hard *not* to, growing up as he had in a near-palace. So, with a "make it or break it" mind-set, he'd planted himself on the eastern seaboard, intent upon living a more

Christ-like existence than he'd ever lived to date.

Maybe Hank had a point; maybe his discontent was rooted in the fact that while Joe *had* most definitely turned certain areas of his life over to God, he hadn't given up control of *himself*.

And he might just have been able to pull it off, this whole "go it on your own" way of living, indefinitely.

If he hadn't met Shannen.

"Thanks, Hank," Joe said. "You've given me a lot to think about, as usual."

"And as usual," his friend said, laughing, "I don't have a clue what you're talking about. But you'll be in my prayers, m'friend."

He got on his knees, right there in the sparsely furnished living room of the apartment above his shop and clasped his hands tightly together. "Dear God, I'm ashamed of the man I've become. . .ashamed of my sins and ingratitude. Will I ever become what You want me to be? Or will I continue to fall?

"It's always been an amazement to me. . .that You could love a creature as weak as myself. Change my imperfections into virtues, my weaknesses into strengths, my doubts into faith. Maybe then I can be all that You want me to be.

"Help me, Father, to do Your will."

Immediately, a sense of "rightness" washed over him, and Joe sensed that Shannen hadn't fled California like a deer with a hunter on its trail for no good reason. There was no doubt a perfectly rational explanation for that front-page story in the tabloid, too.

And he intended to find out *what*.

Shannen got down on her knees and closed her tear-dampened eyes. Tomorrow would start the Christmas holiday with the Christmas Eve service and family gatherings, but tonight she was alone. . .very alone.

"Sweet Jesus," she prayed, "I know that you look upon me as Your child, and I trust that You care about me and love me. But I am afraid, Lord. Afraid of never finding my 'one true love.' I know that as long as You are in my life, I'll never truly be alone. Still. . .I cling to that worldly need to share my life with another.

"So give me courage, Lord; bolster my strength so that if I never find the man You intend me to spend my life with, I won't wallow in self-pity. Never let me forget that You'll stand by me, no matter what happens. . . because You love me, and—"

The doorbell interrupted her prayer. Shannen grabbed a tissue from the box on her nightstand and wiped her eyes as she headed for the foyer. She took a quick peek through the peephole and saw Joe standing on her porch, hands in his coat pockets, and facing the house across the street.

Shannen stood stock-still and silent. *If he thinks you're not home, he'll go away,* she thought. She didn't want to see him, not now, not ever again, because it would simply be a painful reminder of her foolishness.

Shannen had admitted a hard truth last night on the flight back to Baltimore: She'd fallen in love with Joe Malone; a hard truth, because she was certain he could never return her feelings.

It's your own fault that you're hurting, she scolded herself. *You promised never to involve yourself with a non-believer again—just because a man* says *he's a Christian doesn't mean he is.*

As she concluded the thought, Joe turned and rang the bell again, startling Shannen so badly she thumped her head against the door. Another check of the porch told her he'd heard it, for now his dark-eyed gaze was zeroed in on the peephole.

"I know you're in there, Shannen; I can hear you breathing."

Does he realize what the very sound of his voice is doing to me? she wondered. Shannen sighed heavily, then straightened her spine and lifted her chin. This would be the end of it, then, once and for all. She'd tell him, straight out, about her decision to see Christian men only. And when he insisted that *he* was a Follower—as no doubt he would—she'd remind him how he'd behaved at his mother's wedding reception.

She opened the door. "Joe."

"Shannen, have you been crying?"

The look on his face warmed her to the soles of her feet. If only she could believe he was everything he seemed to be. . . . "I often get a little misty when I pray," she admitted.

Their eyes met and held, connecting them one to the other like an invisible cable. Oh, how she longed to throw her arms around him, admit that she missed him, missed him more than she'd ever missed Todd!

Joe's hair was slightly windblown, and it took every ounce of her self-control to keep from gently combing it back into place with her fingertips. There were dark circles beneath his big eyes, too; lack of sleep and too much rich food had taken its toll, but he was still as appealing as ever.

"Come in, Joe," she said in a carefully controlled voice. "I just made a pitcher of iced tea. Would you like a glass?"

"You know me," he said, grinning as he stepped inside, "I'm a sucker for anything homemade. . . ."

Shannen closed the door and led the way into the kitchen. "I suppose you're wondering why I left L.A. so suddenly."

"Actually, I know why you left." Hands still pocketed, he shrugged. "I read your note."

She raised one brow. "It was addressed to your *mother*," was her scolding reply.

"She says to tell you you're a gem." Then he added, "Don't look at me like that. . .I only read it because I was worried about you. Last time I saw you, you were in the arms of that old coot, Ian Cole, don't forget."

"I'll have you know he's a gentleman, through and through."

Joe pulled a folded sheet of newspaper from his shirt pocket. "Well, you can't prove it by this." He handed it to her.

She put the pitcher down and unfolded the tabloid. Eyes wide and mouth agape, Shannen gasped. "They've made it look as though. . ." Another gasp. "What if my *mother* has seen this!" Her gaze darted to the telephone. "I'd better call her, tell her the *real* story."

Joe took her free hand and nodded at the article. "I have a feeling that if your mother had seen that, *she'd* have called *you* by now."

She bit her lower lip. "I suppose."

"Shannen," he said, leading her to the table, "I have

to talk to you."

She chose the chair nearest the sink, and he pulled up a seat beside her. Elbows on his knees, he leaned forward and stared into her eyes. "I haven't been completely honest with you," he began, "and I want to set things right."

"May I explain this first?" she interrupted, holding up the tabloid.

"No need for that. Ian called me last night."

"Ian. . .?"

Joe nodded. "He read me the riot act," he said, grinning, "told me he had a good mind to show me what a fifty-one-year-old man is capable of doing to a guy my age."

Shannen could only shake her head in amazement. *You're a lucky woman,* she told herself, *to have made such a good friend in such a short time.*

"I'd never hurt you—at least, not deliberately—I hope you know that."

He seems genuine enough, she thought. But if she really believed in his sincerity, she'd be in L.A. with him now, returning from after touring the sights. . . .

"I suppose I deserve that silence," Joe said quietly. "I'm sorry I wasn't up-front with you all along."

She got up, filled their glasses with tea, and returned to the table. "And I'm sorry I ran off like a spoiled little girl."

"I'm sorry my behavior made me look like—how did Ian put it?—a wolf in sheep's clothing."

They went back and forth that way for a few minutes, Shannen explaining her fears of making faulty decisions because of her naivete, Joe admitting how he'd been hiding behind doing good works.

"It's about time I put my trust and faith in God instead of myself," they said in perfect harmony.

After another moment of friendly laughter, Joe took Shannen in his arms. "I know we haven't known one another long, and some will say this is premature. . . but I've prayed about this, and. . .and. . ." He held her closer, tenderly cupping her face in his hands. "All my life, it seems, I've been looking for. . .I didn't know for *what*, but I made a lot of mistakes trying to fill the void. It wasn't until I realized I could lose you that I knew what *it* was: I love you, Shannen Flynn, and if you'll have me, I want to spend the rest of my life with you."

Trust God, she told herself. *Just let go and let Him be in charge!* "This is another of those incredible coincidences of ours," she said as tears of joy filled her eyes. "I love you, too, Joe. I love you, too!"

epilogue

one year later

"See there?" Shannen's mother said, pointing to the autographed picture of Ian Cole on the piano in her living room, "There's your namesake!"

The baby gurgled contentedly and bounced up and down in his grandmother's arms. "Have you heard from Ian lately?" she asked Shannen.

"Got a letter from him last week, as a matter of fact," Shannen said, grinning. "He says he'd be delighted to spend the Christmas holidays with us."

Her mother clasped both hands under her chin and flushed, inspiring Shannen's dad to grumble good-naturedly, "I'll never understand what she sees in that man."

Joe went along with the feigned jealousy and slung an arm around his father-in-law's shoulders. "Not to worry, Dad; Ian is harmless."

"Easy for you to say: He was your best man—and it isn't *your* wife he's taken a shine to!"

Shannen and Joe exchanged knowing grins.

"Think we oughta tell 'em?" Joe asked.

She nodded.

They filled the Flynns in on the latest in the movie star's life.

It seemed Ian had a favor to ask of his newly adopted family.

"He's accepted Christ in his life!" Shannen said excitedly. "And after spending a few days with you and Mom," she told her father, "and seeing how happy—and lasting—a Christian marriage could be, he went back to Liverpool and looked up his first love. He discovered that by the grace of God, she'd never married."

"But that's all gonna change on Christmas Eve," Joe put in. "He's bringing her here. . .to make her his wife." He drew his mother-in-law to him with his free arm. "Ian wants to you to play the organ at his wedding, Mom. And Dad, you're gonna be the best man."

Shannen grinned at her brothers. "He'll need to borrow a few of the kids. . .as ushers and flower girls."

"What about Ian, here?" her mother asked, kissing the baby's cheek.

Joe blew a raspberry on his son's chubby tummy. "He's gonna be the fat little pillow where we put the wedding rings," he said, inspiring a giggle from Baby Ian and a round of laughter from the rest of them. "Amazing what a little faith can do."

"*Soprendente,*" Shannen echoed Joe's sentiment in Italian, "*che cosa un po fare potere.*"

Joe's brows rose with confusion. "Huh?"

She shrugged daintily. "It's funny how the very same words can sound so much more romantic. . .in the language of love."

Loree Lough

A full-time writer for nearly thirteen years, Loree produced two thousand-plus articles and dozens of short stories, novels for kids ages eight to twelve (American Adventure), and twenty-plus inspirational romances—including the award-winning *Pocketful of Love, Emma's Orphans, Kate Ties the Knot,* and *The Wedding Wish* (**Heartsong Presents**). She contributed to best-selling anthologies *An Old Fashioned Christmas* and *Only You* (Barbour Publishing), and had her "Suddenly" series released by Love Inspired. Also writing as Cara McCormack and Aleesha Carter, Loree lives in Maryland with her husband and Mouser the Cat ("who wouldn't know a mouse if it handed her a hunk of cheese"). Her office is adjacent to the laundry room "so I can keep alive the illusion that I'm a fastidious housewife. . . ."

Candlelight Christmas

Colleen L. Reece

one

Thy word is a lamp unto my feet,
and a light unto my path.
PSALM 119:105

A wondrous, gift-wrapped Christmas Eve morning dawned over Seattle. Ribbons of sunlight glistened on sodden trees, grass, and shrubs. The waters of Puget Sound sparkled like tinsel, reflecting freshly washed blue skies and clusters of clouds whiter than snowcapped Mount Rainier looming in the distance. Emerald City shoppers clogged streets and stores, freed at last from the rain responsible for Seattle's well-deserved nickname. Joggers filled neighborhood parks and walked the local beaches. "Let's enjoy it while we can," they told one another. "Those innocent-looking clouds can change in a hurry."

On a broad hill overlooking the city, the cream walls of Shepherd of Love Hospital glowed under an unexpectedly warm December sun. Anticipation raced through the corridors, wards, and rooms, all tastefully decorated except for those housing critically ill patients. Doctors and nurses making morning rounds left behind a trail of smiles; all who were well enough would be released before the holidays. Staff members busily cleaned vacated rooms, whisked fresh linens on hospital beds, and prepared for the influx of patients Christmas Eve and Christmas Day inevitably brought.

Similar excitement filled the staff dining room where red velvet bows adorned holly and cedar wreaths on the soft green walls. April Andrews, RN, helped herself to hot muffins, bacon, eggs, and tomato juice at the buffet table. She mumbled to her sister Allison, a step behind, "There should be a law against sickness and accidents at Christmas."

Brown-haired Allison, who at first sight appeared an exact replica of her twin, laughed. "Just how do you propose such a law be passed?"

Mischief danced in April's Puget Sound-blue eyes. She drew herself up to her full five-foot height. "How would I know? I'm an RN, not a lawyer."

"You should have been," Allison stated flatly.

"Been what?" April stared. "An RN? I am. So are you, remember?"

"Not a nurse. A lawyer." Allison's grin couldn't disturb the peace in her steady gaze, a peace that characterized her and set her apart from her twin. "You can talk the birds out of the trees, as Jim always says." A shadow crossed her spirit. Mentioning the tall, brown-haired, brown-eyed man who had been neighbor and friend as far back as Allison could remember brought pain, not joy.

Friend? her traitorous heart taunted. *Jim Thorne, a friend?*

Allison swallowed. Hard. Friend was all Jim could ever be, even though her childish adoration for the substitute brother had changed to a woman's love. The new small-but-perfect diamond on her twin's ring finger sealed Allison's lips and heart. Forever.

The first secret she had ever kept from April lay over Allison like a rain-soaked blanket. If her sister ever suspected the truth, she would unflinchingly sacrifice herself for her "better half," as she called her twin.

Never! Allison vowed. *Better for one heart to be shattered than three.*

"Hurry up, will you?"

April's typical impatience recalled Allison to the present. She selected a piece of toast, poured freshly squeezed orange juice from a frosted crystal pitcher, and followed her sister to a deserted table. Her lips twisted in a wry grin at the symbolism in that short walk. Even though she had entered the world twenty minutes *before* her mother was blessed with a second baby girl, Allison had been following April's more adventurous footsteps since they were toddlers.

Once seated at the white-clad, presently deserted table, April eyed Allison's skimpy breakfast with obvious disfavor. "That's all you're having?"

Allison nearly blurted out she'd be lucky to get even that much past the misery in her throat. "I'm saving up for dinner."

"Not me. It's your turn to say grace."

"You mean not *I,*" Allison corrected. She bowed her head and asked a short blessing before April could reply.

It didn't deter her irrepressible sister. After repeating Allison's "Amen," she smirked and said, "You, I, me, who cares?" She hungrily dug into her breakfast while Allison nibbled toast and sipped orange juice. "I can't wait to get home." She cast an affectionate look around the charming room. "Not that I don't love this place."

Some of Allison's misery lifted. "Everyone does."

"I know." April rested her fork on her plate. Her expressive eyes glowed like twin sapphires. "Shepherd of Love Hospital is as respected as any in the city, and Seattle is internationally known for quality medical facilities."

With the keen insight born of their twinship, Allison knew April was mentally reviewing the incredible history of Shepherd of Love. A man named Nicholas Fairfax had felt led by God to build a hospital where medical skills, faith, and prayer worked hand in hand. A hospital that never turned anyone away, regardless of ability to pay. A hospital free from government restrictions because private funding came unsolicited, from persons who heard about Shepherd of Love and felt directed to contribute.

Words carved into the hospital director's office door set a high standard: *Thy word is a lamp unto my feet, and a light unto my path* (Psalm 119:105). If staff members were unwilling to reflect Christ's example of love as they dealt with patients, they were put on probation. If their conduct didn't improve, they were dismissed. A few weeks earlier, a nurse had been reprimanded for calling a patient a "gomer."

"We used the word in the hospital where I previously worked," she defended herself. "It only means 'get out of my Emergency Room.' We used it to designate street patients who come in again and again, drunk or hurt from fighting or falling down. They clutter the ER and take time from others."

"Shepherd of Love tolerates no such talk," she was

told. "You knew our rules when you came." The nurse received another chance only after promising not to offend a second time.

April's exasperated voice broke Allison's reflections. "If you're going to crumble the rest of that toast instead of eating it, let's go."

Allison looked at the mutilated bread. "Good idea." She straightened her aqua sweater and slacks, the counterpart to April's bright red ensemble. They no longer wore the twin outfits that once kept their friends mystified as to their identities, but occasionally they chose matching clothing in different colors. Allison favored bright pastels. April leaned toward vivid primary colors.

A long, covered passageway connected the staff residence building with the hospital. The girls' two-bedroom, ground-floor apartment was located near the far end of the T-shaped building and done in shades of green. The twins preferred living at the hospital and making frequent visits home to Auburn over expending time and energy commuting, especially in bad weather.

Driving home today validated their decision. Bumper-to-bumper traffic on the city streets, followed by a narrow escape from a three-car fender bender on Interstate 90, left them frazzled. "We'll have to allow plenty of time coming back," Allison warned.

April capably merged onto Interstate 405 South and nodded. "Even though the night shift doesn't start until eleven, I'm glad we planned for a one o'clock dinner with Dad and Mom." She slowed for a pickup that barreled into her lane in front of them. "I hope this snarl clears away by then."

"It should," Allison encouraged. "Rush hour will be

over and most people will be either home with their families or at church." She stared out the window at shining Lake Washington. "This is the second Christmas Eve we've volunteered to work so the married nurses can have time off." She grinned and confessed, "I'm glad we'll both be on duty." A laugh escaped and made her look more like April than ever. "I suspect I'll be sitting around doing nothing on Maternity while you're slaving away in Pediatrics!"

"Just remember: She who laughs last laughs best. *And* loudest. Lots of babies are born on Christmas. Even Jesus." April looked smug.

"When else would He be born?" Allison felt the same warm gratitude she always did when thinking of that first Christmas. "April, do you ever think what the world would be like if Jesus hadn't come to save those who accept Him?"

"Yes. Tyranny and more crime and probably no hospitals." April shuddered and made a face. "The traffic is getting worse. Mind if we don't talk for awhile?"

"Mmm." Allison slid down, readjusted her seat belt, and closed her eyes. In less than an hour she would see her parents. Her face burned with selfishness, but she couldn't help rejoicing over the fact that the Seattle Fire Department's schedule meant Jim Thorne wouldn't be next door and running over to see the Andrews. His engagement to April was still so new Allison hadn't yet reconciled herself to the changed situation.

She sent a prayer for strength heavenward, knowing she must not betray her feelings. She had always recognized that marriage would separate her from her twin, but she never had dreamed it would be like this.

The prayer helped, although fresh pangs assaulted Allison later when April showed their parents her ring. They were frankly delighted and not at all surprised. "We always did want that boy for a son," Mr. Andrews boomed. His eyes twinkled. "I figured he'd probably choose one of you, but I couldn't help wondering how Jim could ever decide which twin to pick!"

Laughter drowned Allison's horrified gasp. Her fingers turned icy. Only the discipline of her profession kept her from losing control. "Jim never thought of me that way," she commented. How could she sound so calm when her stomach and brain churned like an electric mixer on high? She jumped up and headed for the aroma-filled kitchen, willing tears back inside her eyelids. "Hey, when do we eat? I'm starving."

Somehow she made it through dinner. Somehow she joked with the others, telling them how working Christmas Eve had a fringe benefit: the opportunity to join others in candlelight caroling through the hospital before they went on duty. "April and I loved it last year." She cleared her throat of a sudden obstruction. "The appreciative expressions on the faces of patients who couldn't go home for the holidays went a long way toward making up for not being here."

Serious for once, April softly said, "It sure did. I wanted to hug and thank every one of them for their courage." Bright drops dampened her lashes.

The family lingered at the table long after stuffing themselves with traditional Christmas dinner. At last, Allison eyed the shambles and said, "Let's clean up here, then go for a walk. I'll never make it through tonight if I don't get some fresh air and exercise." She started stacking plates.

Dad offered, "If you'll clear and April will put away the food, I'll be noble and do pots, pans, and load the dishwasher."

"What about me?" Mom wanted to know.

Dad grinned at her. "You can watch and later cut the pie."

The twins groaned. "More food? Just what we need," Allison complained.

"She's kidding," April quickly added. "By the time we walk a couple of miles, guess who will be first in line for Mom's pumpkin pie and whipped cream."

"I'd rather play lazy than walk," Mom confessed. "Why don't you girls go while Dad finishes up? We'll visit more when you get back."

The Andrews home near Green River Community College offered splendid walking opportunities. Cul-de-sacs cut down on traffic. A bluff overlooked the Green River and the town. It also afforded an excellent view of Mount Rainier.

"It looks close enough to touch," Allison marveled, when they stood opposite the majestic mountain, even though she had stopped in the same spot and marveled countless times before. She spread her arms wide. "I love this place."

"Me, too." April grabbed her twin and broke into a wild, impromptu dance that reflected her natural high spirits. "I'm also *in* love."

Allison glanced at April's ring finger and muttered, "I would hope so," even though her peace had fled and her stomach felt like it had been hit with a cannonball.

April stopped and anxiously peered into Allison's

face. "My marriage won't change anything. Between us, I mean. We won't let it."

Not your marriage, Allison's rebellious heart protested. *Your marriage to* Jim Thorne. Yet she could not fault Jim. Even if he had known how the quieter twin's childish feelings had changed, who could resist April, sparkling as the month whose name she bore? Had Jim been waiting for April to turn from her many admirers and realize the boy next door was now a man, with a man's love?

Allison took a deep breath and dropped the bombshell that had begun forming with April's engagement. "Things actually may change. A lot. I'm considering spreading my wings after you and Jim are married. Literally. There's an opening with the helicopter rescue service Patti Thompson Sloan and her husband Scott fly for out of Kalispell, Montana. They want me to apply."

two

I will lift up mine eyes unto the hills,
from whence cometh my help.
My help cometh from the Lord,
which made heaven and earth.
Psalm 121:1–2

An eternity of silence followed Allison's startling announcement. She uncomfortably shifted her gaze from April's jolted expression to Mount Rainier, pinkening in the rosy light cast by the setting sun. Her fingers clenched. How would her sister react, once she recovered from shock?

She only wondered for a moment. Then a silvery peal of laughter shattered the quiet. She whirled. April stood clutching her stomach and laughing even harder.

"Sorry," she finally managed to get out between spasms. "It's just that—Allison Andrews, you were so scared when we flew to Disneyland you practically left nail marks on the arms of your seat!" This time she positively chortled.

So much for my attempt at independence, Allison thought sourly. She stubbornly crossed her arms. "Helicopters aren't the same as airplanes."

April fished a tissue from a pocket and wiped her

eyes. "They're a heap sight worse, as Dad would say." She tucked her hand through Allison's arm. "Get serious. Can you honestly see yourself making a career of something you hate?"

"Maybe not, but I also can't see myself. . ." Allison broke off and clamped her lips shut. Why had she allowed herself to burst out like that? Her acting ability just wasn't skilled enough to hide her feelings from either of the two she loved. Jim Thorne's keen brown gaze had always been able to ferret out her deepest thoughts. As for April—Allison inwardly sighed. April Andrews knew her twin better than Allison knew herself. How could she have believed for a single moment she could deceive her twin once April recovered from the initial euphoria of her engagement?

For the third time that day, April's voice brought Allison back to the real, troublesome world. "You can't see yourself doing what?" she demanded. "Staying on Maternity forever? So what? There are a lot of other jobs if you're tired of seeing babies born." April stated the obvious fact with the practicality friends always found surprising because of her bubbly personality.

Allison sagged in relief. Thank God April hadn't connected her sister's dissatisfaction with Jim Thorne! "Forget it. One more look at the mountain and I'm ready for pie, believe it or not."

"Same here." April shifted her gaze toward "their" mountain, as they had called it since childhood. Arms linked, the girls silently watched late afternoon shadows touch foothills, snowfields, and at last, Mount Rainier's spotless, shining crown. When gray gloom obscured the mountain and sent exploring fingers into the valley below, they turned toward home. Neither the radiantly happy April nor her troubled sister had reason to suspect their precious time together would be their last quiet moments for a long, long time or that so much drama lay ahead. Nothing would ever be the same.

Dusk dogged the girls' footsteps from the time they left the bluff. It attempted to overtake them just before they reached the last corner, but it couldn't compete with the hundreds of lighted Christmas decorations that held normal winter darkness at bay. Simple and elaborate trees stood in windows and yards, joined by Santa, snowmen, and manger scenes. Only a few homes remained unlighted. April gave an excited little bounce. "I love Christmas!" She squeezed Allison's arm. "It's so . . .so gladsome."

Some of her twin's depression lifted. She nodded. "Know what my favorite decoration is? That." She pointed to their own home. Dad and Mom had switched on the electric candles in every window facing the street. "There's something special about a light in the window."

"I know what you mean," April said in low tones. "Lighted windows stand for warmth. For welcome and the feeling nothing can hurt you once you're inside. Most of all, they stand for love. I can't remember a time Dad and Mom didn't leave a light in the window for us when we were out."

Allison heard the wistfulness in her sister's voice. She forced back a rush of nostalgia. Most of those times she and Allison had been together double-dating or somewhere with Jim. She resolutely turned her thoughts from him. Christmas Eve was no time to mourn over days long since lived.

April didn't seem to notice the little pool of silence that formed between them when Allison didn't reply. "It's a tradition we can carry on for our families."

"Yes." Allison barely got out. She closed her eyes against an unbidden mental picture of April setting a light in the window when twilight fell. Of Jim hastening home, face aglow with eagerness. Of April flinging wide the door to be caught in her husband's strong embrace. If only she could close her heart, as well!

Fortunately for Allison's state of mind, the bustle of sharing dessert, more visiting, and preparing to start back to Shepherd of Love covered her lapses into silence. Always quieter and more introspective than her twin, the family had long since accepted her reticence. Mr. and Mrs. Andrews never pushed the girls to be copies of each other but encouraged each to be an original. Even the few times in childhood, when Allison secretly wished she could be a little more outgoing, she still accepted who she was as a gift from God and seldom complained to Him.

"You drove down. Do you want me to drive back?" she asked April.

"Not unless you want to. You know me. I love being behind the wheel." April cocked her head to one side and grinned.

"You just like being in control," Allison laughingly accused. "I don't mind. I'd rather play passenger and relax." She yawned. "Wonder what tonight will bring?"

"Have you so soon forgotten your preposterous predictions, Madam Prophetess?" April taunted. Her eyes sparkled with fun. "You're going to lounge around in an empty Maternity Ward while I serve as an angel of mercy to the children in Pediatrics who need all the TLC I can give them."

Allison smirked and bowed low before her sister. "Yes, Your Wisdomness."

"I'll remind you of that non-word the next time you correct my grammar," April threatened. She glanced at her watch. "If we don't leave now, we won't be back in time for the caroling."

"First our prayer," Mr. Andrews reminded. The four joined hands and bowed their heads. "Our Heavenly Father, we thank You. Not only for our many blessings and the joy of being together, but for the wondrous gift of Your Son. We ask protection on the highways for Allison and April this night and for all others who travel. We ask Your guidance as our girls serve those who need their skills.

"Bless us and help us walk in Your Son's steps, reflecting Him and giving You the glory. In Jesus' name, Amen."

How many hundreds of times had they done this, Allison wondered. Sometimes only one of them prayed. At other times, each offered a prayer. Tonight she felt glad she didn't need to pray out loud. The choky feeling in her throat would surely stop any words her grateful heart might attempt to express audibly. Besides, God heard "heart prayers," as Mom called them, not just those that were spoken.

A round of hugs later, the girls climbed into the car and heeded the call of duty. They hit an in-between time for traffic and safely reached Shepherd of Love in plenty of time to don their uniforms and be on time for the caroling. April slid into a soft pink pants outfit. Allison chose blue. She would change into hospital scrubs if a mother delivered.

Tossing warm cardigans over their shoulders, they joined the dozen or more employees who had chosen to participate in the caroling. Each carried a tall, white, lighted candle and they formed a double line. Allison's spine tingled when she felt April's shiver of excitement. They went through the halls side by side and into all wards except those containing critically ill patients, singing, "Joy to the world, the Lord is come" and other carols.

That same joy showed in the eyes of those who watched and listened. Some patients joined in the singing. Treble voices piped up in Pediatrics, where April left the group. Deep and sometimes cracked voices came from senior adults. At last, the carolers began "Silent Night." Touched anew by the blended voices of those desiring to serve the One born in a manger so long ago, Allison found she couldn't sing. Only her heart gave thanks for that silent, holy night more than 2,000 years before when Jesus came to save all who would accept Him.

The last inspiring note faded. The caroling ended. No, not quite. A muffled cry came from the front of the line. "Look, everyone. It's snowing!"

The carolers rushed to the windows, excited as children. Christmas snow seldom visited Seattle. When it came, it rarely lasted. Now a white skiff covered the parking lot. Soft flakes joyously fell to the waiting earth, as though eager to join their companions on the ground.

Allison thrilled at the sight, wishing April were there with her to enjoy it. This kind of snow recalled childish games: fox and geese, building snowmen, making snow angels.

Allison stayed at the window a long time, then reported to Maternity. The quiet she had predicted offered her and her night supervisor the opportunity to catch up on necessary paperwork. Yet the two nurses could not resist the strong call of what lay outside the ward windows. They periodically took breaks to monitor the increasingly heavy snowfall.

Time passed. More white stuff fell. By three o'clock Christmas morning, radio and television weathercasters reported that more than four inches blanketed Seattle, falling at the incredible rate of an inch per hour. Cities and towns to the north had far more and the storm showed no signs of lessening.

Conditions worsened. Rapidly dropping temperatures and a howling north wind joined forces and became the Arctic Express. It swept in with devilish glee, changing beautiful to menacing. Ice pellets mercilessly attacked hospital windows. Although the ward was warm, Allison shivered, glad for her sweater.

Shepherd of Love and every other hospital in Seattle and the Pacific Northwest began to feel the blizzard's inevitable toll. Victims of traffic and various weather-related accidents arrived by ambulance, utility vehicles, anything that could get through. A few came on foot, fighting every inch of the way from nearby homes. The Emergency Room sent out a desperate call for help, summoning all medical personnel who could be spared from regular duty to report to ER immediately. It would take hours for even the most intrepid off-duty doctors and nurses to reach the hospital. In the meantime, the need for help heightened.

"Go," Allison's supervisor ordered. "I'll call you back, if I have to." She gravely shook her head. "God help any woman whose baby decides to arrive in this storm!"

The somber prayer accompanied Allison to ER. She stopped at the door of the waiting room, aghast. In all her years of training and floor duty, she had never seen the chaos that reigned here now. Heart thumping, she surveyed the scene. Triage evaluation of the patients pouring in had already begun. Those who were assessed as ones who could wait were told to do so. Some accepted it calmly. Others raged at the delay.

A man furiously pranced up to Allison and demanded, "What's wrong with this dump, anyway? A hospital is supposed to be prepared. Why don't you do something about this mess? My wife's wrist may be broken."

"I–I think it's only sprained," the meek-looking woman to whom he pointed apologetically explained. "I slipped and—"

"It doesn't matter," her husband interrupted. "She needs a doctor."

"Pipe down, buddy," a burly man growled, holding a blood-soaked towel to his head. He smiled at the timid woman. "Beggin' your pardon, ma'am, but a lot of folks here are worse off than us." She nodded and he turned back to her irate husband. "The Arctic Express didn't send out warnings, even to the weather forecasters. No one knew it was coming, so lay off blaming the hospital."

Someone snickered. Others cheered. The obnoxious man hastily took a seat, but he mumbled in a low tone to his scarlet-faced wife.

Allison sent the hospital's defender a grateful glance and quickly reported for orders. A butterfly or two danced in her middle. She hadn't worked on ER since nurses' training, and tonight it was a far cry from Maternity! As she started work, she caught sight of April applying a temporary bandage to a child who appeared more frightened than hurt. Some time later, she found herself next to her sister.

"Pediatrics was never like this," April said out of one side of her mouth.

"Nor Maternity."

"Some prophetess you turned out to be!" April taunted, then laughed.

Allison's lips curved into a smile. "*I* didn't claim to be one. It was your idea. Besides, I was half right. Maternity made a deserted island look overpopulated."

The lights went out, plunging the hospital into terrifying blackness. A heartbeat later, the hospital's auxiliary power system kicked in and a voice from the doorway riveted attention on the ice-covered figure. "Sit tight, people. You may be here a while. Most of Seattle and the Pacific Northwest has lost power. Downed trees have destroyed hundreds of power and telephone lines. It's going to take power companies hours to repair, maybe days."

April's fingers dug into Allison's arm. Her face turned stark white. "Jim is sure to be out somewhere. There will be fires and people to rescue."

Allison's heart turned to stone. She forced herself to rally for her sister's sake. "God will take care of Jim," she whispered, even though her heart was full with the same torment. Fear and faith battled for mastery of Allison's soul.

three

A refuge, and hiding place from the storm and rain.
ISAIAH 4:6 (NIV)

The grim announcement concerning the winter storm situation intensified the fear in the ER waiting room. Several persons rushed to the windows, but they could see little. Heavy, swirling snow hid everything except bundled-up workers in the ambulance area, frantically clearing away snow to accommodate the steady stream of vehicles bringing more patients.

Allison rubbed her eyes. Was this an endless nightmare? If only she could awaken and find herself safely in bed.

A hard pinch on her arm from April killed the futile hope. "Get out of your trance and get moving," she hissed. "We can't let concern for Jim keep us from our jobs." The pallor of her face contrasted sharply with the courageous words.

"Thanks." Allison shuddered. "I'm just having trouble believing it's real."

"It's real, all right," April grimly said through trembling lips. "Too real. If the Arctic Express is as bad as reported, this may only be the beginning."

"God help us if that's true!" Allison breathed.

"He will, but He's also going to need us to do all we can." April squared her shoulders and briskly walked toward the next patient.

Allison mentally saluted her sister's strength. She herself felt so shaken inside she wondered if she could carry on. April's reminder of their high calling to serve others did help. Thoughts of self, the storm, everything beyond the hospital walls faded. Even concern for Jim took second place, although it lurked just beneath the surface in a dull ache. Allison became her usual competent self and lost track of time. Hours or a lifetime later during a temporary lull, she gratefully accepted a hot drink from the burly man who had spoken up earlier.

"Sit down while you can," he respectfully suggested. Worry lines crossed what Allison knew would normally be a good-natured face. "I don't want to alarm you, but I sneaked out to my truck and caught a weather report. The temperature has dropped ten degrees and the wind chill is a lot lower." He sent a significant glance toward the window.

Allison's gaze followed his. The snow showed no signs of letting up. It formed fantastic patterns from the strong winds before piling up on every surface, increasing the probability of more trees coming down. "I guess no one knows what we are in for or how long it will last." The tired nurse sipped the steaming liquid. "I see someone took care of you." She pointed to the large bandage on his head. "Are you allowed to go home? Or can't you get there?"

He looked sheepish. "I can get there all right. I put studded tires on early and I carry extra weight in the truck bed." He grinned. "Holler if I'm in the way. Otherwise, I'd like to hang around and see if I can help."

"Like squelching complainers and saving thirsty nurses?" Allison teased.

"Yeah." The would-be Good Samaritan shifted from one foot to the other. "My wife and boy were supposed to fly home this morning from seeing her folks in California, so no one's at my place." He looked out the window again. "Fat chance of that happening now. Oh, my name's Bill." He held out a strong hand.

"Allison." She gripped his hand. "How do you think you might help?"

Bill pointed to several unhurt but forlorn-looking children huddled in chairs waiting for their parents. "I'm pretty good with kids." He looked modest. "You know, storytelling and stuff. I even know a few magic tricks."

His warm smile and willingness to help warmed Allison's heart and melted her weariness even more than the hot drink. "Great. I'll help you round them up."

A few minutes later, Bill sat in a corner surrounded by children. Allison lingered long enough to hear him say, "Okay, kids. I've got some tricks and enough stories to outlast any old Arctic Express, but first, we gotta be partners."

His audience perked up right away. "Partners?" a small boy echoed.

"Yeah. Some of my stories are really funny. It's okay to laugh, but not very loud. There's a lot of people here who are sick and hurt. We have to keep quiet and not bother them. Got it?"

"Got it," the children chorused in tones just above a group whisper.

"Thanks, Bill." Allison smiled and turned to leave. The gruff man would change those children's fearful waiting experience into a more pleasant memory.

He looked surprised. "Sure. That's what life's all about, ain't it? Folks helping folks." He leaned into the circle of squirming, eager bodies. "Now. My name's Bill and I'm a truck driver." He held out empty hands, flexed his fingers a few times, and a tiny toy appeared out of nowhere. Ignoring the carefully controlled *oohs* and *ahs,* he said, "I'll tell you a story called 'The Runaway Truck.' It really happened." He chuckled. "If I ever get up nerve, I may just send it to some magazine and see if they'd like to buy it."

A flaxen-haired girl tugged at his sleeve. "Is it a once-upon-a-time story? Do they live happily ever after?" Her enormous brown eyes grew anxious.

Bill grinned. "You have to wait to find out if it's happily ever after, but it does start 'once upon a time.' Here goes." He lowered his voice until it sounded mysterious. "Once upon a time when I first started driving truck, I. . ."

Allison reluctantly tore herself away, knowing the staff had found an ally.

A half hour later, the ER supervisor approached her. "When did you eat last?"

"I think I had a snack a century or two ago." Allison's rumbling stomach verified her statement. "It's been so busy I haven't thought about eating."

"Go now while you can," the supervisor ordered. Lines of weariness sagged her face. "We're going to have to snatch food—and sleep—when we can get it, probably for several days." Her smile looked forced but her gratitude and appreciation were real. "We couldn't have made it even this far without all the help from other parts of the hospital." A twinkle appeared in her tired eyes. "I'm surprised you haven't been called back to Maternity. This is just the kind of day babies choose to enter the world! By the way, your sister's gone to lunch. Pediatrics will be needing her back now that we're admitting some of the kids who came in." She straightened and trudged back to her command post.

Allison hurried to the staff dining room, aware for the first time of how hungry she was and how good it would feel to be off her feet for a short time. Short it was. She barely had time to smile at April and fortify herself with steaming chowder and a king-sized sandwich before a summons came from Maternity.

"Our first Christmas baby this year," she told April. "See you later!" She didn't wait for a reply. Women as far advanced in labor as this one—who had been brought in by ambulance after foolishly trying to drive and getting stuck—didn't wait for nurses to linger over lunch!

Good food and the familiar routine of Maternity after the din of ER rejuvenated Allison. So did the delivery process. When the masked, gowned nurse held the tiny scrap of humanity in her hands, Allison was as thrilled as usual. Birth never became routine. Each child fresh from the presence of God brought new wonder. Allison whispered a quick prayer for the tiny boy and his family, then laid the infant in his mother's arms. Her joy brought smiles from the staff.

Now that the need to keep on keeping on had temporarily subsided, Allison fought exhaustion. If another woman came in to be delivered, could her nurse be alert enough to do her best work? She must. As April had said, God expected and needed everything they could give.

The welcome arrival of a long-delayed maternity nurse and the day shift supervisor offered relief. Allison stumbled downstairs and through the covered passageway to the staff residence hall. Once in the quiet apartment, she headed straight for the shower. Steam and warm water helped wash away fatigue. Ten minutes later, she crawled into bed and dropped into dreamless sleep.

An insistent shaking roused her. In the twilight between sleep and waking, Allison wondered if an earthquake had been added to Seattle's miseries.

The shaking came again, heavier this time. "Wake up, Allison."

She forced open eyelids that felt like stone blocks. "April? What time is it? I don't have to go on duty until—"

Her sister's normally sparkling eyes were dull from lack of sleep. "Yes, you do. Stat. ER needs you again and I have to go back in two hours. Patients are streaming in nonstop. The place is a madhouse."

Fully awakened by the seriousness of April's words, Allison flung back her covers and snatched a spotless green uniform. "How can so many patients get through when doctors and nurses aren't able to report in for their shifts?"

"They're coming as quickly as they can." April giggled nervously. "The doctors and nurses, I mean. Ambulances are better equipped for this stuff, if anything can be." She smothered a yawn and started for the open bedroom door. "Sorry, but I can't stay awake long enough to talk. Or even walk without staggering." She yawned and weaved her way out.

❄

When Allison again entered the ER waiting room, she had a feeling of déjà vu. Had nothing changed at all? Yes. Different bodies occupied the chairs and lined the walls. Different children gathered in the corner around faithful Bill, who waved cheerfully and went on with a story. His voice sounded hoarse now, but he continued ministering to the children as best he could.

Allison's eyes stung, but she managed a smile and plunged back into the business at hand. Never had she seen such an assortment of needs. Traffic accident victims by the score. Falls by persons who should have known better than to go out in such weather. Serious burns for those foolish enough to bring gas barbecues inside their homes in order to cook Christmas dinners. Homeless persons seeking warmth and shelter from the frightful world outside.

Folks helping folks, Bill had said. The words sang in Allison's mind while her skilled fingers checked pulses, applied bandages, gently felt for broken bones. A favorite Scripture quickly followed: *A refuge and hiding place from the storm and rain* (Isaiah 4:6, NIV). Those who had come to Shepherd of Love sought that hiding place, a haven from fear and trouble.

The thought sustained her in the following hours. A bright spot, literally, came with the restoration of electrical power. A muted cheer rose when the brighter light replaced power from the auxiliary system. "Every off-duty power company employee has been called back to help with repairs," Bill informed Allison when she paused beside him. Most of his audience had rejoined their parents. Some had left the hospital. The few others lay asleep on the floor, wrapped in hospital blankets. Bill's face turned somber. "I don't envy them on a night like this. Or anyone else who has to be out in it."

Allison jumped. The pressing demands of her patients had forced concern for Jim from her mind. How incredible that she could have forgotten him for a single moment! "Do you know if there have been any fires? Bad ones, I mean?" Her voice shook in spite of her best efforts to control it.

"I'm afraid so. People trying to keep warm with improper devices." Bill's keen gaze bored into her. "Are you—I mean, are you thinking of someone special, not that it's my business."

Very special, Allison's heart answered, but she only said, "Yes. Dad and Mom will be fine, though. They live near Auburn. We were there. . .good heavens! Yesterday? It feels like an eternity. Anyway, they have plenty of food and a wood-burning fireplace insert to keep them warm." She took a deep breath. "I'm concerned for my sister's fiancé. He's with the Seattle Fire Department."

Understanding dawned in Bill's eyes. He awkwardly patted her shoulder. "I wouldn't worry about him, ma'am. Firefighters are trained for all kinds of situations. He's probably a lot better off than people just trying to cross the street when the traffic lights aren't working. The power companies are doing temporary hookups for hospitals, but most of the city is still without power."

He smiled again. "Some pretty amazing stories are coming out of all this. Neighbor helping neighbor and so on. The latest is that food companies have tons of food ready to send to the shelters. The storm knocked out their ability to get it there." He cleared his throat. "Would you believe hundreds of people who confessed if it were a work day they wouldn't even think of trying to get there, climbed into their four-wheel drives and came to help out? Some drove forty miles each way so the needy could have Christmas dinner!"

"That's one of the finest things I've ever heard," Allison cried. "Too bad it takes a tragedy like this to bring out people's natural goodness."

A disturbance at the ambulance entrance door abruptly ended their conversation. Paramedics wheeled in a prone figure, already hooked up to oxygen and IVs. Allison followed the procession to the nearest examination room, where an ER doctor waited.

"We've got a bad one here," the paramedic muttered. "This guy went into a collapsed home and rescued an elderly woman. She's okay except for shock, but he's going to need surgery. A beam fell. He couldn't get out of the way in time. Unconscious when we pulled him out and has lost a lot of blood. Vitals are. . ."

Allison pushed closer, in spite of a voice inside her that silently screamed, *Stay back.* She clenched her fists and forced herself to look into the unconscious man's bloody, unshaven face below the heavy bandages, dreading what she instinctively knew she would see. With a sinking heart, she recognized him: Jim Thorne. Firefighter, hero, and the man both she and April loved.

four

There be. . .things which are too wonderful for me. . .
which I know not: The way of an eagle in the air;
the way of a serpent upon a rock;
the way of a ship in the midst of the sea;
and the way of a man with a maid.
PROVERBS 30:18–19

Jim Thorne little knew and cared less what was happening outside the walls of Shepherd of Love. Trapped in a never-never land of pain, he relived the incidents leading up to his arrival at the hospital again and again. The details never varied, starting with an unusually quiet Christmas Eve.

"Looks like we may get off easy this year," one of Jim's fellow firefighters had remarked when they returned from a grease fire shortly after their twelve-hour shift began at 8:00 P.M. Fortunately, the only damage was a lot of smoke and a badly frightened woman. She had insisted she had left a frying pan with melted shortening on high "only for a minute." The firefighter added, "I hope it isn't the lull before a storm."

Jim glanced at the large clock on the fire station wall. Ten o'clock. Ten hours to go, unless something unexpected came up. "So do I." He grinned. "My girls are working tonight and part of tomorrow, but God and emergencies willing, we can spend part of Christmas Day together."

"Girls? Plural? Last thing I heard, you were engaged to *a* girl. Uno. One."

Jim's laugh sent gold twinkles into his brown eyes. "Being engaged to April is a little different because she and Allison are so much part of each other. Besides, we all grew up together. They were the girls next door. We spent as much time in each other's homes as we did our own."

The other man gave a mighty yawn and looked apologetic. "Sorry. I'm not bored, just beat. My family and I went tree shopping after I got off work yesterday morning." A grin softened his craggy face. "Nothing would do except that I help decorate, then my boy wanted to open a present." The grin widened. "It naturally turned out to be the biggest package, a train set."

Jim chuckled. "And of course it just had to be set up and you had to show him how it worked and you didn't get any sleep before coming back on duty."

"Who made you so smart?" His friend's expression gave away that was exactly what had happened. "Anyway, it was fun." He yawned again. "Think I'll get some shuteye before we get any more calls."

"Good idea." Some of the other firefighters were engaged in a card game, but Jim relaxed in a comfortable chair and closed his eyes. He needed to think. His reference earlier to childhood days living next door to the Andrews twins had churned up old memories. Some were best forgotten.

No.

Had he shouted the word? Evidently not. No response came from his partner, who like all firefighters on duty, dozed with one ear cocked for an alarm.

Lord, I have to fight out this thing, then bury it forever, Jim prayed. Eyes still closed, a procession of long-dead events paraded through his mind. April and Allison giggling together on their swing set. He and the twins picking berries, hiking, swimming, all the wonderful things kids did during Northwest summers. The lemonade stand they ran one year that went out of business because the youthful proprietors drank up all the profits on hot summer days. The paper route they shared for almost a year before enthusiasm dwindled.

Always together. Always eager for new experiences, especially April.

Childhood images changed to the teen years. A picture of Allison in her first long dress floated into Jim's brain. He had been her escort to a church youth banquet that called for dressy clothing. Even now Jim could see every detail of Allison's fluffy blue dress. Accustomed to seeing the twins in jeans or simple skirts and tops, Jim had experienced major shock. The dress also did something far more significant. Jim's young eyes saw the promise of womanhood in his changed friend. New and strange emotions rose within him.

The entrance of April, fresh and pretty in a daffodil yellow gown, gave him time to recover. Her date arrived and the foursome started out on a special, unforgettable evening. Laughter and silences. A banquet speaker who made God real in the lives of those he addressed. And always the feeling Jim was on the brink of some vastly important discovery.

Jim stirred uneasily. He set his lips in the firm line that warned those who knew him best it was time to back off. If these lingering feelings weren't settled, they would cast a shadow over his and April's life together. "It's simply nostalgia," he told himself.

It didn't help. The days following the banquet had brought denial, then acceptance of what had happened to him in a twinkling. They were some of the hardest of his life. At times he secretly called his feelings puppy love, then cringed at the term and hastily changed it to first love. It would pass, wouldn't it? His heart furiously refuted the idea as unworthy.

If only he had known whether Allison felt the same! Why couldn't he tell? A dozen times he groaned and wondered why his former keen perception into Allison's hidden thoughts had deserted him when he needed it most.

Weeks changed to months. Allison treated him no differently than before, except for a certain shyness and reserve he could not interpret. He dared not question her. Although she remained friendly, Jim felt she was drifting away from him. He also decided something had given her an inkling of his feelings, feelings that disturbed her and were not reciprocated. Creating distance between them rather than having him speak could be her way of avoiding a declaration that would change everything.

Boyish ardor seldom lives forever without some encouragement. Graduation meant partial separation, with the girls away at nurses' training and Jim in college. Jim had long since given his feelings to his Heavenly Father in prayer. The whole thing became dreamlike, a precious memory to cherish but not a foundation on which to build.

April flitted from date to date through the girls' training. She gleefully shared news of each new conquest with Jim when opportunity arose for the three friends to spend time together.

"What about you, Allison?" Jim sometimes asked.

Her quiet smile and downcast gaze gave away nothing.

Her sister wasn't as close-mouthed. "Allison could have ten dates a day if she wanted them," she always retorted.

"I have to study a lot harder than you do in order to get high grades." Allison looked wistful. "Even one date a week would mean flunking my classes and getting kicked out of training."

Nothing could squelch April. "No way. You're at the head of our class while I'm content to be in the top ten percent."

The conversation left Jim no wiser than he had been before. Didn't Allison date at all? If not, why not? No matter how conscientious she was, she couldn't spend all her time studying.

The twins' training ended. Allison stood at the top of her class with April not far behind. Jim rejoiced with them when they both applied to and were accepted by Shepherd of Love. He continued to treat them in his usual brotherly manner. Then everything changed. On a rare occasion when all three friends were home in Auburn at the same time, Jim saw April with new eyes.

She sat on the grass, holding a fallen robin. Perhaps it was the gentleness in her face as she stroked the lifeless body that caught at Jim's heart. Or the lone tear that escaped because she could not save the bird. Absorbed in the backyard drama, April didn't notice her neighbor watching her. Jim quietly backed away, unwilling to intrude. A tenderness formerly reserved for the quieter twin took root and sprouted. Because of April's tendency to change as rapidly as the month for which she had been named, he had failed to detect a side of her often shown by Allison. It endeared April to him more than anything else could have done.

He had strode back across the lawn toward her, making sure to tread heavily enough to warn her of his presence. "I always hate to see a bird die."

She ducked her head. Jim suspected it was to hide more tears. He patted her shoulder. "Jesus said not one sparrow shall fall without His care."

April raised her head and looked into his face. Some-thing flickered in her misted blue eyes, an indescribable expression Jim had never before seen. She reached for the comfort of his strong hand. When he took hers, the feeling he stood at a crossroads beat against his brain.

The next moment it vanished. April dropped his hand and sprang to her feet. She impatiently dashed moisture from her eyes. "Some nurse I am, crying over a bird when there is so much greater sorrow in the world." She threw back her head and smiled, once more the April he knew well.

Jim later told himself he had imagined the look. He failed miserably. Every time he saw April, he caught the elusive, growing awareness in her eyes that their shared sorrow over a fallen robin had created a subtle difference in their friendship. At first it made him feel uncomfortable, disloyal to Allison. He scorned the idea. There had never been anything between them but warm friendship and a boy's unspoken, unreciprocated love.

Jim frankly confessed his confusion to the Lord and in time felt the peace that comes to those who faithfully ask, seek, and find. He received no divine go-ahead, but he began to enjoy discovering more of April's "softer side," as he privately called it. Weeks later, he realized April had fallen in love with him.

That afternoon, Jim had gone to the hospital to visit a burn victim he had helped rescue. Pure impulse and the off chance April could take a break landed him in Pediatrics. She wasn't there, having been ordered off duty to recuperate from a harrowing situation.

"A wild-eyed man stormed in and demanded drugs," the nurse reported. "April kept calm. She stalled him until I could slip away and call Security. Thank God they arrived in record time! The man had a knife, and. . ."

Jim's stomach knotted and he lost the rest. "Is she in her apartment?"

"Under protest." The supervisor grimaced. "You know April!"

"Yes." He hurried away. All the danger he faced in his job hadn't prepared him for losing the girl so dear to him. Heart pounding, he hurried from the hospital through the passageway down the endless hall of the staff residence building and knocked on the twins' apartment door.

She flung it open and stared at him. He stepped inside and automatically held out his arms to the white-faced nurse obviously suffering from delayed shock.

With a little cry, she fell into them and hid her face against his chest. The next moment, she stood on tiptoe and kissed him.

❄

"Hey, buddy, are you dead or just deaf?"

Jim Thorne's eyelids flew open. He stared, feeling as if he had just returned from a long journey.

"Move it, will you?" his friend who had gone for a nap snapped. "We've got a call. And I thought *I* was a sound sleeper!"

Jim started to explain he hadn't been asleep and desisted. All business now that he had been roused from his reverie, he followed the crew to the fire engine and swung aboard. "What time is it, anyway?"

" 'Late, and weather not fit for man nor beast,' as the saying goes."

Jim's first sight of what lay outside the fire station doors sent his heart plummeting to his shoes. Snow, rising wind, and freezing air warned that the hours ahead meant work, heartache, and perhaps tragedy. So much for any hope of getting off at the end of his shift. He'd be lucky to be relieved at all.

When Seattle blacked out from lack of power, Jim and other firefighters who had determinedly battled their way to the station grimly looked at each other. Getting through city streets was seldom easy. Without traffic lights, the difficulty multiplied.

After the first few calls, Jim lost track of time. The storm partially obliterated daylight when it came. Seattle had become a disaster area. "I've lived here forty years and never seen anything like it," a veteran firefighter mumbled. He pointed to trees torn from the ground and wildly waving roots high in the air.

The next caller was almost incoherent. "Help! A tree crashed on my neighbor's house!" the woman screamed. "I know she's home, but the place is kindling and—"

Precious moments fled before Jim could calm the woman long enough to get an address. He cut off her babble with, "Excuse me, ma'am. We'll be there soon. It's not far from our present location." He slammed down the receiver.

Again the wail of sirens. Again the churning of snow from the fire truck's chained wheels. When they reached their destination, sweat crawled up Jim's back. *Dear God,* he prayed. *How can anyone be alive in that?*

With superhuman strength, the firefighters began their job. A curl of smoke warned even more danger lurked inside the shattered walls.

"We have to get in," Jim yelled. "There's a woman inside." A final blow to the front door opened a passage large enough for his body. With his usual prayer for help, Jim squeezed through and stepped inside the broken home.

five

Greater love hath no man than this,
that a man lay down his life for his friends.
JOHN 15:13

Beams creaked ominously from the weight of the monstrous tree that had all but demolished the house. Jim gingerly picked his way through the rubble. Dirt sifted down on him. "Is anyone here?" he called, although the chance of his receiving a response seemed slim. "Ma'am?"

To his joy and amazement a weak voice answered, "Here."

"Don't move. I'm coming," Jim promised. The tree settled a little more, sending down another minor avalanche of dirt. "If we're going to get out of here, it has to be fast," he grimly muttered. Guided by the feeble voice, he finally reached a tear-streaked elderly lady, whose "Thank God you came!" echoed in the firefighter's heart.

"There was a terrible crash," she cried, clutching a blanket around her meager frame. "I–I couldn't find my glasses. I couldn't see to get out."

Jim suspected from the rambling she hadn't recovered from the shock of the crashing tree. "Are you injured?"

"I–I don't think so," she quavered.

A quick check confirmed the statement. Jim wrapped the blanket more securely and carried her to the front door. Her frantic clutch and the debris underfoot hampered him, but at last they stumbled onto the porch. "She's shaken and frightened but doesn't appear to be hurt," he told the paramedics from the ambulance that had arrived at the scene while he was inside. "Take her to the hospital, anyway. She'll need to be treated for shock."

"Right."

To Jim's amazement, the frail woman frantically pushed the paramedics away with surprising strength when they attempted to get her into the ambulance. "No! Leave me alone. I can't leave Toby."

Toby? Jim's blood iced. "Ma'am, is someone still inside?"

She nodded. "Toby. Please get Toby for me. He will be so frightened. . ."

Jim ignored the rest of her plea. He spun on one heel, raced back across the porch, and into the collapsed building. "Toby?"

Only the terrifying sound of splintering wood answered.

"Toby, where are you?" Why didn't the man call out? Or was Toby a child? Not likely. The woman he had carried out was too old for that, unless a grandson had been visiting her.

He fought his way through the nightmare of examining every room. No sign of anyone. Relief filtered through Jim's concern. Toby must have crawled out the kitchen door or through a window. "Please God, let it be so," Jim whispered.

A tremendous crack warned him to get out. *Now.* He turned back toward the front door. A sound like the rushing of a train through the black of night roared in his ears. He glanced up and saw it: a beam torn loose by the weight it had been forced to bear but could no longer hold.

He leaped forward. Too late. Something exploded in his head. Smothering blackness followed—and obliterated all else.

Jim didn't know when his fellow firefighters dug him out from the ruins. He didn't know that many of his fellow firefighters cursed a cat named Toby. A cat that tore out and leaped into his owner's arms seconds before the beam fell. Jim's partner burst out, "Can you beat it? Save a cat and lose one of us?" Others whispered prayers and thanked God it had been a glancing blow. If the heavy beam had hit their comrade squarely, he'd have been killed instantly. This way, he at least had a chance.

Strong and caring hands tenderly lifted Jim into the ambulance. They checked for broken bones and hooked him up to oxygen and IVs. Unashamed tears coursed the cavernous creases in some of the stern faces. "You're carrying mighty precious cargo," one firefighter gruffly told the ambulance driver. "See that you remember it!"

"We will." The ambulance drove away. Moments later, flames leaped from the crushed house. The crew went into action. Thoughts of their fallen companion must take second place to duty. It was the way of their profession, a hard fact they accepted and endorsed. The way Jim would want it.

"This one's for our buddy," someone shouted. A shout of agreement rose, a battle cry against the dreadful storm that had already claimed lives and would claim more. As one person, they plunged into their work of extinguishing the blaze before sparks in the heavy wind could endanger or ignite nearby homes.

❄

Allison Andrews automatically moved out of the way so the highly trained ER team could do their job. All during her training and months of nursing she had sympathized with those whose loved ones were seriously ill or injured. Not until now had she known the full extent of their suffering. Her one glance at Jim Thorne, pale and still, had brought anguish beyond belief. If Jim died, part of her would go with him.

He is not going to die, she fiercely told herself. She repeated the words to April after receiving permission to go inform her sister of Jim's condition. "He is not going to die!" Allison vehemently repeated for emphasis. "God couldn't be so cruel as to take someone who risked his life to save another."

April drove her teeth into her bottom lip and clung to her twin's arm. "God doesn't always spare heroes," she reminded. "Even though they are special to Him." After a moment she whispered, "Jesus said no one has greater love than those who lay down their lives for their friends." Her lips quivered and her eyes reflected the pain Allison knew dwelt in her own. "Don't you think someone who gives his life for a stranger has even more love?"

Allison could only nod. To her amazement, April released her and said, "Others besides Jim need us. Let's pray, then get back to work."

"I don't think I can pray," Allison choked out.

"I will." April took her sister's hand.

Allison knew if she lived to be older than creation she would never forget her sister's simple prayer. Each word fell from paper-white lips, but April shed no tears. "We know You love Jim, Father. Even more than we do. Thank You for being here and for caring for him and all the others in the way You know is best. Help us accept Your choices. In the name of Jesus, Amen." Head high, shoulders straight, she walked away.

Allison watched her through a blur, touched by an impression of armies marching, banners flying. God grant that she, too, could show the courage in the days to come that her sister had portrayed!

❄

The press of work and exhaustion caused the nurses to fall asleep the moment they lay down for short periods. These quick naps saw them through the next grueling hours. Jim Thorne survived surgery, but only God could predict the outcome. In a meeting with his parents, who braved unspeakable driving conditions to reach Shepherd of Love, the surgeon and his assistant outlined what lay ahead. What it came down to was: "We hope for full recovery, but there is always the possibility of impaired vision, even brain damage after such trauma to the head."

The Thornes took the news quietly, then reported it to Allison and April. "We are simply trusting the Lord," they said. "It's all we can do." Allison's heart went out to them. Always close, this new situation bonded the girls to their beloved neighbors even more firmly. Strength and support flowed freely between them, lifting each up to face whatever came.

April had her hands full in Pediatrics and was no longer able to help elsewhere in the hospital, but Maternity stayed miraculously quiet. "We'll lend you out, but don't forget where you belong," the supervisor laughingly told Allison.

"I won't." The nurse's tired heart leaped. Serving as a floater nurse meant working wherever she was most needed. It offered both opportunity and challenge. She might even be assigned to. . . Allison firmly squelched the desire to work in the unit that housed Jim Thorne. Maternity nurses could handle triage for Emergency, but it took specifically trained personnel to provide the specialized care needed by intensive and critical care patients.

Floating didn't keep her from looking in on Jim, however. Against her better judgment, Allison slipped to his side whenever she could steal a moment from duty. If only he would regain consciousness! What wouldn't she give to have him open his eyes, even if it meant she must retreat or betray her feelings to one who must never suspect they existed.

Both Allison and April nearly lost control of their tears when they found two of Jim's comrades hovering outside his room. The girls had already learned of Jim's desperate search for a cat that led to his injury. Hearing it from the ill at ease firefighters made it so much more meaningful. "He's gonna be okay, isn't he?" one of his buddies demanded.

"He'd better, after all those prayers you said you'd been shooting toward heaven," another mumbled. He looked sheepish and hastily admitted, "Not that you're the only one. I said a prayer and so did most of the other guys."

"Thank you." April's smile lighted her weary face. "We have high hopes that he will be fine. It's wonderful to know so many people are pulling for Jim."

"He deserves it." The first man clamped his lips, then his mouth spread in a wide smile. "Say, which one of you is his girl?"

I am, Allison's traitorous heart silently declared. One hand flew to her mouth to keep the words from escaping.

April grinned. "We're both his girls, but I'm his fiancée," she pertly replied.

"Lucky bum." The approval in the man's glance at the twins sent rich color into their faces. "We have to go. You'll let us know if there's a change, won't you?" He shoved his hands in the pockets of his parka. "If he needs anything, the guys will see to it. We've already donated blood." He shoved a workworn hand toward them.

Allison speechlessly grasped it. April shook with his partner, then the firefighters tramped away, leaving their warm concern to surround the girls.

Shorthanded, taxed far beyond their normal limits of strength, the valiant personnel at Shepherd of Love and the other hospitals continued their tasks. So did police, firefighters, those who served at shelters and temporary shelters set up in churches, schools, and senior centers, as well as countless others. Neighbors helped neighbors. Acts of bravery and heroism that would never be recorded in history left an indelible mark in the lives of those involved.

Round-the-clock crews gradually restored power and phone service, but it took time. The snowfall dwindled, raising the curtain of visibility to display a lovely sight. Hundreds of candles originally purchased for Christmas decorations provided light for homes still without power. Many sat in windows; their flickering flames cheered the gloom that still hung over the city.

Briefly off duty at the same time, Allison and April gasped at the Christmas card world outside their apartment window. "A candlelight Christmas," April choked out. "We'll never forget it." She brushed unsteady fingers across wet lashes. "Jim has regained consciousness. Now this." She gestured at the splendor. "God is so good!" The tears kept under rigid control ever since Jim Thorne entered the hospital came like an avalanche. "I was so afraid! How could we live without Jim?" She held out her arms. Their tears mingled.

Long after April lay asleep in her room, Allison twisted and turned in her bed. It was curious that April had used the pronoun *we*. It seemed more logical that she would have wondered how *she* could live without Jim. Was April really and truly in love with Jim? Did she have the 'til death do us part' kind of devotion needed for a lifetime of marriage?

"Dear God, I pray she isn't just in love with love and all the excitement that goes with it," Allison whispered. A wrenching sob slipped from her throat. She hastily buried her face in her pillow. April must not find her sister crying in the night. That sister was at such a low ebb physically and emotionally she would never be able to dissemble, especially when it came to loving Jim Thorne.

It seemed a lifetime since she and April had stood on the bluff overlooking the Green River and Mount Rainier. How her twin had laughed at the idea of Allison taking the helicopter rescue service job! "I have to do something, God," Allison prayed. "As soon as the emergency is over, I'll start looking for a new job. There's no other choice." She paused, then whispered, "Leaving those I love will break my heart. Staying will break April's. And Jim's. Please, God, where do You want me to go?"

God's answer was not audible or in the form of a still, small voice deep in Allison's soul. Instead, a measure of peace stole over her. With it came knowledge. No matter how hard life grew or how far away she might go, she would be a better person for having known and loved Jim Thorne.

A beloved and healing scripture came to mind: *God has said, "Never will I leave you; never will I forsake you"* (Hebrews 13:5, NIV). Allison slept, wrapped in the comfort of the ageless promise.

six

In praise, fame and honor. . .
that you will be a people holy to the LORD *your God,*
as he promised.
DEUTERONOMY 26:19 (NIV)

Snow and ice reluctantly released their death grip on Seattle and the Pacific Northwest. A new front swept in, bringing heavy rain and rising temperatures. Snow became slush overnight, a messy, ugly, sharp contrast to the previous spotless white, terrible even in its beauty.

The warmer weather brought more problems, including massive flooding. Avalanches in the mountains cut off access to eastern Washington and stranded motorists. Crews on Snoqualmie, Stevens, White, and other passes blasted to lessen the danger. Road crews with heavy equipment worked twenty-four hours a day.

Seattle was not exempt from the new problem. Landslides, especially in West Seattle and other areas that overlooked Puget Sound, took full advantage of the water-soaked earth and loosened tree roots. Stunned residents watched homes they had worked hard to buy slip down steep embankments and crash below.

The week between Christmas and the beginning of

a new year had the same number of days as usual, but it felt like forever to the beleaguered citizens of western Washington. "Enough already!" a prominent local newscaster announced when power had been restored to all but a few outlying areas. She underscored the prayer of every man, woman, and child who had suffered in the weather siege and illustrated it with ghastly scenes of the storm's damage.

In spite of the chaos outside the walls of Shepherd of Love, the hospital slowly crept back to normal. "Whatever that is," April Andrews wearily told her sister. Yet in the light of Jim Thorne's progress, the strain they had experienced melted like snow before the warm wind of a Washington chinook. The hospital held its collective breath the first time Jim opened his eyes, hoping and praying he had suffered no permanent side effects, such as blindness or mental impairment.

The answer to those prayers came in Jim's first two words: "Where's Toby?"

Allison happened to be in the room. She stifled the desire to howl with laughter and told him, "Toby's fine. You can see him when you're stronger."

Satisfied, able to relax at last, Jim sank into a deep and healing sleep. Each time he awakened, his gaze became more direct, his mind more alert. Within a few days, he grew impatient. "When can I get out of here? I feel fine," he complained from the depths of a comfortable chair by the window of his pleasant room. His well-worn Bible and concordance lay close at hand on a nearby table.

"That's funny," April innocently said, mischief lurking in her blue eyes. "I heard you nearly keeled over the first time they let you try to walk."

Jim grinned, so like his normal self that Allison blinked back mist. "Who tattled?"

"I'll never tell." April glanced at her watch. "Uh-oh. Break's over and Pediatrics calls." She smiled at him. "Be a good boy, eat your spinach or whatever, and do what the nurses tell you. Remember, I have spies."

"Do you ever! You'll be back later, won't you?" Jim burrowed deeper into the chair and casually added, "I haven't seen Allison lately. She's not sick, is she?"

"No. She must have been in while you were sleeping."

"Oh."

The noncommittal reply so unlike Jim didn't seem to register with April. She dropped a quick kiss on his cheek and hurried away.

Jim turned his chair to face the window. Steadily dripping rain made patterns on the glass. He stared past them to a gray day and an equally gray Puget Sound. So Allison had visited him while he slept. Perhaps that accounted for the dreams that came whenever he closed his eyes. Jumbled dreams, confused impressions of being on a never-ending road that led to—what? In most of the dreams he felt trapped as he'd been trapped in the demolished house. At times, April and Allison stood before him, united by the reproach in their clear blue eyes. Even in his dreams, Jim recognized it as the same reproach he'd seen the few times in childhood when he failed to keep a promise to one of the twins.

Did the dreams hold a deeper significance? The memory of cool hands touching his face, bringing relief, sent a rush of feeling through him. Had those hands belonged to April? Allison? He snorted. The heavy blow and resulting trauma to his head must have scrambled his thinking. Neither April nor Allison would have been assigned to care for him. Yet something about those hands. . .

Jim impatiently turned from the window. Depression attacked him. Must he again fight the battle he thought he had won? "It's silly to believe in dreams," he muttered. "Especially these. They're only wild imaginings born from my mental expedition into the past just before the accident."

No. His heart gave lie to the low-spoken words that rang in his ears like thunder. Jim's hands flew to his suddenly aching head. Painful as it was, he had to face the truth. Not next week or next summer but now. He loved April Andrews deeply, but not in the way she deserved. Knowing this, did he dare marry her? Were friendship and fondness enough for marriage, even if he vowed to make April happy and did his best to fulfill that vow?

The same thought returned again and again in the next few days. Jim was moved from his room to an equally attractive one in the Transitional Care Unit.

He daily regained strength and hounded his doctors and nurses about being released. They proved as adamant about keeping him as he was about leaving.

April scolded. So did Allison, on her rare visits. "Stop being a terrible patient and do as you're told," they insisted. "Take a vacation."

Allison wistfully added, "Wish I could. In all the time I've been here, there have never been so many babies born during such a short period of time. If I didn't know better, I'd think the expectant mothers deliberately held off delivering until after the worst of the storm passed on!"

Jim looked at her shadowed eyes and felt ashamed of his complaining. "You look as if you could use a vacation."

"I know." She scrubbed the back of one hand across her eyes, a gesture Jim had seen dozens of times. "I'll see you both later."

When Jim knew she was out of hearing range, he turned to April. "Is something bothering Allison? I know she's worn out, but—"

April interrupted. "I'm afraid she's getting tired of working in Maternity. On Christmas Eve afternoon, she rambled on about applying for a job with the Montana helicopter rescue service where Patti used-to-be-Thompson and her husband work." A frown marred her smooth forehead. "I thought she was joking. Now I'm beginning to wonder if she meant it."

"Montana! Allison?" Jim felt the color recede from his face. How could he bear it if she went away? A second thought came hard on the heels of the first. How could he stand it if Allison remained? He loved her, eternally, irrevocably. Not with the boyish ardor he'd felt when they both were teenagers. Not with the distant hoping from afar that had haunted him for years. The love surging in his heart like an out of control river made his earlier feelings seem callow.

"Come back, come back, wherever you are," April chanted, ending with a delicious trill of laughter.

Jim stared at her with new understanding and a ton of guilt. His ignorance concerning what lay deep inside him had been like a silken cocoon waiting for the right moment to burst into a gorgeous butterfly—but now it could wreak havoc. Even if Allison could ever learn to love him as he loved her, April would always be between them. Sunny, temperamental April, so much a part of him.

"If you're going into a trance, I'm leaving," she announced. She smoothed the tunic of the peach pants uniform that made her look like a Royal Sunset rose-bud, and trotted away, the picture of insouciance. What would his defection do to her? *Please God, don't let my mistake in thinking anyone could ever take Allison's place with me blight April's life. All of our lives,* he amended.

He quailed at the thought of telling her. A voice whispered in his soul, *Don't be a fool! What makes you think Allison will even care? Don't throw away April's love on the chance Allison will one day care. It will only turn them both against you. You will gain nothing and lose everything.*

Jim clamped his lips shut against the craven suggestion and reached for his Bible, a New International Version. With a quick prayer for guidance, he switched to the concordance and let his gaze aimlessly drift from subject to subject. He might not know what Scripture he most needed just now, but Jim felt certain he would recognize it when he found it.

Honor. Honorable. The bold words fairly leaped from the page. Dozens of references followed. Jim looked them up in order until he came to Deuteronomy 26, verses 18 and 19.

> *And the* LORD *has declared this day that you are his people, his treasured possession as he promised, and that you are to keep all his commands. He has declared that he will set you in praise, fame and*

honor high above all the nations he has made and that you will be a people holy to the LORD *your God, as he promised.*

Praise. Fame. Honor. Jim closed the Bible and let it lie in his lap. He had received praise for simply doing his duty. Bouquets of flowers from persons unknown to Jim graced the hospital room.

Fame? Jim grinned wryly. News of his valiant attempt to save Toby the cat had caught several reporters' fancy. They played it for more than Toby was worth. One arranged for a personal appearance beneath Jim's window and photographed Jim peering down at the now-famous feline, whose only outstanding feature was being in the right place at the wrong time.

The humorous side of the potentially tragic situation only heightened interest. Dozens of cards and letters poured in addressed to the Cat Loving Fireman. One woman sent Jim a proposal, confiding he must be her destiny as she owned seventeen cats. She included a post office box number in case Jim was interested! The twins laughed. Jim raged. He did *not* reply.

Now he read the verses again. Honor. A people holy to the Lord. For better or worse, the die had been cast. His personal creed and commitment to the Lord Jesus Christ demanded his best. Marrying April under the present circumstances would be neither honorable nor holy.

Jim wearily made his way from his chair to his bed. Grown man that he was, he wished he could hide his heated face beneath the pillow until his problems disappeared. His churning brain tried to think of a way through the inevitable sorrow that lay ahead. Nothing came to mind.

By the time a nurse came in to check on him an hour later, Jim had worked himself into a fever. "What have you been doing?" the middle-aged woman demanded after reading the thermometer. "I thought we had this thing licked." She peered into his face. "Are you fretting about something?"

Jim felt his ears redden with embarrassment. "Yeah."

She scowled and placed her hands on ample hips. "You're supposed to leave the worrying to us and to God. Don't you think we can handle it?" she snapped.

It hit him like ice water thrown from a pitcher. To the nurse's amazement and even more to his own, Jim bellowed with laughter. "That's telling me, all right!"

"Just see you don't forget it." She brought a damp cloth and wiped his face. When he confessed he had a headache, she fetched a capsule and watched him down it. "Stewing is for tough old hens, not patients who want to go home."

He laughed again.

Obviously pleased with his reaction and meek, "Yes, ma'am," she marched out after warning Jim, "Young man, if I catch you moping again, you won't get a lollipop when we discharge you."

"Where's all the famous TLC Shepherd of Love patients are supposed to get?" he called after her.

She popped back in, grinning until her face looked like a full moon. "The best tender loving care is doing whatever helps patients get well. It doesn't include endorsing their pity parties!" She shot him a triumphant look and disappeared.

The wise nurse's banter proved to be even more powerful medicine than the capsule that soon relieved Jim's headache. Well, one of them. His major headache remained: How could he tell April their engagement was off?

You're supposed to leave the worrying to us and to God. Don't you think we can handle it? the nurse had demanded.

Shame filled Jim. Those in his profession were used to taking charge, solving tough problems. Jim knew the habit carried over into his spiritual life. He continually fought his tendency to barge in and outrun the Lord. He grimaced and mumbled, "Sorry. I keep forgetting who is in control." A mighty yawn followed. The troubled firefighter fell asleep with a chorus his grandmother used to sing echoing in his mind:

Got any rivers you think are uncrossable?
Got any mountains you can't tunnel through?
God specializes in things called impossible
And He can do what no other power can do.

AUTHOR UNKNOWN

seven

For this cause shall a man
leave his father and mother,
and cleave to his wife.
MARK 10:7

April Andrews sat alone at a window table in the nearly empty staff dining room and stared out at a gray day, perfectly color coordinated to her mood. What was wrong with her, anyway? The after-holiday blahs? Little wonder considering the hectic days and nights she knew would forever remain a blurred memory of duty, worry, and not enough sleep. She sighed. Even the prospect of skiing at Crystal Mountain or Snoqualmie Pass with Jim and Allison, as they normally did following the coming of a new year, failed to cheer her.

"I'm sick, sick, sick of bad weather," April mumbled. Her gloomy thoughts rushed on. If only spring would come! The corners of her mouth turned down. Fat chance. Spring didn't come to Seattle in January, but she couldn't help wishing it would.

Really? a small inner voice asked. *Is that truly what you want?*

April closed her eyes against the dreary day, wishing

she could honestly and enthusiastically answer yes. She couldn't. Spring meant planning her wedding, becoming engrossed with the thousand details necessary to make even a small wedding successful. Right now, even thinking about it left her exhausted.

Why? the little voice demanded. *Brides-to-be are supposed to be excited and happy, not moping about the weather.*

"I'm just tired," April muttered. "Once I get rested, I'll be excited."

"Talking to yourself when you could be talking with me, gorgeous?" a cheerful voice sang out beside her. "Tsk, tsk, what a waste."

April looked up into merry blue eyes. Where had the stocky blond man with the enormous tray of food come from? Who was he, this laughing individual who called her gorgeous without sounding bold?

"In case you care—and I've just discovered I sincerely hope you do—I'm Mike Buchanan, Shepherd of Love's new resident. My medical qualifications are only exceeded by my extreme modesty." He smirked but appeared strangely lacking in conceit, despite his outrageous claim. "May I join you?"

April nodded. The new resident placed his laden tray on the table and sat down next to her. For some unaccountable reason, April's spirits skyrocketed. An involuntary smile curved her expressive lips upward at the open admiration in his eyes. "Are you by chance a mind reader?"

"Not by chance, by profession," he teased. "If you'll excuse me a moment?"

April stared, then quickly bowed her head while Mike gave thanks. He unfolded his napkin and glanced around the pleasant room before tackling a mound of scrambled eggs. "All this and a charming breakfast companion," he said. "Could any mortal man ask for more?"

His teasing but respectful gaze did wonders for April's sagging morale. Her delighted laughter trilled out and her natural joy of living drove away the gloomies. "Thanks, but I'm sure some have been known to do so," she responded. "Of course, I can't think of any just now."

Mike Buchanan's hearty laugh set off rapid and good-natured verbal sparring that continued until Allison arrived. In the interim, April learned she had more than met her match in the witty Dr. Buchanan. He parried every thrust and wholeheartedly applauded when she bested him. How good it felt to laugh and joke after the endless nightmare Shepherd of Love had just experienced!

"April?"

Her sister's voice cut into the thought. "Hi, Allison. Dr. Buchanan, this is—"

The new doctor leaped from his chair, bowed from the waist, and placed a hand on his chest. "Be still, my heart. I am twice blessed." He looked from April to Allison. "Aha! The fair maidens blush at my sincere tribute."

April felt her cheeks turn the same scarlet as her twin's. "Did you swallow a copy of 'The Story of King Arthur and His Knights'?" she demanded.

"Touché!" Mike changed from chivalry to small boy and confessed, "I played the lead in a high school production of *Camelot* and never recovered." He grinned and admitted, "I know God doesn't make mistakes, but if only I had lived in the days of lords and ladies. . ." He let his voice trail off.

"I can just see you riding a white horse and charging into battle," April scoffed. She cocked her head to one side and measured him with an intent gaze. A vision born of her suggestion flickered before her eyes and stirred her heart. Long used to quickly assessing situations and persons, April instinctively knew Dr. Mike Buchanan would be as true to his calling as the fine steel used in the swords wielded by long ago kings, real and fictional.

"There are all kinds of battle," he quietly said. A shadow darkened his blue eyes. "Those in our profession ride into the fray every day of our lives." April felt ashamed of her thrust, but quickly recovered when he straightened, beamed at each of them, and hopefully asked, "As my great-grandmother would say, are you young ladies spoken for?"

April exchanged glances with her open-mouthed sister before holding out her left hand. "I am, but Allison is heart-whole." A pang went through her at the confession. It left her angry: at Mike for his teasing, at herself for resenting the way the new resident's attention left her in favor of Allison. Dr. Buchanan meant nothing to her. In a few months, she'd be Mrs. Jim Thorne. How unspeakably shallow and selfish to keenly feel Mike's loss of interest! Or was it a warning?

Mike's dramatic "The Buchanan luck strikes again" as he bent a blue-eyed stare toward Allison covered April's gasp. Ever since the day Jim found her crying over a dead bird, she had cherished his tenderness. He would be an anchor in life's inevitable storms. She loved him for the strength she had taken for granted but never really recognized or appreciated it. Now the admiring gaze of a stranger quickened her pulses. She could feel her wedding day rushing at her with blizzard force. Her soon-to-be-taken marriage vows loomed, a threat to her freedom. April felt them begin to imprison her in a cage of her own making.

Feeling suffocated, she stood, miraculously hiding her doubts behind a bright, "Excuse me, please. I need to go. You two can stay and get acquainted," and walked out. Even Allison's look of reproach at being left in an awkward situation couldn't hold her twin. She hurried out the dining room door and sped through the covered passageway leading to the staff residence hall. Reaching her quiet, green-walled apartment, she flung herself full length on the living room couch and buried her head in its soft pillows, haunted by a familiar Scripture that came to mind: *But from the beginning of the creation God made them male and female. For this cause shall a man leave his father and mother, and cleave to his wife* (Mark 10:6–7).

She slipped off the couch and onto her knees. "God, something's wrong with me. I'm afraid it's a whole lot more than being tired. If I love Jim enough to marry him, why did I respond like that to Mike Buchanan?" The low-spoken question sounded loud in the empty room. "I thought I could be true to Jim all my life, to cleave to him, as the Scripture says. Now I wonder."

She hesitated. A few tears came to cool her hot face. She impatiently brushed them away and continued. "Is it just that I'm used to masculine attention and thrive on it? Or are You trying to tell me something?"

Seconds ticked into minutes. At last April wearily

rose, prayer unanswered, at least in a way she could interpret. Since early childhood she had been taught to turn to the Bible for help. She reached for a King James Version, then decided in favor of the New International Version. The specific chapter she wanted used the word *love*, rather than *charity*.

April's fingers needed no prompting to quickly find 1 Corinthians 13: *If I speak in the tongues of men and of angels, but have not love, I am only a resounding gong or a clanging cymbal. If I have the gift of prophecy and can fathom all mysteries and all knowledge, and if I have a faith that can move mountains, but have not love, I am nothing.*

Her gaze slid to verse 4: *Love is patient, love is kind. It does not envy, it does not boast, it is not proud.*

April stopped reading. She had certainly envied Allison when Dr. Buchanan wrote off the engaged twin and focused on her sister! She read on. *It* [love] *is not rude, it is not self-seeking. . .it always protects, always trusts, always hopes, always perseveres. Love never fails.*

April silently admitted her feelings were self-seeking, rooted in the comfort and protection Jim offered. "Lord, how can I say my love never fails, when simply meeting a new doctor makes me question it?" she brokenly prayed.

She forced herself to continue, moving to verse 11. *When I was a child, I talked like a child, I thought like a child, I reasoned like a child. When I became a man, I put childish ways behind me.*

A great wave of knowledge rolled over April, encompassing her in the depths of truth. She had not put childish ways behind her. Far from it. At this very moment, thoughts of Allison and Dr. Buchanan together in the staff dining room ran like an underground river beneath April's struggle to know herself. She allowed the Bible to rest in her lap and closed her eyes. Shame and the need to be honest with herself and God threatened to consume her. A long time later, she opened her eyes and read the final verse of the New Testament "love chapter": *. . .these three remain: faith, hope and love. But the greatest of these is love.*

April put aside the Bible and paced the floor of the apartment. She had solemnly promised to be Jim Thorne's wife. He had faith in her. What would it do to him if she confessed the uncertainty growing to gigantic proportions inside her heart? How could she have failed to recognize her love for Jim was mostly comradeship and memories, coupled with the excitement of receiving and displaying his ring?

April disconsolately stared at her ring. It felt heavy, weighed down with implications for the future. She had briefly wondered when Jim kissed her the first time, and her heart continued its steady beat, but she had squashed the thought as unworthy. The thrills and chills she had experienced as a teenager belonged to puppy love. Far more important were the feelings of security and joy in sharing time together. She had also become caught up in the glamour of a beautiful wedding, a home of her own, children someday.

"You have been so stupid," April told herself. "Especially with Dad and Mom as an example of a good marriage. Now what, Lord?" She sighed. "I wish Allison would come. Maybe she can get me out of this muddled mess." Yet April quailed at the idea of confessing. Allison adored Jim. What would she think of her twin's faithlessness? April could picture Allison's clear blue gaze penetrating deep into her sister's trembling soul, her voice scornfully demanding how April could have mixed love and being in love into an impossible situation.

"Would it really be so bad to just go ahead and marry Jim?" April pondered aloud. "It's not like I care for anyone else." She resolutely ignored the interest and attraction she had felt when Dr. Mike Buchanan appeared at her table. "Jim's all those things the Bible says. I already love him a lot. There's no reason I can't work at it and make it grow. All I have to do is put my mind to it."

April set her lips in a firm line, but she couldn't ignore a nagging something that sneered at her reasoning. She deliberately replaced dark thoughts with a picture of herself walking down the church aisle between Dad and Mom. None of this march-in-with-Dad-and-not-Mom for her!

April shut her eyes. The apartment walls faded. She heard the swish of a long, white gown and smelled June roses from her mother's garden. A pink-clad Allison preceded her down the aisle. Jim waited at the front, brown eyes steady and smiling as April slowly moved toward him. The minister began to speak. "Dearly beloved, we are gathered. . ."

April's eyes popped open. What came next? She scrambled from the couch and dug through the stack of papers she and Jim had been given to study in preparation for their premarital counseling sessions. The burning desire to read a wedding service with vows similar to those she and Jim would take resulted in scattered pages and a small pamphlet. She settled back on the couch, heart thumping for no apparent reason. Opening the pamphlet, she could almost hear her minister repeating the words he had voiced countless times before.

> *Dearly beloved, we are gathered in the presence of God to unite this man and this woman in holy matrimony. Marriage is ordained of God and should not be entered into lightly. . .*

April restlessly skipped the rest of the charge and came to the vows.

> *Do you, April Andrews, take James Thorne, to be your lawfully wedded husband; to love, honor and cherish him; for better, for worse; for richer, for poorer; in sickness, in health. . .*
>
> *Do you mutually agree to be companions, forsaking all others, keeping yourselves holy, keeping yourselves for each other and from all others, as long as you both shall live?*

April drew in a jagged breath. She had attended many weddings, even participated in some. Hearing the exchange of vows had never left her so shaken. One thing was certain. Knowing the quality of her love for Jim, she could no more make that sacred covenant than leap over Mount Rainier. Her spirits ballooned at the decision, then thudded to her toes. How could she tell Jim? And Allison?

eight

And we know that all things work together
for good to them that love God,
to them who are the called according to his purpose.
ROMANS 8:28

A search to discover the most miserable people in Seattle would have placed three formerly inseparable friends high on the list.

April suffered incredible remorse after realizing she had been in love with romance and not with Jim Thorne. Sometimes she speculated as to how many others had been fooled by the "white lace and promises" of the Carpenters' classic song, "We've Only Just Begun." Dreary January days limped by. They gnawed at her sense of fair play and urged her to end the impossible situation. April threw herself into her pediatrics nursing duties more fervently than ever. "Doing penance," she wryly confessed to herself when she volunteered for overtime. "I just don't have the courage to face Jim."

An influx of patients gave her a temporary out and tossed a further sop to her conscience. So did Jim Thorne's release from the hospital under the condition he take time enough off work to fully recuperate. He protested but finally gave in and left for home, his dad's chess, and his mother's good cooking.

April felt reprieved. A curious look in Jim's far-seeing brown eyes showed he recognized something was wrong, but he hadn't figured out what. The few times he questioned her, she claimed fatigue and excused herself as quickly as she could.

April did hesitantly approach Allison one evening when they were both off duty. Jean-clad and wearing a bulky sweater over a matching blue knit turtleneck, she eyed her twin. Allison sat slumped in a chair, looked far wearier than April felt. Even her pink sweat outfit couldn't lend enough color to disguise her pallor. She had told April earlier that three women delivered during her shift.

"One experienced complications. For a time we thought we would lose both mother and baby. The delivery required our team's finest medical skills and intense prayer. Thank God they both pulled through." She glanced at April. "What's bothering you? You didn't lose a patient today, did you?"

"No." Aware of her sister's close scrutiny, April debated, then asked, "Do you think most brides have second thoughts?"

An unreadable expression came into her twin's eyes. Allison's face took on a set look. Her lips thinned. "Why? Are you?"

Unprepared for the blunt question, April mumbled, "I just wondered."

Scarlet flags waved in Allison's cheeks. "I can't believe this! A few weeks ago you were dancing around on the bluff overlooking Mount Rainier shouting, 'I'm in love.' " The scorn April feared flashed in Allison's eyes.

"Does this have anything to do with a certain resident here at Shepherd of Love?"

"No. Yes. I don't know." April looked away from the flaming condemnation in her sister's face.

Every trace of fatigue left Allison's rigid body. She sat up straight. "Just what is that supposed to mean?" Understanding crept into her eyes. "You resent the fact Dr. Mike Buchanan asked me out, don't you?"

April hedged. "Are you going?"

"That, my dear sister, is none of your business."

"I just asked," April weakly protested. "We never keep things from each other." She could feel the hairline crack in their close relationship caused by Allison's out of character remark expand into a vast, uncrossable chasm.

"Don't we?"

The unexpected answer triggered off April's volatile nature. "All right," she cried. "You're not going to like this, but you asked for it! I thought I loved Jim enough to marry him. I don't. I never will." She pressed her hands over her eyes. "I'm trapped. I can't stand losing Jim's friendship, but it's wrong to marry a man I only love as a brother."

An ominous silence followed April's outburst. An eternity later, she took her hands from her hot face and stared at her sister. Allison sat with hands clasped, as if the confession had turned her into an ice carving. Her blue eyes looked enormous in her too-pale face. Something flickered in their depths. Pity, dying indignation, and an expression April could not interpret but knew she would never forget.

When Allison spoke, she sounded old. "Are you in love with Dr. Buchanan?"

April shook her head. "I like him. A lot." She didn't add how much she treasured her chance encounters with the brash but respectful resident. Determined to be honest, she slowly added, "I'll always be grateful he came along when he did. I knew my love for Jim lacked something by the way my heart leaped at the sight of a new, attractive man."

Allison rose, her face a mask that successfully hid the way she really felt. "You have to tell Jim. Right away." She walked toward her bedroom door, steps heavy on the carpeted floor. "You've put in enough overtime to ask for time off. Go to Auburn and tell Jim, April." She stepped inside and closed the door.

April had the feeling more than one door had closed between them. Would Allison ever forgive her for breaking Jim's heart? Desolation filled her. Although they had shared childish squabbles, she had never before felt so completely separated from her twin. And it was all her own fault.

Please, God, give me strength to do what I must, she silently prayed. Fortified by the knowledge He would never leave nor forsake her, April resolutely marched out of the apartment, through the passageway, and to Pediatrics.

"May I take a couple of days off soon?" she asked her supervisor.

"Of course." The supervisor checked the duty schedule. "How about early next week?" She grinned. "We don't seem to have any emergencies scheduled!"

April nodded, but she felt let down. Now that she had chosen to face up to her problem, she had hoped to get it over with much sooner. Would her high resolve last through the hours and days before she could travel to Auburn—and Jim?

While April struggled with the delay, Allison lay on her bed and stared at the pale green ceiling. Her heart pounded until she thought it would deafen her. The interview with her sister had caused her to run the gamut of emotions from disgust and disappointment in April, to unreasonable hope. "Don't be stupid," she fiercely told herself. "Just because Jim can't have April doesn't mean he will turn to you. Even if he did, you'd always know you only had a secondhand love." The thought hurt unbearably. So did the knowledge Jim might well turn against both of them. Being around Allison would surely be a painful reminder of the charming butterfly Jim had lost.

Exhausted by her uncontrollable emotions, she dropped into an uneasy sleep. She dreamed she and Jim walked in a field of flowers. Far ahead, a yellow-clad April flitted through the blossoms, laughing, careless, ever distancing herself from the two who followed at a slower pace. Soon Jim forged ahead. Although he never caught up with April, he left Allison far behind, alone and sad.

She awoke feeling depressed. Sometimes dreams came true. God grant that this one didn't. She slipped from her bed, locked her door—something she never did—and poured out her heart in prayer. A verse came to mind, Romans 8:28: *And we know that all things work together for good to them that love God, to them who are the called according to his purpose.*

How can good come from this? she rebelliously cried. Yet the verse stayed in the back of her mind, comforting her when she felt like running away from the whole miserable problem. It helped still her turmoil, even when April returned and reported the time lapse before she could make her confession.

A cryptic message from Jim the next day further complicated the twins' tension. It read:

Dear April,

We need to talk. When will you have time off?

Love,

Jim

"D–do you think he suspects something?" Dread filled April's eyes and nibbled at Allison's heart.

"How could he?" She clutched icy fingers. "You haven't done anything to arouse suspicion or gossip, have you?"

April shook her head vehemently. "Absolutely not!" Tears glistened in her lashes. "I care too much about Jim for that."

"But not enough to marry him." Allison bit her lip, wishing she had swallowed the accusation instead of hurling it toward her unhappy sister.

April wilted until she resembled a homeless waif. "No."

Days later, Allison hugged her sister and huskily said, "Drive carefully. I'm praying for you." *And Jim.*

The unspoken words lay between them.

April drove away, haunted by her twin's worried face. "Not for long," she vowed. "No matter what happens, having it settled is better than this. I can't let this come between Allison and me." She merged into traffic and concentrated on her driving. Time enough when she faced Jim to decide what to say.

❄

Allison never clearly remembered the hours in between April's departure and her arrival back at the hospital. Her trained hands and mind performed her duties. Her heart traveled with her twin, the part of herself that faced the end of an era. When she finished her shift, she trudged to the apartment, prepared to spend a lonely evening. April wouldn't be home until the next day.

The sound of a key in the lock later that evening startled her out of the haze of misery into which she had drifted. April burst in, face shining. "It's all right," she babbled. She seized Allison and waltzed her around the room. "Everything is all right. Oh, Allison!" Her tone spoke volumes.

"What happened?" Allison hoarsely demanded.

"Jim. He's wonderful! He's—you'll never imagine. . ." April clamped her lips tight shut. "He wants to see you."

"He what?" Allison shook her sister. Hard. "Why should he want to see me?" Her heart felt like lead. Had her changeable sister reconsidered?

"That's for him to say." April went into a fit of giggles, then sobered. "It really, truly is all right. The way it was always meant to be. Jim will tell you so."

"You confessed and he forgave you? It would take a saint to do that!"

April blinked. "He's a saint, all right. He's also waiting for you in the hall." Her voice softened. "Listen to him, Allison." She tremulously smiled at her sister, threw wide the door, and stood aside to let Jim enter.

The door closing sounded like a death knell. "So you forgave her," Allison said flatly.

"There was nothing to forgive. I only wish I'd known long ago." A lovely light came into Jim's brown eyes. "Allison, I hope you will believe the strange story I'm about to tell you." He gently drew her to the couch and sat beside her. "Even though it's incredible, every word is true. Please try not to interrupt until I'm finished." His fine lips twisted. "I know you will want to stop me."

She wordlessly nodded, hating the position in which April had placed her but feeling obligated to do as he requested. Jim took her hands in his. She didn't have the strength to pull away. Or the desire. It might be the last time she could ever be with him, despite April's confident reassurance everything was all right.

"Once upon a time I loved two girls more than life itself," Jim began. "One day something changed." His fingers convulsively tightened on hers. "A girl in a fluffy blue dress walked straight into a young boy's heart." Old memories crept into his eyes.

Allison shook her head to clear it. When had April worn a fluffy blue dress? She favored yellow. Surely she wouldn't have forgotten a dress so important it knocked the boy Jim had been head over heels!

His eyes glowed and he continued, "I didn't dare show how I felt, for fear of spoiling the wonderful friendship the three of us shared."

Pain shot through her. It must have been for her sake. Dear Jim! Remaining silent all those years when he adored April. Her admiration and love deepened, and she fought tears at the thought of how he must have suffered.

Jim's steady gaze never left Allison's face. "The girl I loved with all the intensity of first love grew shy and reserved around me. In time she drifted away. I decided it must be because she didn't care for me the way I did for her. I gave my feelings to God and went on.

"Weeks passed. Months. Graduation and college brought inevitable separation, but I kept in touch when possible. One day I found April crying over a fallen robin. It was the beginning of a special friendship." He smiled at Allison, who thought her heart would break. "I convinced myself I was in love with her."

Allison could remain still no longer. "Convinced yourself? When you had cared for April all those years?" She jumped up and glared down at him.

Blank dismay greeted her question. Jim's eyes darkened and he leaped from the couch. "Not April. You, Allison. Don't you remember your blue dress?"

She sagged and would have fallen if he hadn't caught her. Joy and disbelief clamored for supremacy. A moment later, disillusionment came. "Jim Thorne, I wouldn't have believed you would pull such a shabby trick!" she raged. "April throws you over and you come whining to me with this unbelievable story of–of. . ." Allison couldn't go on.

"Of loving you always," he finished for her. "I felt you could never care, so I told myself April and I could be happy. But I couldn't go through with it."

How could he stand there and lie? It cut her to the quick.

Jim's intense gaze bored into her. "Have I ever deceived you, except by failing to let you know I loved you as a boy and even more now?"

She shook her head. Her heart leaped until she thought she'd choke. All this time, Jim had loved *her,* not April? If it were true, and she'd never known Jim to lie, what anguish each had needlessly gone through!

He tilted her chin with a strong hand and softly said, "Allison, do you believe me? I'm not asking you to love me. I just want you to know the truth."

"I believe you, but—"

"So did April." His joyful laugh settled deep into Allison's heart and glowed like the diamond she knew April would never again wear. "You can't imagine how glad I was to learn she had mistaken fondness for love! I've struggled for weeks knowing I had to tell her. That's why I sent word saying we had to talk." Jim reached in his pocket and pulled out a crumpled envelope. "I wrote this letter days ago but I decided mailing it would be a coward's way out. April cried when she saw it. Then she laughed and confessed why she'd been avoiding me. May I read it to you?"

Allison nodded. The crushed page Jim withdrew from the envelope and carefully smoothed out promised significance far beyond the boldly scrawled words. A new timbre touched Jim's voice as he read the short message.

Dear April,

I don't know how to tell you this, but I must. I love you dearly and always will, but not with the love necessary between man and wife. I thought we could make a good life together. Perhaps we could, if I didn't love another.

Even though she may never care for me, I will be untrue to you, her, myself, and most of all to God, if I allow our engagement to continue.

You probably never suspected it, but I fell in love with Allison the night I escorted her to the church dinner. I honestly thought I'd put that love out of my heart long ago. Now I know I had not.

If you can't forgive me, at least try to understand. Allison knows nothing of this. She never has. For all of our sakes, please don't tell her. She will never care for me except as a dear brother. I hope one day you will find the man God has chosen to enrich your life.

He let the page fall to the floor.

Allison gave a small cry. "You were wrong, Jim!"

He looked somber. "I know. I should never have let it go so far."

She took a deep breath and gathered her courage. "I don't mean that. You were wrong about my. . .my never caring."

Jim's face lighted. First with incredulity, then with hope. He placed his hands on her shoulders. "You mean in time you might care? Enough to become my wife? It's a lifetime job."

Allison slid her arms around his waist, feeling she had at last come home. Love made sweeter by the long years of waiting shone in her eyes, brighter than a leaping flame. "Not someday, my darling. Now."

❄

A few months later, April and Allison walked up the candlelit aisle of the church they had attended since childhood. April wore yellow. Allison was radiant in spotless white. She and Jim joyously repeated the solemn vows that made them one—the vows that had awakened April to what lay in her heart.

The maid of honor closed her eyes and silently gave thanks. God had truly brought good from all the trouble and misunderstanding. Then she stole a glance at Dr. Mike Buchanan. The unguarded look in his eyes curled into her heart and hinted at a bright and blessed future for the twin who was now free to follow her heart.

Colleen L. Reece

Colleen is a prolific writer with more than 100 books to her credit. In addition to writing, Colleen teaches and lectures in her home state of Washington. She loves to travel and, at the same time, do research for her inspirational historical romances. Twice voted "Favorite Author" in the annual **Heartsong Presents** readers' poll, Colleen has an army of fans that continues to grow, including younger readers who have enjoyed her "Juli Scott Super Sleuth" series for girls aged nine to fifteen.

Debra White Smith

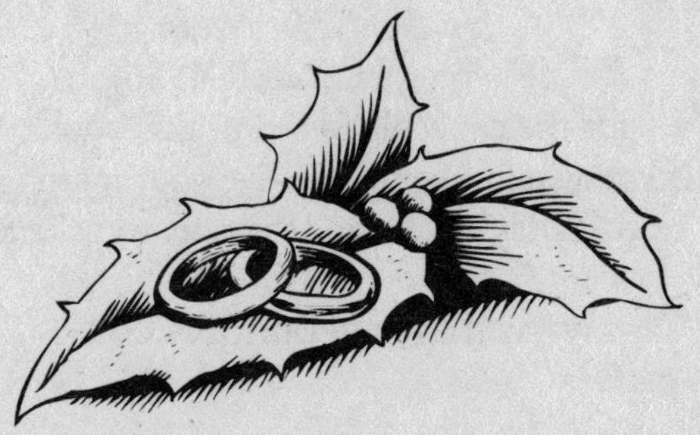

Dedication

To my critique partner,
Dr. Bob Osborne,
for keeping me accountable to
always produce my best.

Author's Note:

I am deeply indebted to Willard F. Harley's
His Needs Her Needs
(Fleming H. Revell, 1986)
for the concepts found in this book.
If you would like to improve your marriage,
read Harley's book and visit his website at:

www.marriagebuilders.com

one

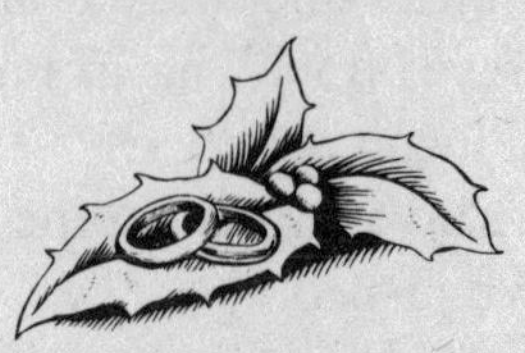

Hands shaking, Katelyn Grant examined the phone book under the "G" listing until she came to "Jake Grant." Her ex-husband. Feeling as if she were about to jump off a cliff, she picked up the cordless phone and dialed the number. Nearly a year ago, she had heard that Jake moved back to Mena. Thankfully, she hadn't bumped into him. In a town as small as Mena, Arkansas, that was nothing short of a miracle. Her heart pounded as if she had been running laps with her high school P.E. class. Would her ex-husband be home? Desperately, Katelyn hoped Jake wouldn't answer the phone; with equal urgency, she hoped he would answer.

As the phone began its ringing, she bit her lips and stiffly sat on the edge of the wicker love seat. Shortly after Katelyn found Christ as her Savior six months ago, the Lord began leading her to contact Jake and take responsibility for her part in their divorce. After weeks of resisting, Katelyn finally acquiesced to God's prompting this Saturday afternoon. With each of the phone's rings, her nausea grew. She had conjured every ounce of bravado she possessed to dial the number. If Jake didn't answer, could Katelyn ever find the courage to call again?

Just when she thought Jake wouldn't pick up, the ringing stopped and an all-too-familiar voice came on the line.

Her throat constricted, and no words formed. She hadn't spoken with Jake since the day of their divorce decree; the day he drove off with his mistress, Diane South. Were the two still living together?

"Hello?" Jake said again, this time more abruptly.

"Jake?" Katelyn rasped.

Silence. Elongated, pregnant silence.

"Katelyn?" he replied, a note of incredulity in his voice.

"Yes. It's me."

"I was just thinking of you."

"Oh, really?" Katelyn's palms produced an annoying film of sweat. And she lambasted herself for being pleased that he thought of her. "Were you using my picture for dart practice or something?" Her attempt at humor came out more like a weak squeak.

"No, nothing like that," he said with a chuckle.

She remembered that deep, under-the-breath laugh. Oh, how she remembered it. For five years that laugh had been a part of her world. But Jake preferred another woman. The old wound produced a familiar ache, despite Katelyn's resolve to forgive him.

"So. . .what's new with you?" he asked, the curiosity spilling from his voice, a curiosity that proclaimed, "Why are you calling me?"

"Uh. . ." Katelyn eyed the ten speed hanging in its usual spot on the living room wall of her duplex apartment. A lot was new with Katelyn. Her main "newness" stemmed from her radical encounter with Jesus Christ. That experience revolutionized her life, leaving her alive in a way she had never experienced. But her spiritual journey was by no means pain free. After Katelyn's initial euphoria, God began nudging her toward confession, repentance, and restitution. This phone call to Jake was a part of God's nudging. Katelyn knew that she must face Jake in person. Every time she thought of writing a letter or just talking on the phone, a still small voice prompted her to a face-to-face encounter.

"Uh. . . ," she said again. "There's a lot new with me." Katelyn nervously cleared her throat. "I. . .um. . .I actually was–was calling to ask if we might could–could meet for dinner this eve–evening?" Her last question came out in the voice of a trembling teenager.

As Jake's silence stretched indefinitely, Katelyn wondered why she couldn't control her vacillating emotions. This was Jake, for pity's sake. Just Jake. Her ex-husband. At one time, the two knew each other inside out. Why did Katelyn suddenly feel like she was talking to a stranger?

At last, Jake spoke, "Yeah. Dinner sounds great."

Katelyn thought she heard a momentary quiver in his own voice but quickly dismissed the notion. Three years ago, Jake made it painfully clear that he held no interest in Katelyn. Mentally. Emotionally. Physically.

"We can meet at. . ." The first eating establishment she thought of in Mena, Arkansas, was Audrey's Bed and Breakfast. Audrey's served gourmet sandwiches all day and was Jake and Katelyn's favorite romantic restaurant during their marriage.

Katelyn quickly dismissed the idea and decided on McDonald's. There was nothing romantic about McDonald's. She certainly didn't want to give Jake the wrong impression. For after she confessed what God had laid on her heart, Katelyn planned to turn her back, walk away, and never—absolutely never—see Jake Grant again. She opened her mouth to suggest McDonald's, but Jake beat her to a suggestion.

"Why don't we meet at Audrey's?" he asked softly.

"Uh. . .I was thinking more in terms of McDonald's," she countered. "I haven't had a Big Mac in a month, and you know me and Big Macs." Her pulse pounded in her throat. This was insanity. Pure insanity. Perhaps Katelyn should have never called Jake.

Another chuckle. "That's fine. McDonald's it is. Is 6:00 okay?"

"Yes. Six is fine."

After the appropriate adieu's, Katelyn hung up and flopped backward. The few inexpensive ornaments of an otherwise austere decor joined the rest of the room in a disconcerting spin. The whole apartment reflected Katelyn's personality. Practical. Uncomplicated. Straightforward. A lover of sports. But presently, her various sports trophies, ten-speed, and collection of autographed tennis balls jumbled together as the room tilted.

Katelyn shut her eyes to get a better grip on her emotions. At once, she cried out in the simplicity of a babe in Christ, "Lord, You're the one who got me into this. If I'm going to make it through dinner with Jake, I'll need Your strength. Please, please, let me get through the whole thing with my dignity intact."

❄

Like a man obsessed, Jake dug through the bottom drawer of his rustic dresser. At last, his search ended when his fingers grasped a taped-shut shirt box. Impatiently, he ripped off the lid, releasing a scattering of photos of himself and Katelyn. For some reason he hadn't been able to throw them away as his mistress had demanded. When Diane left a year after Jake's divorce, he hadn't possessed the courage to open the box.

Today's phone call gave him that courage.

As if he were seeing his ex-wife for the first time, Jake sorted through the pictures, drinking in her wholesome beauty. Some would call Katelyn plain. But her straight red hair, pale skin, and scattering of freckles, never left Jake thinking she was plain. He possessed a weakness for redheads. Katelyn had told him early in their college courtship she possessed a weakness for blond athletes. So Jake thought he had met the woman with whom he would spend the rest of his life. But that didn't happen. Their marriage failed.

He picked up photo after photo which brought back so many forgotten, happy days. Katelyn, early in their marriage with their first puppy Fred. Katelyn and Jake on vacation in Montana. Their second Christmas together when Jake put a big red ribbon on the new sports coupe he bought especially for Katelyn. Earlier today he had mused that yet another Christmas was soon approaching. Another empty Christmas without Katelyn.

Finally Jake collected the scattered photos from the hardwood floor, placed them back into their container, and set the box on the end of the poster bed his parents once shared. Immediately, the old farmhouse seemed forlorn, empty, lifeless. Jake moved into the ancient, yet well-kept homestead last year when his mom and dad decided to buy an RV and travel. Jake left his forestry job in northern Arkansas to take a forest ranger's position at Queen Willa Mena State Park. Shortly after his move back to Mena, he began having recurring thoughts of Katelyn. How was she? What was going on in her life? Did she ever think of him? How could he have been so stupid to throw away what they shared?

All morning, Jake's mind dwelt on the last question. Then when he picked up the phone and her trembling voice greeted him, Jake almost dropped the phone. Did she want to rebuild their marriage? Could Jake be that lucky? In three short hours he would know.

Jake rushed to the small bedroom closet, whipped open the door, and began examining his limited wardrobe. Nothing seemed appropriate. As a forest ranger, his uniforms were supplied. Therefore, the rest of his wardrobe consisted of precious more than sports shorts, jeans, and a few pair of worn dress slacks. In minutes, Jake decided to make a quick trip to the men's store in Mena. He never worried much about clothing, but something in Jake insisted he look his best that evening.

❄

Katelyn put off getting dressed until 5:30. She purposefully chose a pair of blue jeans, a long floppy sweatshirt, and a pair of jogging shoes. Then she pulled her straight shoulder-length hair into a casual ponytail and chose not to apply her usual sporty touch of makeup. She refused—she simply refused—to get dressed up for Jake. Katelyn didn't want to give him even a hint of the wrong idea. This dinner date was about obeying God. Period. Nothing more.

She locked the door to her duplex and settled into the red sports coupe that had been Jake's Christmas gift to her many years before. Several times after the divorce,

Katelyn thought of selling the vehicle. But the thing was paid for and P.E. teachers in small Arkansas towns didn't make much money. So to be practical Katelyn kept it.

Steering through Mena's streets, she occasionally glanced toward the bluish mountains that stretched across the western horizon. During the last year, Katelyn often stared toward those mountains, wondering if Jake perhaps got a job as park ranger for Queen Willa Mena State Park. It would make perfect sense.

All last year, she had rehearsed what she might say to Jake were they to incidentally see each other about town. Thankfully, that never happened. But now Katelyn had arranged a face-to-face meeting. With tired resolve, she drove into the McDonald's parking lot and warily scanned the cars to see if Jake might be awaiting her. She saw no sign of him and decided to sit in her car and pray until he arrived. Not a day went by without encountering the fact that being a Christian took a lot of courage. She needed all the supernatural bravado she could muster for this confrontation.

Jake drove his all-terrain truck into the parking place beside a familiar red car. So Katelyn never sold the car. He didn't know if this was a sign of her continued loyalty to him or a sign of her lack of finances. Even though his heart wanted to believe the former, Jake's common sense insisted on the latter.

He slid from his truck and into the brisk November air. The smells of French fries and hamburgers met him as he closed his door and peered through Katelyn's passenger window into the driver's seat. She sat with her forehead propped against the steering wheel and wore her favorite clothing—a floppy sweatshirt and blue jeans. At once Jake felt overdressed in his pleated cotton pants and stiff new shirt.

He walked around her car and lightly tapped on her window. Her head snapped up and she turned teary eyes to him. Why was she crying? As their gaze lengthened, Jake resisted the urge to whip open the door and blot away the tear that trickled down her cheek. Jake's heart raced as if he and Katelyn were in one of their collegiate matches of mixed doubles tennis. At once, all the old attraction spilled through Jake like an overwrought river long held at bay. He must have been crazy to divorce Katelyn. How would he ever survive this encounter without trying to take her in his arms?

Deftly, she dashed away the tears and opened the car door. "Hi," she said with a sad smile.

"Hi." To keep himself from touching her, Jake jammed his hands into his pockets. "You've been crying. . ." He trailed off, his voice full of concern.

"Oh, that. . ." She locked the car door, closed it, and turned toward the fast-food restaurant. "I was just praying."

Praying? Jake fell in step beside her. Since when did Katelyn pray? The whole time Jake had known her she was an agnostic at best. Even though Jake possessed a belief in God, he never put much stock in talking to Him, much to his mother's distress. He and Katelyn specifically agreed early in their relationship that neither of them cared to make religion a part of their world. What occurred in Katelyn's life to change that stance? Something within Jake stirred, a vague longing which recently had become his tormentor.

As he opened the door to McDonald's, he felt as if he were opening the portal gate to a new chapter of his life. Perhaps the chapter would involve Katelyn and maybe Katelyn would tell Jake about prayer.

two

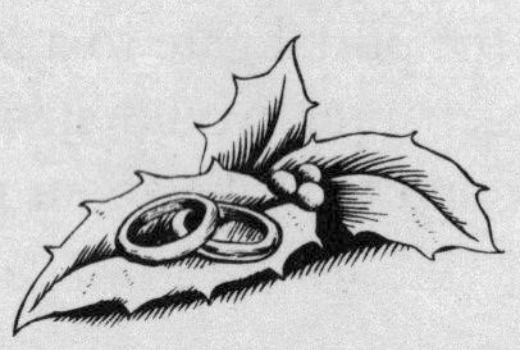

Katelyn sat across from Jake in the corner booth. She eyed her Big Mac and fries, but her churning stomach refused to allow her more than a few sips of cola. Other than their initial eye contact, Katelyn managed not to look Jake in the eyes again. For looking into his eyes had proven entirely too dangerous. Having not talked with him in three years made her feel as if she were seeing him for the first time. The lock of straight blond hair hanging just above those mesmerizing eyes and the patrician nose commandeered her attention as strongly as they had on their first date. But despite the fact that he could still stir her pulse, Katelyn refused to even consider ever rebuilding their relationship. In short, Jake Grant trampled her heart. Katelyn didn't want to experience that hurt again. Besides, he was probably married to Diane by now anyway.

As she stared at the untouched meal, a strained silence settled between them. Her hands shook uncontrollably, and Katelyn tucked them under her thighs to stop their shaking. She groped for a beginning but couldn't find the words to start. Jake was watching her. She could feel it. *Oh, Lord, why did You have to get me into this mess?*

"Well, hello, Katelyn," a familiar male voice called.

With an inward groan, she turned a faint smile

toward her new pastor and his wife. How would she ever explain why she was having dinner with her ex-husband when they didn't even know she had an ex-husband? "Hello, Pastor Steve," she said.

His petite wife smiled her greeting, and the tall pastor laid a caring hand on Katelyn's shoulder then politely extended his hand to Jake. "I'm Steve. Steve Anderson. And this is my wife, Sophie. We were just out for our Saturday night date."

Sophie laughed. "Yeah. Steve always chooses the most romantic spots."

"Well, we're on a budget," he said with a teasing shrug. "If you wanted steak and candlelight, you should have married somebody with more money."

"You're just fine for me," she replied, latching onto his arm.

Katelyn often envied their wonderful relationship, something she and Jake never had. Not really. Even though they shared chemistry from the start, they never shared the depth of love Katelyn readily saw in her pastor and his wife.

Momentarily, an awkward silence settled between them, and Katelyn felt pressed to introduce her male companion. At first, she resisted then decided she might as well plunge in. "This is Jake Grant," she supplied, choosing not to add any explanation of his relation to her.

Sophie twirled her finger in a circle. "And you two are. . . ?"

"I'm her ex-husband," Jake supplied.

"Oh." Sophie's dark eyes registered all kinds of questions.

Katelyn suppressed another groan. Already, she felt obligated to tell her pastor and wife why she was out with her ex-husband. Since Steve and Sophie recently moved to Mena, their friendship with Katelyn had swiftly deepened. Something in Katelyn couldn't leave them just hanging. This confession and restitution business was not by any means an easy road.

"Well, we'll let you two get on with your meal," Pastor Steve said, tugging his wife's hand. "I've got a romantic drive up to Queen Willa Mena State Park planned to round off the evening."

"Oh, so you did have romance in mind after all," Sophie teased as they left.

"They seemed nice," Jake said casually.

Without thinking, Katelyn forgot her former resolve to avoid eye contact and looked into the depths of Jake's gray eyes. She saw a barrage of questions waiting to be answered such as, "Why did you invite me here? Why are you attending church?"

"Yes, they are nice. I really enjoy having them at our church."

"So, you're going to church now?" Jake said, munching a fry.

"Yes. I. . .I started about six months ago."

"Why? I didn't think you much believed in God."

"Uh. . .that's part of the reason I wanted to talk with you, actually." She took a cleansing breath, darted yet another heavenward plea for courage, and began to say the things God required of her. "I know this may be hard for you to believe, but I had a radical encounter with God about six months ago. I accepted Jesus Christ as my Savior, and my life has been totally changed."

"Oh, really?" Jake asked mildly, as if he were intensely interested but trying to hide it.

"Yes." She toyed with the wrapper on her Big Mac and remembered that moment when she heard the Lord calling her name. "Like you said, I always doubted that there even was a God, but one day, I found a New Testament a student left in the gym. I picked it up and had a sudden curiosity about the whole concept of religion. I started reading that New Testament and couldn't put it down. By the time I got through with John, I knew that I had encountered truth—real truth—for the first time in my life."

As she told her story, Katelyn's shaking eased. Somehow recalling her conversion brought her new strength, new resolve. Still studying her untouched meal, she continued. "And that's basically the driving force in the reason I asked you to dinner."

"Oh?"

Katelyn glanced at him and new feelings exploded in her chest. She cared for Jake, cared very deeply. The knowledge that he was spiritually lost and didn't even know it overwhelmed her.

"I—" She cleared her throat as these unexpected emotions seemed to snatch the very words from her mind. "I—being a Christian is a wonderful life, Jake, but I'm learning that there are things God requires of His children. One of them is. . .is this issue of confessing sins to Him, repenting, and then making restitution with the ones we've wronged."

She paused, forcing herself to slowly meet Jake's gaze and hold it. The moment of truth at last. Katelyn desperately hoped she could squeeze the words from her tightened throat. "God has. . .has shown me that you weren't the only one to. . .to blame for our failed marriage. And I—" She cleared her throat but still held eye contact. "I felt that I needed to tell you in person how sorry I am for my part in our divorce." There. The words were out! A new peace engulfed Katelyn. A peace that said her heavenly Father witnessed and approved her obedience.

Jake stared at her in stunned silence as if the words hung between them and he were trying to absorb their meaning. At long last, he spoke. "I never dreamed I could be so lucky. When you called, I only dared to hope that. . .that. . ." He covered her hand with his as more words spilled forth. "Katelyn, I don't think I ever stopped loving you. I would have given my right arm for you just to agree to seeing me, but to say that you want to rebuild our marriage is—"

"What?" Katelyn exclaimed. Snatching her hand away, she rubbed at the betraying tingles. "I never said I wanted to rebuild our marriage."

A new wave of emotions marched across Jake's expressive face. Confusion. Uncertainty. Pain. "But you implied that you—"

"Well, I didn't mean to imply that," she whispered, feeling the stares of a family in a nearby booth. "I told you the reason I wanted to see you. It was just to confess that. . .that I was in the wrong as well. Now I've done that, and—"

"But that's crazy!" He tossed his napkin onto the table as if he were trying to come to terms with Katelyn's reasoning.

"Would you *please* lower your voice," she insisted,

leaning forward. "I don't want the whole town to know our complete conversation by sundown."

"So what if they do?" he replied, clearly agitated. "I feel as if you're playing some kind of game here, and I want some answers."

"I've already told you why I wanted to see you. Now I've admitted my fault and I'm ready to move on with my life, both spiritually and physically. That's the beginning and end of it."

"Well if all of this involves your finding religion, it sounds like being a Christian is about the most hair-brained way to live I've ever heard of," he challenged.

"It isn't, actually," Katelyn defended, her own volume rising. "The more I confess and make restitution, the more peace I have. There's something very freeing about coming totally clean with God and your fellow man." Grabbing her pocketbook, she stood and issued her own challenge. "You should try it sometime."

As if her last words were the final trump card, Jake stared at her as though she had truly given him food for thought. "So that's all you have to say?"

"That's it." Feeling light as a cloud, Katelyn turned to walk away. But something made her turn back around. Katelyn didn't stop to ponder whether that "something" was a perverse urge to mischief or her own heart's desire to know if Jake's mistress was still in his life. "And by the way, tell Diane I said 'hello'." Diane and Katelyn had been friends long before Jake had had the affair with her. The whole ordeal left Katelyn feeling betrayed on all sides.

"Diane and I haven't been together for two years," he said flatly. "She moved back to California."

"Oh." By now the nearby family had stopped eating and shamelessly scrutinized Katelyn and Jake.

"Katie," Jake said, standing. "There's something I think I need to say here."

The contrite note in his voice made Katelyn want to run. As long as Jake had been her enemy, she knew how to handle him, but now. . .now. . . And what had he said earlier about giving his right arm just for her to agree to seeing him? Was Jake really still in love with her after all the misery he put her through?

"I think I just need to go home," she muttered, rushing for the door.

"Katie. . .Katie. . ."

Feeling as if she were running for her emotional life, Katelyn dashed across the parking lot and fumbled with inserting the key into the car's door lock. *Please, God, please let me get away before he catches up with me.* But Katelyn heard Jake's rapid approach and knew that was one request God chose not to grant. With a desperate whimper, she inserted the key into the lock. A second later Jake gripped her shoulders and gently turned her to face him.

"Listen. . .listen to me," his words were a cross between a plea and a demand.

Biting her lips, Katelyn stubbornly stared over his shoulder and tried to suppress the tears stinging her eyes. Never had she imagined Jake would so desperately want to rebuild their marriage. What had she gotten herself into?

"Look at me," he said softly. Jake gently tugged on her chin until her gaze met his. "I need to say 'I'm sorry,' too. I was wrong, Katie. More wrong than you. I knew that only months after our divorce. And I've been kicking myself ever since. I thought being single would be a riot. But it isn't. It's a hard, lonely existence. And I—"

The tears would be denied no longer. With a muffled sob, Katelyn covered her mouth as turbulent emotions jerked her into their gripping current.

Jake's arms wrapped around Katelyn, enveloping her into his warmth. "Oh, Katie, I am so, so sorry."

Momentarily, she yielded to his embrace, glad for any source of strength in her tempest of tears. But those tears eventually subsided and Katelyn was aware—far too aware—of his masculinity. All those intimate moments they once shared flooded her mind, leaving her weak-kneed and breathless.

His hold tightened, and Katelyn knew he, too, felt the old chemistry. "Katie?" he said on a sigh.

Katelyn, relying on more willpower than she knew she possessed, abruptly broke Jake's embrace and turned her back to him. "I meant what I said, Jake," she said, her tone sounding less than convincing. "I never intended, and I still don't intend, to renew our relationship. I don't ever plan to remarry or date again. Not you or anybody. Not after what you put me through. I simply needed to confess to you. That's the beginning and end of it."

Painful silence, the kind that throbbed with heartache, engulfed them, trapping them in a world all their own. Despite the passing cars, the occasional honks, the sounds of children in the McDonald's play area, Katelyn felt as if she and Jake stood isolated on a deserted island.

After what seemed an eternity, he spoke, "Well, if that's the way it is, I guess there's nothing more I can do." His voice held a disillusioned edge.

"There's nothing more," she said firmly.

As if he were waiting to give her time to change her mind, Jake didn't move. "Katelyn. . ."

"I'm sorry," she stated simply. "I. . .I just c–can't."

Finally, she heard him walk away and slowly get into his truck. Katelyn didn't change her position until he drove away. Her heart pounding in sorrow, she unlocked her car door and slipped into the seat. Weakly, she propped her forehead against the steering wheel and began her prayer of thanks for surviving the encounter. But her prayer seemed to go no farther than the top of her car as a very disturbing thought entered her mind. Never once had Katelyn consulted God about whether or not she should renew her relationship with Jake.

The drive home took only five minutes, but it stretched into a reverie of years. Every place Katelyn passed brought memories of days filled with joyous expectation, days which eventually brought loss. Katelyn dragged herself to her front door and, through the mist in her eyes, fumbled to insert the key in the lock. The door opened grudgingly. Katelyn searched the living room for some sight of warmth or consolation. The Spartan room looked back with a cold, dispassionate stare.

Throwing her pocketbook on the wicker love seat, she walked to the electronic keyboard in the corner. Katelyn didn't consider herself an accomplished pianist. During her teen years her interest in sports had dominated piano lessons until there was no longer room for them in Katelyn's burgeoning schedule. However, she loved to chord the classics, pop tunes, and recently, church hymns. As she sat on the padded stool, the instrument seemed to challenge her to release the emotions raging through her soul. The internal churning exploded in the form of an angry pounding on the keys that sounded more like a hard-rock tune from Katelyn's teen years. Once her initial fury spent itself, her fingers slowed their flight across the keys and eventually produced hymns and choruses. Those sacred tunes tumbled from her thoughts until one stunned her mind. "Have thine own way, Lord. . .mold me and make me after Thy will. . ." With swift jerking execution, she turned off the keyboard.

Katelyn plodded toward the kitchen to eat a piece of cold chicken and drink a glass of milk. They did nothing to lower the fuming in her soul, the thoughts plaguing her mind. *Jake. Jake. Jake.* How could he have ever ended their marriage? A cool shower and a good book in bed might put a swift end to her mental torment.

She stood in front of the dresser mirror and considered the image looking back. The reflection gave no indication of any feeling, just an empty gaze. Katelyn jerked the sweatshirt over her head and slammed it on the floor. The mirror changed. Her counterpart appeared cool and aloof. She tore at the cotton undershirt she wore for warmth and tossed it against the sweatshirt. Katelyn studied the image. The voiceless specter looked hard and unyielding. She slipped off her jeans and added them to the heap on the floor. A relentless change flowed through her reflection. Cracks of selfishness appeared along with smudges of bitterness. With the removal of each piece of clothing the image grew worse. Finally nothing covered her. Katelyn shivered at what she saw.

Retreating into the shock of the cool water, Katelyn allowed the numbing effect to hide her fears. She dried without looking into the mirror. The rubbing did nothing to warm her shaking body. Tears streamed down her cheeks as she struggled into a faded nightshirt. She flipped off the final light and groped for the bed. Falling across the thick comforter, she grasped a fluffy brown teddy bear which Jake gave her for their first Christmas together. Other than the car, the bear was the only gift from him she had kept. It warmed her as Jake never did.

three

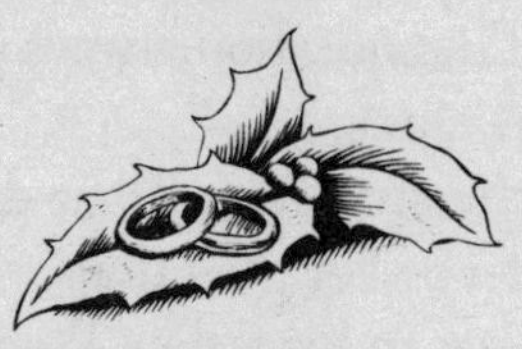

There's something very freeing about coming totally clean with God and your fellow man. You should try it some time.

Katelyn's words haunted Jake all week, even during the Thanksgiving dinner he shared with his parents. He had to admit that he *did* notice a change in Katelyn, despite his wanting to deny it. Her eyes sparkled with a new tranquillity Jake longed to experience. But how? Jake hadn't attended church since junior high. He felt lost; he didn't know what to do to make peace with God.

That question led him to begin scanning through the Bible his mother gave him last Christmas and ultimately led him to ask around town until he discovered where Katelyn's minister Steve Anderson pastored. Jake now stood outside the pastor's office door in a church hallway which smelled of hymnals and new carpet. The smells brought back old memories from his distant past. Jake's mother took him to church from childhood until his early teen years. But his father never put any value in church or God. By the time Jake turned thirteen, he'd adopted his father's attitude—the ways of the father became the path for the son. Only in recent years had his father expressed an interest in the things of God. Several times, he tried to talk to Jake, but Jake refused to listen. Instead, he challenged his dad with, "If church and God are so important, why didn't you go with me all those years?" That question always put an abrupt end to his father's questions.

Standing in the shadows of that dimly lighted hallway, Jake felt as if a pall of guilt draped over him because of his abrupt answer to his father. Perhaps, like Katelyn, his father simply didn't understand the importance until later in life. With new resolution Jake lightly tapped on the door. He had a 10:00 appointment, and he was a little early.

A smiling Steve, tall and dark, opened the door. "Jake. Come in. I've been waiting on you." Jake expected the pastor to be in a formal suit and tie, but was pleased to see he wore jogging gear, like Jake. "I usually take Saturdays just to make sure my sermon is ready for Sunday, but I'm glad you asked to see me today anyway."

Jake entered the immaculate office lined with books and wished his life were as neat. Right now he felt as if his life were a mess—a huge mess. Could God repair what Jake had destroyed?

Steve arranged two seats around a circular table in the corner and produced steaming cups of coffee. Jake felt completely at ease in this man's presence. He figured Steve to be in his early thirties, about Jake's age, and the two soon discovered they shared much in common, including a love for tennis.

After the usual pleasantries, an awkward silence settled around the two men. Jake cleared his throat and began in halting words. "I guess Katelyn has told you about our divorce—why we divorced, that is."

"Actually, no." A trace of curiosity danced through

Steve's dark eyes as he pushed his glasses up the bridge of his nose. "We've only lived in Mena a couple of months. Even though Katelyn and Sophie and I—well, especially Katelyn and Sophie—are developing a close friendship, we didn't even know Katelyn was divorced. We just assumed she never married. After meeting you last week, Sophie and I knew that Katelyn would eventually tell us about the divorce, but we wanted it to be in her time, not ours. So we haven't pushed."

"Well, the divorce was my fault mostly, if you want the truth," Jake blurted. "Last week at McDonald's she said she felt God asking her to confess that she was to blame too."

Steve nodded as if he understood Katelyn's motive perfectly.

"But I'm the one who had an affair. Not her." Jake awaited some show of judgment to play on the pastor's face but surprisingly none came.

"That's a temptation I think every man alive wrestles with. Even me."

Jake tried not to gape. "You mean even you've been tempted to—"

"Of course," Steve answered without a blink. "Sexual sin is a man's weakness. And Satan attacks us at our weak points. But as a man of God, I've committed myself solely to my wife, and I stay on my knees every day to keep that commitment alive."

"Oh." Jake was too taken aback to form another thought.

"If your and Katelyn's story is like a lot of stories I've heard, I think what God has probably shown Katelyn is that she was partly to blame for making you even weaker on the point of sexual sin. Let me guess. . ." Steve squinted his eyes. "Early in your marriage, your sex life was great. As the years rolled on, Katelyn turned you down more and more until your sex life was almost non-existent. Then, you met a woman who seemed more than willing to fulfill your sexual needs, and you gave in."

"How did you know?" Jake said, astounded.

"It's the same story over and over again. I've heard it many times. I've come to the conclusion that most of the time when there's an affair, it's a much larger story than just the man—or woman, for that matter—who betrays a mate. That doesn't mean the affair is justified or that the wife is to blame. Sin is sin, and we must take responsibility for our actions. But there's often a whole set of dynamics that comes into play."

As Steve's words penetrated Jake's mind, he stared at his sneakers in thoughtful silence. At last, he spoke. "Well, I've really blown it on all fronts. That's the bottom line."

"If you want the truth again, I almost blew it too, early in our marriage. There were plenty of things I didn't understand about Sophie's needs—like the fact that she needs to be courted all the time, not just before the marriage."

Once again, Jake was taken aback with Steve's frankness. Never did he anticipate a pastor who would be so openly human. Somehow, Jake thought he would encounter somebody who had it all together and had all the answers. Even though Steve produced some answers, there was nothing haughty in his demeanor.

"How long have you been a Christian?" Jake asked,

wanting to steer the conversation to the reason he came —to hopefully discover the peace he saw in Katelyn's eyes.

"I found the Lord at twenty. I was in college, actually, in pre-law classes."

"Oh?"

"Yes. And I met a young woman who refused to go out with me because I didn't share her faith.

"Sophie?"

Smiling, Steve nodded. "You got it. So I started attending church in hopes of getting her to change her mind. After awhile, I lost all hope that Sophie would go out with me but kept going to church anyway. I felt that something was missing from my life. And, to make a long story short, I had an encounter with Jesus Christ one Sunday morning that blew my socks off."

"I've been reading the Bible some this week, and I think I want an encounter with God like yours—and like Katelyn's," Jake said in a raspy voice.

"Of course you do," Steve answered practically. "Every person alive does, whether he admits it or not. That's the reason Christ died on the cross. He did the hard part. Our part is simple. All you have to do is admit you've sinned, ask God to forgive you, and believe in Jesus Christ as your Savior."

"That's it?"

"That's all." Steve placed his doubled fist over his chest. "But it needs to be a heart thing, not just a head thing." He paused while the meaning sank in.

Jake wasn't certain he understood all the particulars. Nonetheless, he was ready to do anything to escape the misery of his guilt and experience the freedom Katelyn mentioned. At last, he spoke. "I'm not sure I completely get everything, but I do know that I want whatever it is that Katelyn has. She seemed so at. . .at peace."

"Would you like me to pray with you?"

Jake nodded his ascent, and the two men knelt together. Steve laid his hand across Jake's shoulders in brotherly support and led Jake in the prayer of faith. As the words formed in his soul and exited his mouth, Jake felt as if his spirit soured to the heights of the stars. At once an incredible peace flooded his whole being, and Jake knew he was experiencing a supernatural encounter with the Creator of the universe. All the guilt from his sins with Diane seemed to vanish, replaced by a joyous song he recalled from his childhood church days, a song of relinquishing all broken dreams to Jesus. One by one, he extended those dreams to his Lord, and God filled the wounds with peace. Jake didn't even realize he was sobbing until Steve shoved a fistful of tissues into his hands.

"Just stay on your knees every day, Brother," Steve encouraged. "Stay on your knees. I know if I don't, I fall flat on my face."

As the two shared a supportive, masculine embrace, one driving thought formed in Jake's mind: He must see Katelyn. See her now.

Despite the chill of early December, sweat drenched Katelyn as if summer were at its peak. Her daily ten-mile bicycle journey took her up and down Arkansas hills and normally left her invigorated. But not today. As she pumped her ten-speed onto her street, Katelyn felt as if she were pulling a burden of rocks behind her.

All week she had been distracted by her encounter with Jake. Several of her students asked if she were depressed. One girl even bought Katelyn a funny greeting card to cheer her up. But nothing seemed to help. All Katelyn could hear was Jake's hurried admission that he still loved her. All she could see was his crestfallen face when she'd refused his offer to rebuild their marriage. All she could think was, *I never prayed about whether or not God wanted Jake and me back together.*

And upon the heels of that thought came another thought: *Would I be willing to remarry Jake if that was God's will?* The very idea left her nauseous. The last thing —the very last thing—Katelyn wanted was to set herself up for more heartache. Furthermore, Jake wasn't a Christian. And the thought of being in a physical union with him yet unable to share her spiritual union with Christ was no longer Katelyn's idea of a good marriage. All week, tormenting thoughts disturbed her and disrupted her morning prayer time.

Laboriously, she pedaled up the last hill toward her small duplex. The day stretched before her like an endless eternity. During the week, Katelyn's coaching job distracted her, exhausted her. But today was Saturday, a supposed day of leisure. Immediately, Katelyn determined to call Sophie Anderson and see if the church would mind if she purchased some poinsettias to decorate the sanctuary. That would give her something constructive to do, and the chore would hopefully take her mind off of Jake Grant.

With renewed determination, Katelyn steered toward her duplex, only to see a familiar green truck in the driveway and a familiar man ringing her doorbell.

Katelyn's stomach dropped to her knees. Why was Jake at her door? Was he going to push her into trying to renew their relationship? The thought left Katelyn wanting to run. Jake obviously didn't see her. Katelyn could pedal around the neighborhood and give him time to leave. Then, she could avoid another confrontation with her ex-husband.

But the same soft voice that challenged Katelyn's lack of prayer regarding her relationship with Jake propelled her to face him. Running wouldn't solve a thing. As determined as Jake had always been, if he didn't see her now, he would be back later.

With a resigned sigh, she rode into her yard, stopped the bicycle, and produced a hoarse "hello."

four

Jake turned to face Katelyn, a hesitant smile playing on his features—the same type of smile he showered her with before they married. Despite her determined effort to drain emotions from her thoughts, Katelyn's pulse jumped. She instantly wondered if she had been crazy not to run when she saw him standing at her door.

"Hi," he said, casually slipping his hands into the pouch pocket of his sweatshirt.

Katelyn rolled the bike closer, glad that it produced some form of buffer between them. The thought of Jake trying to touch her made Katelyn shiver, whether with dread or anticipation, she couldn't define. The closer she got the more she noticed his eyes were a bit red, as if he had been crying. But Katelyn had never seen Jake cry. Perhaps he had a cold. What in the world did he want anyway? She had made it painfully clear that she wasn't interested in a relationship. Couldn't he take the hint?

As the silence stretched between them, Katelyn debated over whether or not to ask him in. She certainly didn't want to, but she felt somewhat pressured into doing the polite thing. They couldn't stand out here all day.

"Care for some hot chocolate?" she asked, wheeling the bicycle toward the front door.

"Sure." Jake deftly took the bike while she unlocked the door. In minutes, she directed him to hang the bike on the living room wall. Jake looked around the room as if he were absorbing every detail. "You haven't changed much, have you?" His right brow angled upward. "Still up to your eyeballs in sports."

"Yeah. You know me—all action." She crossed her arms, desperately wishing Jake would get around to his reasons for coming. For the longer he stayed, the more Katelyn remembered every detail of that moment he took her into his arms outside McDonald's. The familiar warmth of him. The smell of his aftershave. The rapid beating of his heart.

Only God knew how much she missed him. The first year after the divorce had been almost unbearable. But as time wore on, Katelyn convinced herself she was better off without him, especially if he couldn't be true to her. In recent months the peace God gave had eased her aching for Jake so much that Katelyn erroneously presumed she was over him. Last week's encounter defied that assumption, and today obliterated it. Why had God asked her to contact Jake? She would have been so much better off to continue her life as it was.

Jake walked toward her entertainment center and examined her collection of autographed tennis balls on one of the shelves. His intense demeanor announced that he had something important to say. Taking his precious time to speak his mind always annoyed her beyond endurance. Better to change location than get angry.

Silently, Katelyn went into the petite kitchen and prepared their hot chocolate. Since she had been sweating, Katelyn didn't really want a mug herself but she prepared one anyway. Without thinking, she automatically heaped several extra marshmallows in Jake's cup, just as he always liked it. When she turned around, he was only inches behind her. She jumped and sloshed the hot liquid on one of her hands.

"Ouch."

"Here, let me take that." He took the mugs, set them on the counter, and helped her clean up the mess with a dishtowel. "I'm sorry. I thought you heard me."

"I never hear you when you do that. Why are you always so persistent in sneaking up on me?" she demanded, her tone reflecting her taut emotions. Katelyn didn't realize until her words were out that she was talking in the present—as if they were married and sharing the same home.

"I didn't know I was still persistent," he said with a hesitant grin.

Katelyn, completely taken off guard, grappled with a response—any response. When she met Jake at McDonald's, she never intended to rekindle their relationship. She still didn't. Just thinking about the possibility pained her. There was no way she would ever trust the man again. Period. Suddenly, the whole situation became too much for Katelyn.

"Why did you come here?" she rudely snapped.

His eyes narrowed a bit, and Katelyn felt as if he bit back the first response that came to him. After several silent seconds, he spoke. "I've been to see Steve Anderson," he supplied evenly.

"My pastor?" she squeaked out. "Whatever for?"

"I wanted what I saw in your eyes last week," he said with an edge to his voice.

"You mean you've become a Christian?" she asked, not even bothering to hide her gape.

"Don't look so surprised. Good grief, Katelyn, the way I understand this thing, God forgives everyone who asks."

"And you asked?"

"Of course I did. That's part of it." His voice rose a few decibels. "I know I've messed up my life, but you don't have to act like I'm a hopeless case."

"Who says I'm acting like you're a hopeless case? I'm just shocked, that's all." An unpleasant thought struck Katelyn. Perhaps the whole thing was an act to get her back. Would Jake lie about an encounter with God in order to get her to consider dating him? But his eyes were red, as if he had been crying. Had he, like Katelyn, shed tears when he felt that sudden surge of supernatural peace entering his soul?

"You don't believe me," he said flatly.

"I never said that."

"No, but I see it on your face." A red flush crept up his neck. With an exasperated growl, he stalked toward the living room.

Katelyn remained in the small kitchen, arms folded, watching him from where she stood. His back to her, he placed his hands on his hips and stared out one of the picture windows facing the tree-lined streets decorated in Christmas cheer. Despite herself, the winds of admiration blew through Katelyn. Jake Grant was still just as handsome as he'd ever been.

She noticed him the first day of her junior year at the University of Arkansas. What amazed Katelyn was that he seemed just as interested in her as she was in him. Once they were branded "an item" on campus, Katelyn received many envious glances from female students. Those glances didn't stop once they got married and started their careers.

Apparently, that was part of the problem. Jake never had trouble finding women who were interested in him. Katelyn knew about the affair with Diane. But looking back, she wondered if there had been more affairs and Jake just covered his tracks. At once, she wanted the answer to that question.

"Was Diane the only one?" she asked stiffly. "Or were there more I just never found out about?"

Jake didn't move. The question seemed to reverberate around the room like a misplaced echo. For once in her life, Katelyn knew she had taken Jake by surprise.

At last, he slowly turned to face her and spoke through tightened lips. "Diane was the only one."

A surge of guilt splashed against her soul like a bucket of ice water, leaving a frigid ache in its wake. Her first thought was to apologize, but that seemed crazy. Why should she apologize? He was the one who had the affair. Then Katelyn remembered her very words to him at McDonald's, the words God had required of her, the words acknowledging that she was partly to blame for their divorce. She also remembered that resurgence of bitterness that accompanied her home from McDonald's and glared back at her from the dresser mirror.

Her eyes stung. Her lips trembled, and Katelyn pressed them together. For a lack of nothing else to do, she grabbed a mug of hot cocoa and swallowed a mouthful of the liquid. Unfortunately, she swallowed too fast and began to cough as if she were drowning.

Jake rushed to her side. "Are you okay?" He placed a hand on her back.

Immediately Katelyn stepped away from his touch. As things stood, she was able to control her tears. But any physical contact with her ex-husband might leave her nothing but a sobbing bundle of nerves. Once the coughing began to abate, Katelyn felt she should apologize for her caustic remarks. Her attitude had not been Christlike and did nothing to reflect the forgiveness she had extended to Jake.

From the corner of her eye, she saw him standing near the breakfast bar, as if he wanted to say more but didn't quite know how to say it.

"I'm sorry I've been. . .um. . .waspish," Katelyn said to the tiny Christmas tree sitting in her kitchen window. "I shouldn't have brought up Diane again. And. . .and if you say you've accepted Christ, then. . .then I believe you," she said, her voice strained yet sincere.

Even though Katelyn never looked at Jake, she felt him relaxing. Several minutes lapsed in which the refrigerator's humming produced the only noise in the room.

At last, Jake spoke again, "The reason I came over here was to tell you about what happened to me today—about my accepting Christ—and I also wanted to see if there was any way at all that you would reconsider. . ." He trailed off meaningfully. "I know what you said at McDonald's. But I just can't get away from feeling like we should give it another try. I've felt that way all week. But today after praying with Steve Anderson the feeling is stronger than it's ever been."

"So are you asking me to remarry you. . .n–now?"

Katelyn refused to look at him. She couldn't. The whole thing was beyond overwhelming. She didn't trust her reaction, not in the least. If Jake tried to wrap his arms around her and whisper who-knew-what in her ear, Katelyn would melt on the spot.

"No, I'm not proposing," he said at last. "I already tried that, remember, in front of a captive audience at McDonald's."

The touch of a smile in his voice drew Katelyn's gaze. Sure enough, Jake was grinning as if he were a cat who had eaten a dozen mice. His smile always had been a charming occasion, with just a touch of cockiness to round the whole thing off. Katelyn bit her bottom lip to stop herself from automatically returning the smile. What had gotten into her? One second she wanted to sob uncontrollably and the next second she wanted to grin.

"So, what are you suggesting?"

"I'm suggesting that perhaps we start seeing each other again."

The word "no" poised itself on her mouth, but she couldn't seem to get it out. Something stopped her—a haunting voice that suggested she had yet to consult God about her answer. All week Katelyn rebelled against thoughts that perhaps it was God's will for her and Jake to rebuild their relationship. Jake wasn't a Christian, she kept reasoning. Now that excuse had been dashed aside. Jake claimed to have found the Lord. The question was, could Katelyn trust him? Or better yet, had she truly forgiven him? Her musing created an uneasy stirring in her midsection.

Not sure exactly what to say, Katelyn started to speak, but Jake held up his hand. "I promise I won't pressure you in any way. We can just start over as friends, if you like."

"We never were friends," Katelyn said with a hint of irony.

"Maybe that was part of the problem," Jake said, shrugging. "Maybe if we just started over, Katelyn. . . would you consider it?"

She chewed her thumbnail and wondered if there were a way she could view Jake Grant as "just a friend." Friends didn't usually make her pulse race. Furthermore, she and Jake had shared too many intimate moments for Katelyn to be able to simply forget them.

Daringly, she peered into the depths of his sincere eyes, contemplating his offer. Last week Katelyn never dreamed she would actually consider dating Jake once more. But the longer she looked at him, the more she knew there was only one right answer to his question.

"Yes."

He blinked in surprise then produced another of those smiles that knocked Katelyn off her feet the first time she met him. "Yes, you'll consider it, or yes you'll agree to it?"

"Yes, I'll. . .I'll—" She hesitated. Something in her soul beckoned her to completely agree, but Katelyn's human side still hedged. What if he hurt her again? Could she emotionally survive another episode of Jake's cheating? "I'll consider it. I'll pray about it," she added as if she didn't already know what God thought on the subject.

"Okay. . .that's better than nothing." He tucked his hands into the front pocket of his sweatshirt. "When will you let me know?"

"Um. . ."

"The reason I'm asking is because I. . .er. . .sorta thought this afternoon would be a great day for a picnic up at Willa Mena Park. The sun is coming out, and it's supposed to be in the lower sixties. We could pack the picnic basket Aunt Fran gave us—uh—you do still have that basket, don't you?"

"Yes. I've got it," Katelyn said slowly, never anticipating Jake would ask for an outing so soon. She hadn't even given him a definite "yes" yet.

"So, what do you think?" His eyes pleaded for her acceptance.

Katelyn began chewing her other thumbnail and she trembled from the inside out. At McDonald's Jake told her he never stopped loving her. Was that the truth? Or was it merely a product of his not enjoying being single? If he weren't lonely, would he be here now?

So many questions buzzed through her head, Katelyn finally wondered why she was trying to analyze it all. Why couldn't she just give the man a chance? If she were honest with herself, that was what she wanted in the deepest recesses of her heart. But one date would lead to another and another and. . .could she trust him?

"I'll get the picnic basket ready," she finally blurted, wondering if she had lost her mind.

"Good. I'll run to Audrey's and buy us some sandwiches," he said, rushing for the door as if he were afraid she would change her mind.

"Oh! And pick up some sodas while you're out."

"I will," he said, closing the front door behind him.

The whole scene brought back memories from their marriage. Jake dashing to the store. . .Katelyn calling out one last item to remember. . . The realization left her collapsing onto the bar stool. What had she gotten herself into? She must be half crazy to even stay in the same room with Jake Grant, much less agree to a date.

five

Jake took the last bite of his ham on rye and tried to act casual, tried not to stare at his ex-wife. Inside, he was as nervous as a schoolboy infatuated with his teacher. Wearing jeans and a sweater, without any makeup or jewelry or perfume, Katelyn still arrested Jake's attention. The bright December sunshine did amazing things to her red hair, making it seem all the brighter. Katelyn was just Katelyn. And that's what Jake liked the best about her. Why had he ever let her get away?

He sat across from her on a striped blanket atop Willa Mena Mountain, overlooking a wide expanse of Arkansas peaks and valleys, covered with a collection of evergreens along with oaks and maples and hickories, now barren from autumn's frost. A crisp breeze played tag with the surrounding trees and merrily rushed to and fro like a frolicking youngster.

Jake had prayed like crazy before knocking on Katelyn's door. He prayed like crazy the whole time he was at her apartment. And he was still praying like crazy. But not exactly practiced in the art of prayer, Jake could produce only one heavenward plea, "Lord, please work this out between us. I've really blown it." So he kept repeating this simple message over and over in his mind. Just the fact that Katelyn agreed to come on the picnic itself seemed a miraculous answer to prayer.

Yet Jake desperately needed to do something, to move around. The thought of relaxing on the blanket with Katelyn so close left his mind to wander in directions it shouldn't. They had been married once. The chemistry they shared early in their marriage was still there. But at this point Jake felt he had no right to even so much as hold her hand. The wariness in her expressive eyes supported his assumption.

"Wanta go for a hike?" Jake asked while Katelyn put away the picnic leftovers.

"Sure," she said as if she were relieved to have some form of physical activity.

Within minutes they placed the picnic basket in the back of Jake's truck and followed the trail down the side of the wooded mountain. Neither spoke, and Jake followed close behind her as they crunched through the fallen leaves, enjoying December's crisp air. The trees seemed to enclose them in a world of their own, and Jake relaxed as the smells and sounds of the approaching winter met his senses. A squirrel's agitated barking. The scent of pine. The clean Arkansas wind.

"Do you have a Bible?" Katelyn asked softly, the words sounding as if they rode the breeze stirring the trees.

"What?" Jake hadn't expected the question.

"A Bible. Do you own one?" Pausing on the trail, she turned to face him.

"Actually, yes, I do. Mom gave me one last Christmas. At the time I thought she was being pushy. But I started thumbing through it last week. And today, after all that's happened, I'm glad for it."

"Good. You're going to need one." Her honest brown

eyes were more candid than Jake ever remembered them being. "I'm not exactly a Bible scholar, but I suggest you start reading with Matthew and Psalms. Read a chapter a day from each. That's what I did at first. It's a nice introduction to the whole book."

"Thanks." Remembering his experience with God that morning, Jake desperately wished he could feel more religious. But all he could think about was how much he wanted to take his ex-wife into his arms.

Only when it was too late did Jake understand that she and he had indeed become one when they married. Once he divorced her, Jake felt as if half of himself were missing. Oh, he tried to cover the loss with parties and Diane, but the truth of the matter was that Katelyn was a part of him. Even now, Jake felt more complete than he had in years.

When a faint flush spread across Katelyn's cheeks, Jake realized he was staring at her. Suddenly he felt as if she had somehow read his mind. Was his expression that obvious? If so, Jake decided he might as well speak his heart. "I know I'm the one who ruined our marriage, Katelyn, but I'm only half a man without you. I threw away my most treasured possession, and if there's any way—"

As the flush on her cheeks increased, Katelyn held up her hand. "Please. . .please, Jake. I. . .I can't talk about it right now." Silently she ducked her head and walked farther up the trail.

Jake lambasted himself for rushing her. Why couldn't he learn not to push? It seemed he had always pushed his way through life. It worked great in sports, but relationships were another story. Maybe that was part of the problem. Perhaps his new relationship with God would somehow teach Jake not to shove ahead without thinking.

He fell in behind Katelyn and tried to enjoy the beauty of the surrounding forest—the very woods in which he worked. He knew this hiking trail as well as he knew the creases in his own palm. But today Jake felt as if he were in a maze of uncharted wilderness. Where would he and Katelyn go from here?

By sunset exhaustion claimed Katelyn. She and Jake finished their hike then played a few rounds of golf at the putt putt course near the hotel atop the mountain. They ended the day with a trip through the small zoo of injured animals, next to the golf course. Now they settled on the striped blanket once more, munching the leftovers from their lunch and gazing toward the bejeweled sunset which invited cooler temperatures and turned the rolling mountains into a canvas of splendor.

Even though they smiled often and talked lightly, their every word seemed strained. In short, Katelyn felt as if she were in a time warp all afternoon. Every time she glanced into Jake's eyes she relived scenes from their marriage. The intimacy they shared. The laughter. Then, the pain. There were issues between them that divided just as greatly as their divorce decree had. Would Katelyn ever be able to completely relinquish her feelings of resentment? She had told God over and over again that she forgave Jake. But would Katelyn still feel so defensive about the whole ordeal if her forgiveness were complete?

His accepting Christ only complicated the situation.

Presently, the peace Katelyn witnessed in Jake's eyes, the glow on his face, convinced her his conversion was sincere. Nobody could fake what an encounter with Jesus Christ did within the soul. Jake wasn't faking. And Katelyn knew they now shared not only a physical attraction, but also a relationship with the Lord. Nevertheless, none of that deleted their past.

She felt him sitting close to her, felt his warmth against the cold breeze, even though he wasn't touching her. Did she want that warmth back in her life? When she remembered his words of regret on their hike, a part of Katelyn cried out in desperation for the man whom she once called "husband." Another part of her wanted to run.

As the sun continued its descent and the crows began their evening calls, Katelyn felt Jake's silent appraisal. She didn't dare look at him. What was he planning? If he tried to kiss her, would Katelyn have the willpower to pull away?

"Well, I guess we should get ready to go," he said. "It's going to be dark in a few minutes."

"Okay," Katelyn replied without looking at him. She began to stand, but Jake beat her up, gripped her hand in his, and pulled her to her feet—the first physical contact they shared all day.

As if she were caught in a slow-motion flashback, Katelyn remembered another time they shared a picnic. On their honeymoon, the week after their marriage. Jake, always wanting to picnic outdoors, had prepared provisions in their Colorado cabin while Katelyn slept in one morning. He surprised her with a steaming cup of coffee and a rousing, "Wake up, sleepyhead. It's time for a picnic." They had hiked through the woods, much like they did today. But then, they held hands and exchanged kisses sweeter than honey. On the way back to the cabin, Jake scooped Katelyn up in his arms and carried her back to their bed. They made love and napped in each others' arms.

As she stood mere inches from her ex-husband, the whole scene swept over Katelyn, leaving her breathless. Why had Jake trampled her love? Katelyn would never, absolutely never, have broken their wedding vows. Her thoughts only heightened the ache in her heart and left her biting her lips to stay the tears. Nevertheless, one stubborn tear escaped to trickle down her face.

Before she realized Jake's intent he gently brushed his lips against the tear's trail. That mere gesture only melted the iron determination Katelyn had exercised all day. Without preamble, a muffled sob erupted from her throat, and Katelyn leaned toward Jake.

"I am so, so sorry," Jake breathed. "I don't know what else to say. I don't know how to make it all right. I only wish you could somehow forgive me."

Katelyn relaxed against Jake, allowing him to gently rock her. As the sun continued its descent, the shadows about them deepened. Katelyn felt as if those shadows were a reflection of the dark corridors of her heart. She realized she had never stopped loving Jake. But she also realized she had yet to completely forgive him, despite her taking responsibility for her part in their divorce. She knew she hadn't been the perfect wife, but on the other hand, Katelyn had been much better to him than he had been to her.

With the emergence of that thought she abruptly

broke their embrace, brusquely grabbed the picnic basket, and began walking toward Jake's truck.

"Katelyn?" he called, a disillusioned edge to his voice.

She stopped but didn't turn to face him.

"You haven't even started to forgive me, have you?"

Her spine went stiff. Who was he to ask her such a question? She stood for several seconds while a lone owl serenaded the oncoming darkness. Katelyn felt Jake's gaze boring into her spine. She wished she had never agreed to this outing. When the tension grew unbearable, she rushed toward the truck without a backward glance.

Their return trip to Mena was fraught with emotion. Katelyn forbade herself to look at Jake again. She had lived with him long enough to know he was holding his anger at bay. That only made Katelyn angrier. Who was he to be mad at her? He was the one who destroyed their marriage!

When Jake pulled into her driveway, Katelyn slid from the truck and retrieved the picnic basket without a word. Feeling as if she were escaping an airless void, she marched into her duplex, deposited the picnic basket on the breakfast bar, and gripped the edge of the kitchen counter until she heard Jake's truck purring up the street.

❄

Jake pulled to a stop in front of the family homestead, pounded his steering wheel, and swallowed an expletive. He knew enough about his new commitment to Christ to understand that he needed to begin cleaning up his language. But Lord help him, Jake had never been so tied up in knots in his life.

Was this thing with Christ about forgiveness or wasn't it? All last week he scanned through the Bible. Vaguely he remembered a reference to forgiveness in the New Testament. . .something about God not forgiving us if we don't forgive others. If Katelyn was a Christian as she claimed, then how could she continue holding a grudge against Jake? He hadn't fully realized until this afternoon just how eaten up with unforgiveness she actually was. Why had she even contacted him to "admit her part in the divorce" if she still held a grudge against Jake? None of it made sense.

Like a bewildered child, Jake began a broken prayer to his heavenly Father, "Oh Lord, I've messed up big. You know that. Can You salvage anything from what I've destroyed?"

Jake didn't know what else to say, but just that simple prayer seemed to ease his exasperation. And something his mother said shortly before Jake's grandfather's death flitted through his mind. . .something about turning the whole thing over to the Lord and asking His perfect will to be done. As he got out of his truck and entered that empty, lonely house, Jake breathed that prayer. He grabbed his Bible from the antique lampstand and breathed that prayer. Determinedly he plopped onto the couch, opened his Bible to Psalms, and breathed that prayer.

six

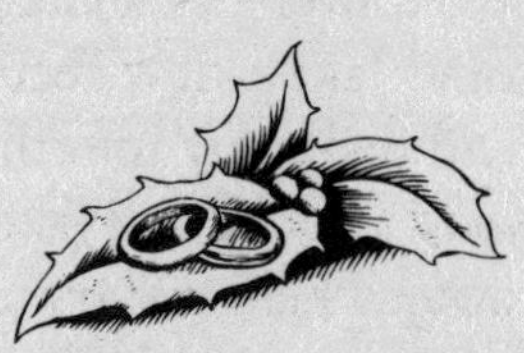

Never did Katelyn expect Jake at her small church the next morning. But there he sat, three rows from the back, his attention riveted on Pastor Steve behind the pulpit. Katelyn sat on the same side of the Christmas-wreath-bedecked sanctuary in the very back row where she collapsed upon seeing her ex-husband. He had yet to spot her. Katelyn possessed no earthly idea what congregational songs they sang or what the message was about. All she could do was relive her picnic with Jake the day before and his final words, "You haven't even started to forgive me, have you?" Those words had haunted her all night. And they were true. Katelyn knew for certain, that, despite her verbal homage to forgiving Jake she still harbored unforgiveness in her heart.

But whether she could forgive him or not was immaterial when considering the likelihood of rebuilding their relationship. Katelyn knew after yesterday that she could never go back to Jake. His betrayal could never be erased. Katelyn simply wasn't prepared to set herself up for more heartache. Jake Grant meant heartache.

When the final benediction was said, Katelyn rushed toward the exit for an obligatory shaking of the pastor's hand. Much to her frustration, the exit door was jammed by a cluster of little old ladies discussing the annual Christmas potluck dinner with Sophie. Frantically, Katelyn looked over her shoulder and glimpsed the blond, handsome Jake a few feet behind her. She wanted to groan and disappear into the new plush carpet. She knew beyond a doubt that Jake spotted her. Her red hair gave her away. There was no use trying to hide.

Was Jake planning to attend this church from now on? If so, Katelyn envisioned week after week of trying to worship with him breathing down her neck. The thought left her almost nauseous.

By the time she was shaking Pastor Steve's hand, she felt Jake mere inches from her. Her hair virtually stood on end as Steve appraised her and Jake, a question in his eyes.

"Good to see you this morning, Jake," Steve said. "I was hoping you would make it."

"It's a pleasure to be here. Your sermon was fantastic. And I'm definitely interested in the Thursday night Bible study. I've got a lot to learn."

"Would you two like to join Sophie and me and the kids for lunch?" Steve asked. "I think Sophie made a roast."

"Uh. . .we didn't come together," Katelyn rasped, her heart pounding as if she had ridden her bicycle to Montana and back.

"I know." Steve shrugged. "Doesn't matter."

"I really don't think—" Jake began.

"Oh, but please do," Sophie interjected as she turned from the elderly ladies and toward Steve's conversation.

Compulsively Katelyn stole a glance toward Jake. He looked as desperate as she felt. However, another emotion churned in his eyes. Pain. The realization hit her like a punch in the gut.

"Okay, Sophie, if you insist," Jake said at last. "I'll join you for lunch if Katelyn will."

With Sophie, Steve, and Jake looking at her expectantly, Katelyn felt pressured into accepting. "That's fine," she choked out, her frustration growing.

"Great!" Sophie produced one of her million dollar smiles. "I'll go home and get everything ready, then. Want to walk to the parsonage with me, Katelyn?"

"Sure," Katelyn said quickly, relieved to escape Jake.

"We'll just leave you two big, strong men over here to lock up the church and corral the kids while we talk about girl stuff," Sophie said with a wink.

"Oh, brother," Steve groaned, rolling his eyes.

Katelyn, following Sophie across the church lawn, wondered how she and Steve kept such a spark in their marriage. They just celebrated their tenth anniversary and had an eight-year-old boy and a six-year-old girl. Something in the deepest recesses of Katelyn's soul longed for a marriage like Steve and Sophie's.

But Jake certainly wasn't the person to have that type of marriage with. Even considering his new belief in Christ, Katelyn doubted that the two of them could maintain a spark for long. She couldn't deny that Jake still stirred her, but Katelyn also couldn't deny that his affair was beginning to torment her as never before.

"A penny for your thoughts," Sophie said, as she opened the parsonage door.

Following her friend past the family Christmas tree and into the cute country kitchen which smelled of savory roast beef, Katelyn pondered what to say. She wanted to be completely candid but she held back for some reason. Sharing her true feelings about Jake with Sophie left Katelyn feeling uncomfortable. She hated to admit how much she resented him.

"I'm sorry," Sophie said, donning an apron. "I didn't mean to pry."

"It's okay. I guess I was just miles away, that's all." Even though the statement was true, Katelyn felt a bit peevish in not sharing her heart. But, simply put, she couldn't. "What do you need me to do?" Katelyn asked with a smile.

In a matter of thirty minutes, the table was set, the men and kids claimed chairs, and Sophie and Katelyn seated themselves as well. Katelyn tried her best to maintain some level of propriety, even though her insides churned with all the emotions raging through her.

She sat directly across from Jake. The children, having fallen in love with the tall stranger, each claimed a spot on either side of him. As Jake continued animated conversation with the children, Katelyn couldn't deny that he would make a great father. They had wanted children, but each passing year saw their plan deferred for one reason or another. Katelyn momentarily pictured a hospital room, her in bed, holding a precious bundle and Jake, a proud father, standing nearby. They could have experienced the joy of a newborn, perhaps several times, if Jake had simply stayed true to her. She gripped her tea glass and sipped the cool liquid in an attempt to ease her overwrought nerves.

When they first sat down, Katelyn was relieved that she didn't have to sit right next to her ex-husband. But as the meal wore on, she discovered she would have been better off next to him than across from him. As things stood, she seemed to be forever making eye contact with Jake. In those gray eyes, she saw memories of their outing yesterday. Shadows of that moment when Jake held her in his arms. The heartache of their broken marriage which seemed forever hanging between them.

With each minute Katelyn's nervousness grew. She barely nibbled her food and strained to keep herself focused on the conversation. The meal seemed to wear on for hours, but at long last the dessert was finished and everyone began standing.

Steve invited Jake to watch the football game, and Katelyn assisted her hostess with cleanup. As Sophie prepared a tray laden with mugs of hot cocoa, Katelyn debated whether or not she could slip out the kitchen door so she wouldn't have to traipse through the living room and face Jake once more. Would Sophie understand?

As if to answer her question, Sophie gently squeezed her hand. "You're really uncomfortable, aren't you?"

Katelyn silently nodded and bit her lips. "I know it probably looks to you like Jake and I. . .like we. . .um. . . but. . .well. . .I just—I don't know if I can ever. . ." She breathed deeply in an attempt to calm her raw nerves.

"Steve told me everything yesterday after Jake's visit. I understand the whole thing must be terribly hard for you."

"It is. I think Jake wants us to get back together now, and I don't think. . ." Katelyn trailed off as the tray of hot chocolate blurred.

"If I'd known this was going to be so hard on you, I'd have never asked you. But after seeing you two together at McDonald's I just naturally assumed. . ."

"Yes, I'm sure you would." Katelyn felt as if she

wanted to dissolve right onto the immaculate kitchen floor. Her face heated, and she knew from experience that a red flush was probably creeping up her neck and onto her cheeks.

"Would you just like to slip out the kitchen door?" Sophie asked gently.

"Would you mind?" Katelyn begged, thanking God her friend was so sensitive.

"I don't mind in the least."

Without another word, Katelyn grabbed her purse and silently stepped out of the kitchen and into the crisp day.

She rushed from the house and across the church's parking lot as if a pack of wolves were nipping at her heels. Determinedly Katelyn forced her trembling hands to open her car door and crank the engine. She didn't realize Jake, too, was quietly leaving until she saw Steve and him standing on the front lawn. The last Katelyn saw of Jake, he was watching her drive away. The scene twisted Katelyn's heart and brought back gut-wrenching memories of a time when she watched Jake driving away . . .with her friend Diane.

Jake longingly peered after Katelyn as she sped off, his heart sick. He knew her too well not to recognize just how nervous he made her. The last thing he needed was to push Katelyn further from him than she already was.

So he had quietly asked Steve if he could leave. Steve, seeming to understand the whole ordeal, solemnly agreed and escorted Jake onto the lawn.

"Please pray for us," Jake said, staring forlornly at a row of Christmas lights lining the flower beds.

"I have been," Steve said. "Ever since we met you in McDonald's. I started praying then. When you called to talk with me yesterday, I considered it an answer to prayer."

Surprised, Jake glanced up at his new friend. "Thanks," he said, feeling hopeful for the first time since the picnic. "Maybe there's a chance in all this after all."

"Maybe." Steve gripped Jake's shoulder. "Just keep praying and don't give up. God is in the business of working miracles. We're examples of that. Right?"

"Yeah. You're right," Jake readily agreed and prayed that somehow the Lord would work yet another miracle in his life.

seven

The letter awaited Jake Tuesday afternoon when he arrived home. As usual, he had pulled his truck to the roadside mailbox, opened it, and retrieved the day's mail. The top letter obliterated all thoughts of any potential Christmas cards. He would recognize the neat oversized script in the midst of thousands. Why had Katelyn written? She could have phoned. Jake felt hollow, and the cold autumn wind rattling the surrounding trees only added to his sense of loneliness. At once his prayers for a miracle seemed to mock him.

Without even pulling his truck into the driveway, Jake tore open the envelope. The short message twisted his gut and made him want to roar in frustration. Simply put, Katelyn politely asked him to stay on his side of town and she would stay on her side. She wasn't ready to rebuild their relationship.

Jake quickly wheeled into his driveway, turned around, and pressed his foot on the accelerator. Katelyn most likely was still at the high school. Jake had a few choice things he wanted to say to her.

"Okay, that's enough for now," Katelyn called across the gym to the girls' volleyball team. They had stayed after school for their usual Tuesday afternoon practice, and

Katelyn was shortening it.

"Okay, Coach," they called, curiously glancing at her.

Normally if Katelyn compromised their usual quitting time it was because she was keeping them over, not letting them go early.

But Katelyn was ready to go home. Her head ached. Her heart ached. Her soul ached. Inside her heart she felt as if she had rolled around in a dirty gym locker. As she dejectedly trudged through the smelly locker room and down the short hallway toward her office, Katelyn speculated why she felt so rotten inside. All her unforgiveness for Jake seemed to have emerged from the spot in her soul where she had skillfully stuffed it. Now that unforgiveness covered her whole heart. She was so distraught she could hardly even pray. How did one go about relinquishing unforgiveness anyway? The dark emotion seemed to have sunk its ugly talons into Katelyn and wouldn't release her. In short, she felt as if the unforgiving spirit possessed her instead of her taking charge of it.

Ready to tidy her office and leave as soon as the locker room cleared out, Katelyn opened her office door. She felt Jake's presence before she saw him. With a gasp, she peered up into gray eyes that looked as angry as the churning mass of a tornado.

She stopped on the door's threshold as her knees suddenly grew weak. "What are you doing here?"

Jake held up the letter. "You didn't think I was going to take this sitting down, did you?" he demanded.

"It's my choice," Katelyn countered. "And yes, I did believe you would honor it. This is America," she added sarcastically. "You don't have much of an option."

"I want to know if you prayed about this?" He tossed the letter onto her cluttered desk.

His question took Katelyn off guard. She hadn't prayed much about it. She couldn't. Katelyn was afraid of what God might show her, of what had haunted her all week. If it were God's will for her to rebuild her relationship with Jake, would she? Katelyn was having extreme difficulty in putting aside her natural aversion in the face of God's direction.

"I can tell by your expression that you haven't prayed about it at all," he challenged.

"Since when are you such a spiritual giant that you have any right to question what I have or haven't prayed about?" she bit out.

"I never said I was a spiritual giant," he returned, his volume increasing. "I'm really new at all this, and you know that as well as I do. But I've already read enough of the Bible to understand that Christians are supposed to pray about decisions as big as that one." He pointed to the letter atop her desk.

Katelyn could form no response. As they began a hostile stare down, she realized the locker room had gone from a den of noise to tomblike silence. Compulsively she looked over her shoulder, down the hallway. She couldn't see the girls, but she could feel them listening. Only the Lord knew what they were thinking. Gritting her teeth, Katelyn stepped farther into the office and closed the door behind her with more control than she felt.

"I've made my decision," she said through gritted teeth. "You're going to have to live with it."

As Jake stared at her, pain and anger marring his

face, something within Katelyn shriveled from her own actions. Her heart felt as if it were being squeezed of all life. And something within her spirit protested her every word. She knew beyond doubt that she had never stopped loving Jake, that she never would stop loving Jake. Even now a part of Katelyn wanted to wrap her arms around him and beg him never to leave. But she could never trust him again. So what choice did she have?

"And what about what Matthew says?" Jake finally said.

"Matthew who?" she snapped, grasping for his meaning.

"Matthew in the Bible. Last week I read something about God not forgiving us if we don't forgive others."

"I never once told you I haven't forgiven you."

With a sarcastic snort, Jake threw his hands into the air. "You don't have to tell me. It's all over you!"

Katelyn's heart shriveled all the more, and the very words she had spoken to Jake at McDonald's mocked her: *There's something very freeing about coming totally clean with God and your fellow man.* At the time Katelyn thought she had come totally clean with God and man. Now she saw that there had been an ugly, slimy monster hiding within her which she shut away in the dungeon of her soul. God knew that monster was there even though Katelyn had been in denial about it. The longer she was with Jake, the more prominent that ugly monster became.

"Well what about Exodus?" she finally flung at him, desperate to do anything to divert the conversation.

"What about it?"

"The Ten Commandments. One of them is 'Thou

shalt not commit adultery.' " For added emphasis, she scooped up her letter, tore it in half, and dropped it into the trash basket. When she glanced back up, all color had drained from Jake's face. Something in Katelyn desperately wanted to take back her hateful words. Immediately, she felt further from Jake and God than she had since the beginning of either relationship. Trembling all over, Katelyn crossed her arms and turned to examine the trophy shelf lined with proof of her athletic achievements.

The only noise in the office was the muffled sounds of lockers being closed and calls of good-bye. The girls were finally clearing out. And the office walls seemed to be gradually closing in on Katelyn.

Inside, she felt cold and lonely and swept away in a sea of confusion. Something in her heart desperately longed for Jake's arms around her once more. She remembered all the nights early in their marriage when they swayed to soft music with the lights low until their love found full expression. Then the intensity gradually wore off of their passion until it seemed Katelyn was pursuing her life and Jake was pursuing his. How much energy had she really put into pleasing Jake the last two years of their marriage? If she were honest, truly honest, Katelyn would have to admit that somewhere in all her pursuits of coaching and cross-country biking and . . .and. . .she had stopped including Jake in her life. How often had she let him go to bed alone? How often had she made excuses when she really didn't want to join him in the woods on a Saturday outing?

But by the same token, Jake had never really taken an interest in what Katelyn had to say, in who Katelyn really was. He had been more interested in her fulfilling his physical needs than he was in talking and sharing from the heart. If perhaps Jake had taken time to understand Katelyn. . .if. . .if. . .if. . .

At once the room seemed full of "if's." When Jake walked toward the doorway, Katelyn kept her back to him.

"If you ever change your mind, you know my phone number," he said in a hollow voice. The office door clicked shut, and a hot tear trickled down Katelyn's cheek.

Hovering like a bewildered puppy, Katelyn suppressed the urge to run after him. Eventually the forceful urge overcame her and she rushed from her office. Not sure what she would do with him once she caught him, Katelyn raced toward the parking lot. But she was too late. Jake's truck sped along the drive and onto the street.

Tears drenching her cheeks, Katelyn stumbled back to her office, closed the door, collapsed into her chair, and draped herself upon her desk. Never had she been so miserable. She knew in her heart she was wrong, just as wrong as Jake had been when he committed adultery. But Katelyn didn't know exactly how to correct the problem.

"Oh, God, help me," she gasped through her tears.

eight

O*h, God, help me. . . . Oh, God, help me. . . . Oh, God, help me. . . .* Katelyn prayed that prayer for three weeks. And during those weeks, she chose to attend another church because she knew Jake was attending her church. Sophie called a couple of times, but Katelyn couldn't share with her. The whole thing was too painful. She sensed that Sophie knew exactly what was going on, and Katelyn was thankful that her pastor's wife didn't push, only promised to pray for her.

Every night Katelyn sobbed herself to sleep as she journeyed through the pain of her divorce. At long last she understood why God impressed her to contact Jake. Katelyn had yet to allow herself to explore all the issues of her failed marriage. But seeing Jake in person, staring face-to-face with her past, allowed God to begin a new level of purging within Katelyn. And, oh, what a painful process it was.

At last her fits of sobbing became less intense, her heart less heavy. Finally Katelyn realized she could do nothing to rid herself of the wretched monster of unforgiveness. She must rely on a source much more powerful than her for deliverance from that ogre. Her job was to relinquish the past and allow God's supernatural power to heal, purge, and deliver. Still she struggled with that relinquishment.

She awoke Sunday morning, Christmas Eve, at 4:00 A.M. with only one thought on her mind. *Jake.* His initial plea for them to rebuild their relationship. His gentle kiss after their picnic. His stricken face when he left her office.

As she stretched in bed and snuggled deeper into the covers, Katelyn finally saw with vivid clarity that even though Jake had sinned against her and God, his sin was no worse than hers. In order to cling to her unforgiveness she had deluded herself into believing that she was better than he was. But she wasn't. She never had been. She never would be. They were both a product of sinful humanity, and they both desperately needed Jesus Christ. Not only had Katelyn been unforgiving, she had also rejected God most of her adult life. Only in recent months had Katelyn turned her life over to Him. Up until that point, she had been living for herself. Would her marriage have turned out differently if she had believed on Christ earlier?

Undoubtedly.

The answer blazed through her mind like a bolt of lightning, and Katelyn sat straight up. She thought of all the times her college friends invited her to church, of all the times her sister tried to share the Lord. But Katelyn had rejected each invitation, each attempt. If she had turned to God ten years ago, she might well have influenced Jake to turn to God, just as she recently influenced him. In turn, they would have focused their marriage upon Christ. How different it would have been.

Without another thought, she hunched forward, covered her face, and began calling out to her Creator, "Oh, Father, I am so sorry for not coming to this point sooner. Oh, Lord, I need you to take this unforgiveness from me. Please, please give me the strength and courage to relinquish the whole nasty mess to you. Please give me a new love for Jake. You know that down deep inside I'm tired of living alone and I'm tired of waking up in this bed by myself every morning of my life. Please don't let me grow into an old, embittered woman who never got past this heartache. . . ."

Katelyn continued to cry out to her Lord. She prayed until she knew she had touched the throne of God, and He in turn had truly touched her. Finally she completely released her unforgiveness, her heartache, her emptiness. She released them, and God in turn flooded her with forgiveness, mercy, and love. Yes love. Love for the man who had betrayed her. And she knew beyond all doubt that what she suspected was indeed true. The Lord *did* want her to rebuild her relationship with Jake because that was what God was about. Healing. Reconciliation. Making people and relationships whole.

Overflowing with praise for her Savior, Katelyn looked at the digital clock to see that she had been praying just over an hour. This whole ordeal had taken weeks to work through and hours to pray through. But Katelyn had survived the battle. Not only did she survive, she victoriously overcame.

As she mopped her face with the bed sheet, Katelyn wondered if Jake was up. Probably not. He always liked to sleep until the last minute, and the Christmas Eve church service didn't start until ten. Katelyn figured he probably stayed up late watching a ball game on the sports channel, and he would sleep until nine. But that was fine. His late sleeping would give her plenty of time to get ready for church and surprise him. During their picnic he told her he had moved into the Grant family homestead—the very place Jake proposed to her. What a perfect place for Katelyn to accept his most recent proposal.

❄

Jake groggily opened one eye and peered at the alarm clock. Seven A.M. With a groan, he rolled over and wondered what had awakened him at such an early hour on a Sunday morning. He normally liked to sleep in on weekends because he started his day so early during the week. With a yawn, Jake covered his head to block out the weak December sunshine spilling through the row of bedroom windows.

Jake desperately wanted to go back to sleep and escape his aching heart. He dreamed about Katelyn. They were back together. She forgave him, wrapped her arms around him, and confessed her love. But the more time marched on without her contacting him, the more Jake doubted they would ever be reconciled. In desperation, he poured his heart out to his pastor, and Steve encouraged him to keep praying. Still new at all this, Jake hoped that Steve knew what he was talking about when he claimed that God could work a miracle.

If God didn't work a miracle, Jake had decided to leave Mena and start a new life elsewhere. Living in the same town with Katelyn simply wouldn't work for him. Every day he felt her presence as if she were living next door. Although she wasn't next door, Katelyn was only fifteen minutes away. Her proximity left him aching as if his heart itself had been removed.

Just as Jake teetered on the brink of sleep, a vague bumping noise teased his mind. He rolled over and listened. Perhaps that noise had awakened him in the first place, whatever it was. Occasionally a few deer strayed from the surrounding woods, and Jake had even witnessed two bucks locking horns in his backyard last year. Was that what he heard?

Thoughts of the noise vanished when a familiar smell began filling his nose. Gourmet coffee. Irish Creme to be exact. His favorite. But Jake hadn't bought any in weeks. Why was he smelling gourmet coffee? Had his stress over Katelyn begun to make him hear and smell things?

He sat up and tried to clear his senses with a deep breath. But the coffee smell only gained potency.

Then that noise again. This time accompanied by something which strongly resembled the sizzling of bacon.

At last it all made sense. Jake's parents must have arrived during the night and slept in the guest room. They were due in, but not until Christmas day. Why didn't they call and tell him they would be early? This wasn't like them. His curiosity mounting to mammoth proportions, Jake swung his feet out of the poster bed and grabbed his flannel robe. By now the aroma of bacon mingled with the coffee in an alluring way, and Jake's stomach responded with a resounding growl. His mother was undoubtedly outdoing herself.

Yawning, Jake ran his hand through his rumpled hair and trudged through the homey living room. As he passed the fireplace, he opted to throw a couple more logs on last night's leftover coals. That ought to take the chill out of the air.

The closer he got to the kitchen, the more clearly he began to hear a faint rendition of “Have Yourself A Merry Little Christmas.” He ambled into the kitchen of knotted pine, fully expecting his plump mother and her ready smile. Instead he saw a thin young redheaded woman, her back to Jake, checking on a pan of biscuits in the oven, humming to the tunes flowing from the portable radio Jake kept in the kitchen.

Katelyn!

Jake gaped and rubbed his eyes to make sure he wasn’t hallucinating. But no, Katelyn was indeed in his kitchen. Once she closed the oven, she busied herself turning the snapping bacon. Jake recalled similar scenes from early in their marriage when Katelyn arose early to make his favorite breakfast of bacon, eggs, and biscuits. Often she would serve him breakfast in bed, and he would in turn cook dinner. They had a comfortable routine in their marriage for a while—before things started falling apart.

Jake gulped. Why would Katelyn be cooking for him? And how did she get into the house?

“Er. . .excuse me, Little Red Riding Hood, but how did you happen to find your way here?”

Katelyn, placing the last piece of bacon on a plate, stilled and kept her back to Jake. Little Red Riding Hood. Jake began calling her that early in their acquaintance because of her hair color.

In all her planning of this surprise breakfast, Katelyn had yet to come up with the words to begin what she wanted to say. She swallowed hard and turned to face him. He stood in the doorway, leaning against the frame, hair rumpled, arms crossed, that charming smile in place. He looked like a boy who awoke on Christmas morning to discover a mound of toys, all just for him. And Katelyn's throat went dry.

At last she discovered some words tripping through her mind. "Uh. . .you always liked to keep a key hidden outside the front door when. . .when we were married. I f–figured you still did that. So I. . .I just looked until I found it."

Jake stepped into the kitchen, his eyes churning with a multitude of questions. But he didn't voice one of them. Not one. As if they did this sort of thing every morning, he turned to the kitchen cabinet, grabbed a couple of mugs, and poured two cupfuls of coffee. She watched as he prepared hers, exactly the way she liked it. Two teaspoons of sugar and a dollop of milk.

Katelyn continued to stare at him, to drink in the image of him. She longed to throw herself into Jake's arms and pour out her heart, but Katelyn felt so uncertain of herself and him that she held back.

"I think I smell your biscuits. Are they ready?" he said, darting a glance at her from the corners of his eyes.

"Oh. The biscuits," she said blankly. How long had she been staring at him? "I just checked them. They should be ready by now."

"Here, I'll get them." Jake and Katelyn simultaneously reached for the pot holder lying on the counter. Jake's hand wrapped around Katelyn's, and she didn't dare pull it away.

His hand tightened around hers as if he had just discovered the rarest of jewels. Katelyn, overwrought with emotion, silently begged Jake to pull her into his arms.

"Katelyn?" he rasped, hesitantly tugging her toward him.

"Oh, Jake," she said over a broken sob. She flung herself against him, wrapping her arms around him, opening her heart to his love.

Neither spoke as the years melted away and they were once more newly in love. For what seemed an eternity, Jake gently rocked her, then he trailed featherlike kisses from her ear to her mouth then hungrily crushed her to him. At long last he lifted his face from hers to breathe in her ear, "Oh, Katie. . .Katie. . .I've missed you so much. I've prayed like mad that you'd return to me. Please, please tell me you'll give our marriage another try. I. . .I want to try again so badly. I did so many things wrong—"

"But you weren't the only one." Katelyn raised her head and peered into his eyes. "I was so wrong in so many areas, Jake. I think I was in our marriage for me more than for you. I see now where I set you up for an affair—"

"But it was my sin, Katelyn, not yours. I can't let you take the blame for—"

"Yes. It was your sin. But my own sin of selfishness and. . .and not turning my life over to God weakened you to the point of—"

"But if I had been more attentive to your needs, you probably would have been more attentive to mine. I was selfish too, and I said 'no' to God just like you did. Can you ever forgive me, Katelyn? I so want to make it all right."

"I already have forgiven you, Jake. I promise. I just hope you can forgive me, not only for what I did wrong in our marriage, but for being so resentful lately."

"I forgave you when God forgave me."

Katelyn felt as if God Himself wrapped His arms around the both of them and sealed their renewed love with the witness of His spirit.

"Merry Christmas," Katelyn said, resting her forehead against his.

"It's going to be the best one of all," he muttered before sealing their renewed love with another kiss.

This time, their marriage would last forever.

Debra White Smith

Debra White Smith lives in east Texas with her husband and two small children. She is an editor, writer, and speaker who pens both books and magazine articles and has over twenty book sales to her credit, both fiction and nonfiction. Both she and her novels have been voted favorite by **Heartsong Presents** readers. Futhermore, Debra holds a B.A. and M.A. in English, and her Barbour novellas appear in *Only You, Season of Love,* and *Spring's Promise.* Her **Heartsong Presents** titles include *The Neighbor, Texas Honor,* and the coming series books: *Texas Rose, Texas Lady,* and *Texas Angel.* A portion of her earnings from writing goes to Christian Blind Mission, International.

You can write to Debra at P.O. Box 1482, Jacksonville, TX 75766, or visit her web site at www.getset.com/debrawhitesmith. She loves to hear from her readers!

A Letter to Our Readers

Dear Readers:

In order that we might better contribute to your reading enjoyment, we would appreciate your taking a few minutes to respond to the following questions. When completed, please return to the following: Managing Editor, Barbour Publishing, Inc., P.O. Box 719, Uhrichsville, OH 44683.

1. Did you enjoy reading *Winter Wishes*?
   ❑ Very much, I would like to see more books like this.
   ❑ Moderately—I would have enjoyed it more if __________

____

____

2. What influenced your decision to purchase this book?
   (Check those that apply)
   ❑ Cover ❑ Back cover copy ❑ Title ❑ Price
   ❑ Friends ❑ Publicity ❑ Other __________

3. Which story was your favorite?
   ❑ *Dear Jane* ❑ *The Language of Love*
   ❑ *Candlight Christmas* ❑ *Love Renewed*

4. Please check your age range:
   ❑ Under 18 ❑ 18–24 ❑ 25–34
   ❑ 35–45 ❑ 46–55 ❑ Over 55 ________

5. How many hours per week do you read? ____________

Name ____________________________________

Occupation ________________________________

Address __________________________________

City ________________ State __________ Zip _______